BURNING BRIDGES

Morehouse remembered that he still had something to talk to Webb about. He turned to the writer. "You ever get any threats when you wrote those stories about Tammany Hall?"

"Almost every day."

"You take 'em seriously?"

Webb ran a finger over his mustache. "Not usually. Tammany was just used to getting its way; it controlled the police, the courts, and the politicians. But it couldn't control the press. So when my articles were published, I think they just had to lash out somehow. They threatened everything from getting me fired to drowning me in the East River. Why?"

"Oh, I was talking with a plug-ugly I know; he runs one of the roughest gangs in Brooklyn. And he doesn't know this for a fact, but he's guessing that the bullets that killed Joshua Thompson might have been meant for you." He looked to see how Webb would react. "Puts things in a different light, doesn't it?"

Webb kept his eyes straight ahead. His jaw barely moved as he answered softly, "Yes, I suppose it does."

BURNING BRIDGES

TROY SOOS

KENSINGTON BOOKS
KENSINGTON PUBLISHING CORP.
http://www.kensingtonbooks.com

KENSINGTON BOOKS are published by

Kensington Publishing Corp.
850 Third Avenue
New York, NY 10022

All Kensington titles, imprints, and distributed lines are
available at special quantity discounts for bulk purchases for
sales promotion, premiums, fund-raising, and educational or
institutional use.

Special book excerpts or customized printings can also be
created to fit specific needs. For details, write or phone the
office of the Kensington Special Sales Manager: Kensington
Publishing Corp., 850 Third Avenue, New York, NY 10022.
Attn. Special Sales Department. Phone: 1-800-221-2647.

Kensington and the K logo Reg. U.S. Pat. & TM Off.

First Printing: October 2004
10 9 8 7 6 5 4 3 2 1

Printed in the United States of America

CHAPTER 1

The mental fog was slow to lift. It was some minutes—she couldn't gauge how many—before Rebecca Davies was even aware that she was awake.

Struggling to work her sluggish brain, Rebecca tried to get her bearings. That normally simple task proved to be such a challenge that it almost seemed insurmountable. She was so drowsy that she was barely able to ascertain whether she was in the real world or in a dream. Then she forced her senses to focus on her immediate surroundings, one object at a time, in an effort to determine where she was.

Pale moonlight, filtered through the lace curtains of her small bedroom window, cast familiar shadows about the room; the light was so faint that it did little more than outline basic shapes, but Rebecca's memory filled out the details. She first noticed the rails and knobs on the footboard of her brass bed. A sideways glance revealed the curved back of the Martha Washington chair in the corner; over the chair was draped her silk dressing robe. A sudden flutter of the curtain let in a fleeting trickle of moonlight that reflected off the oval mirror above the washstand. Another stray moonbeam briefly illuminated the hand-painted porcelain vase atop her bureau, prompting Rebecca to recall that the vase held a bouquet of tea roses that Marshall had given her two nights ago. She inhaled deeply, and thought she could detect their delicious scent.

The sights and smells led Rebecca to one conclusion: she was at home, secure in her modest bedroom on the second floor of Colden House. All was calm and nothing seemed amiss.

Rebecca then prodded her slumbering mind in a backward direction, trying to determine what had awoken her. Had she been startled by a particularly disturbing dream? She couldn't recall anything about what she'd been dreaming. Since her pulse and breathing felt normal, though, she assumed there had been no nightmares—on those rare occasions when she had suffered from bad dreams, she usually woke shaky and with a pounding heart. Had it been a noise that awakened her then? If so, its echo had long since faded. She attuned her ears, almost straining to detect any unusual sounds. Other than the soft, rhythmic ticking of her bronze mantel clock, all was quiet. She did notice that it was the serene, insulating kind of silence that exists only during the hour or so just before dawn.

The narrow island of Manhattan was crowded with more than a million and a half inhabitants, and most of them would find it difficult to believe that any spot in the bustling city could be so tranquil no matter what the hour. Colden House was in a unique location, though, at the southernmost point of the island. Rebecca's window overlooked Battery

Park, beyond which were the waters of New York Harbor. In the daytime, tugboats, ferries, and barges rent the air with their horns, whistles, and bells; but, at night, harbor traffic was much lighter and Rebecca found the occasional nautical tones more soothing than jarring.

Nestling deeper into her pillow, Rebecca pulled the soft cotton bedsheet up to her chin and tried to drift back to sleep. She had only an hour or so before she would have to get up and begin organizing another busy day at Colden House, and she wanted to spend that precious hour asleep. As balmy summer air wafted in through the half-open window, Rebecca tuned her ears to the distant sounds of the harbor. She tried to imagine herself at a seaside far away from New York. A mental picture of a South Sea lagoon soon formed in her mind, and Rebecca hoped it would lead to a dream about such a distant, idyllic place. She began to drift into slumber, clinging to the image of blue waters and palm trees and coconuts.

Rebecca had barely gotten her toes into white tropical sand when she was rudely brought back to consciousness and to New York City in the sweltering summer of 1894. This time, the hammering on the front door continued until Rebecca was fully awake and could identify the sound.

"No, not now," she groaned as she slid out of bed and into her slippers. It wasn't unusual for desperate young women to show up at Colden House in the middle of the night—providing a refuge for them was why the home had been established in the first place and why Rebecca had devoted herself to running the shelter. But that didn't mean she enjoyed having to get out of her comfortable bed, especially when she knew there was no chance of getting back to sleep.

As the pounding continued, Rebecca quickly slipped into her robe. She tied the belt as she padded down the stairs. Through the door, she heard a muffled male voice blurt, "Somebody's coming. Let's go!" Rebecca took the remaining steps even faster, so fast that she almost lost her balance as she got to the foyer and reached out to pull the door open.

The first thing she noticed was a pair of well-dressed young men pushing their way into a large carriage stopped at the curb. The lighting was dim—provided by a sputtering street lamp and a gray sky that signaled dawn would soon be coming—but several things were clear to her. The enameled black brougham, with glittering lamps and fixtures, was an especially fine one, harnessed to a pair of equally fine chestnut horses. It was a probably a private carriage—there was no lettering on the door, no number on the side of the lamp, and it was more expensive than vehicles typically available for public hire. Judging by the giddy laughter and speech from within the coach, Rebecca guessed there were four or five passengers, both male and female, and all of them fairly young—perhaps college students. One of them cried, "Drive! Drive!" and the liveried driver in front snapped his whip, causing the horses to lurch forward.

It was only a few moments from the time she opened the door until the carriage was rattling away along State Street. Rebecca noticed from the reflections on the cobblestones that the street was wet; it must have rained during the night. She then directed her attention to the woman who was half sitting, half reclining on the high stoop of Colden House. The woman emitted a low, unintelligible moan.

Rebecca leaned down to see if she was injured, then jerked back when she got a whiff of her clothes. It was a noxious combination of brandy, smoke, and vomit—mostly the latter. More cautiously, Rebecca looked her over, aided by the softly glowing electric light next to the front door.

The girl, who probably wasn't yet twenty years old, wore no hat or coat or even a shawl. Her stringy brown hair showed signs of having been painstakingly set in curls, but most of them had become limp and several locks were clinging to her damp, fleshy face. The girl's eyes were barely open, her breathing was wheezy, and drool trickled from a corner of her thick lips. Rebecca could see no signs of physical injury, though—no blood or bruises. She glanced over the young woman's clothing; her elegant shirtwaist and flowing skirt were of the latest fashion but tailored too tight for her rather stout body. And they were now ruined—probably no laundry could clean the heavy stains from the girl's sickness.

Rebecca put her hand on the girl's shoulder to pull her head upright. "What's your name?" she asked her.

The mumbled response was incoherent, something about "pigeons," "big feet," and "Newport."

"Are you sick? What's the matter?"

Rebecca thought the girl replied, "Nothing" before she heaved again.

Probably nothing more than drunk, thought Rebecca. "Let's get you up," she said, putting her hands under the girl's arms.

The pudgy young woman was like dead weight, though, and made no effort to support herself as Rebecca tried to lift her. After several unsuccessful attempts, Rebecca was almost ready to leave her on the stoop to sleep it off.

Rebecca stepped back, put her hands on her hips, and took a deep breath of fresh air before renewing her efforts. Orange was beginning to tinge the horizon, and Rebecca could hear work beginning on the waterfront. Soon, street traffic would increase and pedestrians would be crowding the sidewalk. She couldn't just leave this girl helpless on the front stoop, so she'd try again, and if she again failed to lift her she'd just have to go inside and get some help.

As she got another grip on the girl, Rebecca heard a metallic clattering behind her. She looked back to see a familiar wagon lurching up the street, the milk cans it carried clanking against each other with each bump in the pavement. The driver, dressed in a clean white uniform, pulled to a stop in front of the house. "Can I be of assistance, Miss Davies?" he called.

"Yes, please, Mr. Culpepper." As he stepped off the milk truck and onto the sidewalk, Rebecca added, "Very kind of you to offer."

He touched the visor of his white cap and a smile briefly brightened his dark features. "My pleasure, ma'am. What's the problem?"

Rebecca explained that she wanted to get this young woman inside the house and upstairs to the infirmary. Culpepper, a strapping man of about thirty, with muscular arms accustomed to lugging five- and ten-gallon milk cans, succeeded in lifting the young woman and bringing her inside. He wasn't particularly delicate about it, handling the woman as if she were a large sack of flour—which she indeed resembled—but under Rebecca's direction, he safely maneuvered her up the stairs and into a small whitewashed room that served as an infirmary.

"Thank you so much," Rebecca said, once the groaning woman had been laid out on a bed.

"No trouble at all, Miss Davies." Culpepper wrinkled his substantial nose and looked down at the girl. "Rather a mess, ain't she?"

"I'm afraid so. I hope you didn't get anything on you."

Culpepper ran a hand over his white shirt, which was still spotless. "No, ma'am." Obviously affected by the stench, he began backing toward the door. "I'll fetch your milk cans now. Put 'em in the kitchen?"

"Yes, thank you." Rebecca was becoming acutely aware of the odor herself. "Oh! What do I owe you?"

"Your bill's all paid up, Miss Davies." Culpepper began his way down the stairs. "Good day, ma'am."

Rebecca wasn't used to hearing that she had no debt. For years it had been a struggle to keep Colden House in operation. Often, Rebecca didn't know if she would be able to buy food for one more day. It was only last year that regular funding was arranged to support the place, and after such a long hand-to-mouth existence Rebecca was still adjusting to the new circumstances.

Following Culpepper down the stairs, she went into the kitchen while he went out to his wagon for the milk. Once in the large kitchen, designed to cook enough for thirty residents, Rebecca first filled the old cast-iron stove with firewood and lit a piece of kindling. As black smoke curled up through the loose grate, she thought perhaps it would now be possible to buy a more modern coal-burning range.

Culpepper came in with a five-gallon can of milk and set it down next to the icebox. "Same order for tomorrow, Miss Davies?"

"Yes, please." To thank him for his help with the young woman upstairs, she added, "I could have coffee ready soon, if you'd care for a cup."

He smiled his appreciation. "Thank you, but I better get on with my deliveries, ma'am." Before he left the room, Culpepper added, "I hope the girl is going to be all right."

"I'm sure she will," Rebecca murmured, again thinking that excessive drink was probably the girl's only problem. But she'd better check on her, she thought. After seeing that the fire in the stove was burning as it should, she headed back up to the infirmary.

The "infirmary" was almost indistinguishable from a small bedroom—which it once was. It didn't contain any real medical equipment, but a couple of cabinets were stocked with basic supplies—bandages, headache powders, and miscellaneous salves and ointments. There were two narrow iron-rail beds, a ladder-back chair, and a washstand with a large enamel basin. All of the furnishings were painted the same antiseptic white as the walls.

Rebecca pulled the chair next to the bed and looked over the girl, whose mouth was now agape as she snored like an old man, and tried to figure out what had brought her here. She couldn't remember anyone ever arriving at Colden House in the manner that this young woman had.

Rebecca's family had established Colden House more than fifty years ago as a place for female paupers to find safe lodging and warm food. Recently, ever since the financial panic of the previous year had sent the economy plummeting, more and more homeless young women were showing up; almost every night, all thirty beds were taken. In addition to the destitute, there were girls who had been injured in sweatshops, abused by husbands or fathers, or worn down by working in the city's thriving vice industry. Rebecca thought about some of the girls now sleeping upstairs, recalled their tragic stories and limited resources, and grew increasingly resentful of wasting a bed on an obviously affluent girl who was merely drunk. The evidence of that drinking was becoming overwhelming; the only thing that masked the smell of liquor and vomit was the odor of exceptionally vile cigars.

To reduce the stench, Rebecca filled a washbasin with water and sponged off the girl's soiled shirtwaist. The material, she noticed, was Japanese silk; and the summer-weight wool skirt was a similarly expensive cut of cloth. A gold ring—not a wedding band—was on one of the girl's fingers and a pearl necklace was around her throat. Rebecca shook her head in puzzlement, again wondering why she had come to Colden House of all places.

When she sat back down and stared at the girl's slack, pasty white face, it occurred to her that it might not have been her idea to come here at all. The young woman hadn't said a coherent word since she'd arrived on the doorstep—so how could she have directed the carriage driver to bring her here? Perhaps she been out with her friends, drunk too much, and her companions thought it would be a

fine prank to drop her off at the door to Colden
House.

Giving her the benefit of the doubt, Rebecca
felt a little more hospitable to the young woman.
She moved her into a position that appeared more
comfortable and tucked a pillow under her neck.
She then lifted her arms to pull a cover over her.
When she did, Rebecca noticed the woman's hands.
The chubby fingers were soft, as might be expected of someone who did no physical labor, but
under the long nails of her right hand were small
pieces of skin and clots of dried blood. Wherever
this girl had been before her arrival at Colden
House, she'd been involved in something more
than sipping champagne in the Astor ballroom.

CHAPTER 2

"How does this sound?" Keith Hopkins cleared his throat as if he were about to recite the Gettysburg Address, and proceeded to read from the sheet of paper on which he'd been working for the past hour. " 'Clayton Mills Dead at Fifty-five! After a year of declining health and a bleak prognosis, Clayton Mills finally succumbed last week. The tragic death was attributed to starvation—the company was starved for cash and could receive no additional credit from banks. For decades, Clayton Mills produced fine-quality paper goods used throughout the world. The deceased paper mill leaves behind eight hundred employees. Its passing will be mourned by the many Schenectady residents who depended on Clayton for their livelihoods.' "

"That's good!" said Marshall Webb, trying hard to sound like he meant it. "One of your best yet."

Hopkins, an unassuming man of about forty with a penchant for tweed suits, beamed at the compliment. Then he suddenly sneezed and brushed a crumpled handkerchief over his droopy mustache. The straggly red hair cascading over his upper lip matched the sparse strands combed over his scalp. "That's just first paragraph," he said, sniffing. "I'm putting in a history of the mill, too."

Webb smiled but hoped he wouldn't have to hear any more of the piece. Hopkins, one of three writers with whom Webb shared a rather bleak office at *Harper's Weekly*, reported on financial matters for the periodical. A year ago, the country had experienced what was called a financial "panic" that had since evolved into a full-blown depression. After reporting on an unending succession of failed banks, bankrupt businesses, violent strikes, and plunging stocks, Hopkins had become depressed himself. Recently he'd adopted a gallows humor and started reporting on the economic woes in the forms of limericks and obituaries. Hopkins never actually turned these efforts into his editor, writing them primarily to amuse himself. Unfortunately, he'd lately begun sharing them with Webb for no obvious reason other than that Webb's desk was closest to his. The only thing Webb liked about the mock obituaries was that they were better than Hopkins's awful limericks.

Hopkins sneezed again and cleared his throat. He suffered from hay fever and this summer had been a rough one for him. "So what are you working on, Webb?" he asked hoarsely.

The truth was: not much. Webb had freelanced for *Harper's* for several years, contributing occasional articles of little interest. Then he'd begun a series on Tammany Hall, police corruption, and election fraud in the city of New York. As a result of his exposé, the state had begun its own investigations headed by the Lexow Committee. The series also brought Marshall Webb some measure of fame and earned him a regular position at *Harper's*. The only thing it didn't bring him was a new challenge. It seemed there was nothing more for him to report about Tammany Hall that the daily papers weren't already covering. Justice was currently being meted out by the Lexow Committee: crooked politicians were being publicly exposed, criminal charges were being filed, and corrupt police officers were leaving the force. Even the once-invincible head of Tammany, Boss Richard Croker, fled the country for Ireland at the start of the committee's work. Unable to compete with the ability of the dailies to cover so many events, the editors of *Harper's* decided that the weekly's primary role would be to remind the public that it had been *Harper's* that initiated the efforts to clean up city government. Webb didn't want to be part of that, nor did he want to merely report the news. Marshall Webb was interested in bringing about change—something that would improve the lives of ordinary people. His exposure of city corruption appeared likely to accomplish that— at least to some degree—and now he wanted to find a new subject.

Hopkins cleared his throat again, this time to remind Webb that he was waiting for an answer.

"I'm thinking of covering the Pullman strike," Webb finally replied. "Maybe go to Chicago and see what's happening for myself."

Hopkins snorted. "You'd better do it quick, then. Looks like that strike is as dead as Clayton Mills." He then went back to work on his "obituary" of the paper mill.

Unfortunately, to Webb's way of thinking, Hopkins was probably right. The Pullman Company, which manufactured the sleeper cars used by railroads all over the country, had responded to the financial downturn by cutting its work force in half and reducing wages for the remaining employees. But it didn't lower the exorbitant rents workers had to pay to live in the company homes. As a result, Pullman's workforce was reduced to a state of virtual slavery. Employees responded by joining the American Railway Union and going on strike in May. The strike proved to be an effective one, so effective that President Cleveland stepped in by ordering federal troops to break it up. Union leaders like Eugene Debs were placed under arrest, workers were threatened, and as a result Pullman cars were now moving again. It appeared that the remaining holdouts carrying on the strike would soon have to concede defeat.

The office door swung open and Harry M. Hargis stepped inside. The *Harper's* senior editor paused for a moment, puffed on the long cigar clamped between his teeth, and surveyed the room. Hargis's elegant attire—smartly tailored vicuna suit, crimson silk cravat with a diamond stickpin, and stiff wing collar—was in contrast to the room's plain décor. Hargis didn't focus on the furnishings—the beige walls and boxy oak furniture didn't merit any scrutiny. Instead, he was studying each of the four writers, one by one. Since all of them except Webb had made themselves look busy the moment the door handle turned, Hargis seemed satisfied that they were all working with sufficient dedication.

The editor strode over to Webb's desk and smiled for the first time, causing the waxed tips of his dainty mustache to lift. It was a mark of Webb's new status with the publication that Hargis was coming to see him—when he wanted to see any of his other writers, he sent them an imperious summons to come to his own plush office. Webb's series on Tammany Hall had done much to boost *Harper's* prestige, and even more to boost sales, so Hargis made a point of treating him almost as deferentially as he liked to be treated himself.

"I just got this from our artist," Hargis said. "Thought you might like to see it right away." He held out an ink sketch for Webb's inspection.

Webb looked it over. The drawing was a portrait of a fleshy-faced man with a walrus mustache so large, and dark eyes so small and close-set, that it was almost a caricature. He was in the uniform of a New York City police captain. Above the portrait was the heading ONE FOR THE ROGUES' GALLERY and below it was the officer's name, CAPTAIN DAVID J. START.

"Captain Start has just been dismissed from the force," Hargis said. "For 'neglect of duty and accepting money to protect a disorderly house.' This is going on the front page of the next issue."

"Looks good." Webb nodded approvingly. "I just hope he won't be the only one to lose his job."

"He won't," Hargis replied cheerfully. "With the information that the Lexow Committee's uncovering, we can be sure Start won't be the only crooked cop to lose his job—maybe some will even go to jail." He tapped the portrait with a manicured finger. "And every one who falls is going to get a picture like this in *Harper's.*" He quickly added, "And we have you to thank for this."

Webb merely nodded. Happy as he was that his investigations were having an impact, he wasn't satisfied with that success. Hargis was apparently content to remind readers on a weekly basis of the publication's role in the exposé, but Webb wanted to move on. "I'd like to work on something new," he finally said.

"Quite understandable," said Hargis. "How about a summary of the payments Captain Start received from the bawdy house—and include something about his connections to Tammany Hall?"

"I did that months ago." Webb tried to sound appreciative of Hargis's suggestion. As far as the editor knew, Webb was happy with his full-time position. But the truth was that Webb had preferred working as a freelancer, where he could stay at home and secretly write lucrative dime novels under a pseudonym. "I would rather begin working on something other than Tammany."

"Well . . ." Hargis drew on his cigar but it was no longer burning. He took it from his mouth and looked at the dead ashes with some annoyance. He then glanced around at his staff and appeared even more annoyed that no one jumped to offer him a light; of course, they couldn't even see he needed one since they were all hunched over their desks absorbed in their work. Hargis turned back to Webb. "As a matter of fact, I do have something new. I was going to assign it to someone else, but it's a political story so you might be interested." He put the dead cigar back between his teeth and began chewing the end.

Webb actually found politics to be of little interest. Most politicians, he'd found, were power-obsessed men more interested in getting themselves elected than improving people's lives. "What is it?" he asked warily.

"The consolidation campaign." Hargis paused to

peel a shred of tobacco from the tip of his tongue. "Looks like the battle is really going to be heating up."

That could be interesting, thought Webb. The most important ballot issue that New Yorkers would vote on in November was whether the cities of New York and Brooklyn, along with Queens, the Bronx, and Staten Island, would consolidate into one city. "That's a big story," Webb said. "How do you want it covered?"

"Joshua Thompson is giving a speech in Brooklyn tomorrow night—he's really been stirring up opposition over there. We need somebody to be at the meeting—you, if you're interested."

Webb noticed that Keith Hopkins had looked up from his desk, curious to hear the answer. "I am," Webb answered. But he remembered that he and Rebecca were planning to have dinner Friday night. "What time is the speech?"

"Seven-thirty. At Canarsee Hall." Hargis took the cigar from his mouth and rolled it in his fingers. "This could tie in nicely with your Tammany Hall series. Consolidation would weaken Tammany even more, and I want *Harper's* to keep pounding away on them."

With a pang of regret at having to cancel his plans with Rebecca, Webb said, "I'll be there."

Buck Morehouse stood in the shadow of the "el"—the King's County Elevated Railroad—to avoid the late morning sun. It had been a blistering hot summer in Brooklyn and although it wasn't quite noon today's temperature was already approaching ninety degrees. Morehouse could feel sweat dampening the armpits of his shirt and the head-band of his derby was already soaked, permitting rivulets to run down the back of his neck. He noticed a white-clad city sanitation worker sweeping horse manure with a long-handled broom along bustling Fulton Street; he envied the uniform, which was certainly cooler than Morehouse's own somber brown sack suit. But then a detective of the Brooklyn Police Department couldn't very well go around dressed like a garbage man just for the sake of comfort.

Trying to absorb the shade of the el as if it were a cloak he could wear to ward off the sun, Morehouse turned his attention to the main entrance of Namm's Department Store. He could smell the foods proffered by the vendors at City Hall Park; there were carts that sold oysters, others laden with bags of peanuts, and several doing a brisk business selling ice cream and lemonade. Morehouse gave thought to lunch, specifically to the free lunch counter at Grady's Saloon a couple of blocks away on Myrtle Avenue. Cold ham and a couple of nickel beers—which Grady served free to police officers—would really hit the spot about now. But Morehouse decided to remain vigilant. He dug into the small paper bag stuffed inside his coat pocket and drew out a couple of licorice gumdrops; he popped them into his mouth and chewed slowly. They were no substitute for lunch but would tide him over a while longer.

A dozen gumdrops later, Morehouse spotted a short frumpy woman exiting Namm's. As fast as his bulk would allow, he darted across the busy street, successfully evading two streetcars and a delivery wagon. Brooklynites were often called "trolley

dodgers" by their Manhattan neighbors because of
the maze of tracks that crisscrossed the city; it was
a term intended to be derisive, but Morehouse
prided himself on his ability to negotiate the chaotic
streets of Brooklyn with speed and agility.

Huffing from the brief exertion, Morehouse
blocked the path of the woman, who was wearing a
bulky wool overcoat that must be torture in this
heat. A frayed and stained straw bonnet was tied
atop a pile of greasy hair that was almost all white.
She could easily have passed as the old crone in
fairy tales. Without tipping his hat, he said, "Looks
like you've been putting on weight, Annie. Don't
tell me you're in a family way."

"Flatbush Annie," who was booked as "Annie
Tegeler" during her numerous arrests, smiled a
gaping grin that revealed the only two teeth left in
her mouth. "Naw. You know I'm saving myself for
you, Bucky. I just happen to like my beer." She chuckled and stuck out a hand to poke Morehouse in
the stomach. "And look who's talking about gaining weight. Looks like you been suckling at a keg
yourself."

Morehouse laughed and patted his belly. For
someone of his short height he was rather proud
that he'd been able to grow a belly of such prominence. "I confess," he said, "I like my beer, too."
Then he adopted a more serious demeanor. "And
if it wasn't for you, I'd be at Grady's right now. So
tell me, Annie: what's your haul?"

The woman looked as if he'd stabbed her. "Bucky!
How can you ask me such a thing? I just been
shopping."

Morehouse pulled a handkerchief from his
pocket and wiped the back of his neck. "It's too

hot to stand here and play with you, Annie. What's under your coat?"

She smiled again, in a manner that might have been coquettish had she been forty years younger. "You'll have to take me dancing if you want to find out."

"Well, I can take you in to the station house to have you frisked."

Annie appeared unperturbed by the prospect.

Morehouse pointed to a tall patrolman in a summer gray helmet standing at a call box on the corner of Hoyt Street. "Or I can have the officer there take you to the Raymond Street Jail. They do a *thorough* search there."

She blanched at the mention of the notorious jail. "Can't you take a little kidding, Bucky?" she whined in a wounded tone. "You know I was just playing with you."

"I know, Annie. I guess I've been out here in the heat a little too long." Morehouse offered her a gumdrop, which she declined. "So what ya get out of Namm's?"

"Nothing much. A few gloves."

"How many?"

"Three or four pair." When Annie noticed Morehouse glancing skeptically at the odd bulges in her jacket's midsection she corrected herself. "Come to think of it, maybe more like a dozen pair. Just trying to make a living, Bucky."

Morehouse nodded. "We all got to do that. I'll tell you what, Annie: you can keep your gloves."

The old woman brightened. "Hey, that's swell of you." She shifted the bunch of gloves under her coat. "Say, you got a lady you might want to give a pair? They're real nice—genuine kid gloves."

Morehouse briefly considered the offer. He wasn't averse to accepting an occasional gift, and as far as he was concerned Namm's clerks were the ones responsible for protecting their goods. But he had no need for a pair of gloves. "No," he answered. "You keep 'em all—because you're gonna have to make this haul your last. You won't be 'shopping' in my precinct for a long time. Not here, not at Loesser's, not anywhere in downtown Brooklyn."

"But—"

"Go over the bridge. Do your 'shopping' on the Ladies' Mile for a while."

"That's five cents to go across the bridge!" Annie squawked. "You think I'm rich?"

"Got no choice, Annie." Morehouse shook his head. "If you want to stay in business, you got to go over to New York. My captain's really been after me lately—there's somebody breaking into these stores, taking gold and diamonds, and *I* gotta put a stop to it."

"I don't steal no gold and diamonds!"

"I know that, Annie. But you pass the message on to everybody you know: until the jewel robberies stop, *everybody's* business is gonna be hurting."

Annie shook her head sadly. "I always thought you was a fair man, Buck Morehouse—ask anybody and they'll tell you I said you was a good man for a copper. But this just ain't right. On account of somebody else stealing jewels, I can't steal a trifle here and there to keep a roof over my head and a bite of food on my plate?" She slowly shuffled away, a protective hand over the gloves bulging under her coat. "It just ain't right," she muttered.

Morehouse briefly watched her leave. He knew

she wasn't responsible for the jewel robberies, and he didn't begrudge her a chance to make a living. But he had no leads in the jewel heists, and had to stir things up a little. He knew that Annie would pass his message on to every shoplifter, pickpocket, and fence in Brooklyn—not as a favor to him, but because she'd want to complain to everyone she knew about the injustice that had been done to her.

After dabbing his neck once more, he shoved the handkerchief back into his pocket and headed off toward Grady's for the beer he'd been craving. He'd walked these Brooklyn streets for many years, most of them as a street cop. Unlike his counterparts over in Manhattan, who got their positions on the NYPD by making the requisite payments to Tammany Hall, Buck Morehouse had spent more than twenty years working his way up from patrolman to detective. He intended to keep his position, no matter how hard he would have to work. It might be more difficult now, with the idiotic plan to merge Greater New York into a single city— Morehouse knew that some in the Brooklyn Police Department were already making contact with New York officials to ensure their positions in a reorganized police force. Morehouse, however, had neither political connections nor the money to buy them. He would have to keep his job by clearing every case that was put on his desk—no matter what methods he might have to employ.

Rebecca Davies wiped a glob of strawberry jam from her palm with a dish towel, then stepped back to look over the kitchen. Except for the stacks of dishes that needed washing, the post-breakfast cleanup was completed. But this provided no satisfaction; it merely signaled that it was now time to make preparations for lunch. Cooking at Colden House was almost a round-the-clock production. With about thirty residents to feed, and antiquated equipment in the kitchen, as soon as everything had been cleared from one meal it was time to begin preparation of the next. She looked at the old cast-iron cooking stove, which was the first thing she wanted to replace; keeping its furnace filled with firewood, and keeping that wood burning with an even heat, was a daily battle. Rebecca considered that it might finally be time to purchase a new coal-burning unit.

"Miss Davies!" The thin voice came from the hallway, but sounded as if it originated upstairs.

Rebecca tossed the dish towel on the table and quickly strode to the hallway. She'd been hoping to have a cup of tea before getting on to the next chore, but it sounded as if that would have to wait. She was just out of the kitchen when the voice called her name again, more urgently.

When she got into the hallway, she saw Stephanie Quilty standing on the landing, leaning over to call through the railings of the banister. "Hurry, Miss Davies! There's a girl making an awful fuss up here." Stephanie was such a wisp of a girl she could almost be mistaken for one of railings; her tiny figure, cloaked in a faded gingham dress of a girlish style, made her appear about twelve years old, five years younger than her true age.

Rebecca hurried up the stairs, wishing that her

assistant, Miss Hummel, were here to help manage
things. Unfortunately, Miss Hummel was taking a
much-deserved vacation to visit her sister in Boston,
leaving Rebecca to handle everything at Colden
House.

When Rebecca reached the landing, Stephanie
said in a hushed voice, "I'm sorry to trouble you,
Miss Davies. But there's a girl I never seen before
making a lot of noise about needing the toilet. I
told her where it was, but she just started yelling."
Stephanie's sad eyes were wide and fearful, and
her careworn face was that of a woman in middle
age. The young woman had been at Colden House
for more than a month, but it never failed to surprise Rebecca that Stephanie Quilty could look so
young from a distance and so old up close.

"It's no trouble," Rebecca replied. "Where is she
now?"

Before the frightened young woman could answer, there was a banging sound and a muffled
curse. Rebecca continued up to the second-floor
hallway, where the woman who'd been dumped on
the doorstep was lurching unsteadily, knocking on
each door she came to and demanding to be let
in. There were no answers, and no other women in
the hall, since most of the residents were either
out looking for work or in classes.

Rebecca called to her, "What do you need?"

The pudgy young woman turned around and
put one hand against the wall to keep her balance.
"I need a lavatory."

"It's right here." Rebecca walked over to her and
gestured to a door a few feet away.

"I looked in there," the woman said, her nose

crinkling. "It's hardly suitable for a lady. What kind of girls you have staying in this awful place?" Her speech was slurred and her eyes didn't appear to focus.

Rebecca tried to contain her anger. This young woman had arrived uninvited, drunk, and soiled with vomit—and now she was being insulting. "If our accommodations are unsuitable," she said sarcastically, "feel free to go elsewhere, Miss—"

"I will. Soon as I—" She clutched her stomach and groaned, then made a dash for the toilet. Apparently, the need was now great enough that the décor was no longer of concern.

Stephanie Quilty cautiously came into the hall-way and joined Rebecca. "Is the lady all right?" she asked.

"Probably just the effects of overindulgence," answered Rebecca. "And so far she doesn't seem to be much of a 'lady.' "

"I think she's in some pain," said Stephanie with concern in her voice. She was more sympathetic to the demanding woman than Rebecca was.

Rebecca decided to give the woman another chance. Perhaps her manner was indeed a result of illness. When she stepped out of the lavatory, Rebecca asked her, "Are you feeling better?"

"Washbasin's empty," was the reply. "I need a wash-basin—with rose water, if you have it." She then looked around with disdain, as if doubtful that such a humble place would be so supplied.

The second chance was now over, Rebecca decided. "What's your name?" she demanded.

"Miss Lucy Robatin. And you're Miss Davies, I presume?"

"I am. And I'll have you know, Miss Robatin, that Colden House is not a hotel. Why did you come here?"

"Your sister invited me. She told me I was welcome at any time. Alice Updegraff *is* your sister, is she not?"

Rebecca was astonished by the answer and it was a moment before she replied. "Yes, Alice is my sister. She told you to come here? Why would she do that?" Alice had married into one of the oldest and wealthiest families in New York, and had recently arranged for her husband to provide badly needed financial support for Colden House. But she had never sent anyone to the home before.

"My parents object to some of my, uh, social activities," said Robatin. "They left instructions with the servants that I am not to be allowed into the house after midnight, nor will the coachmen pick me up. Alice is a friend of my mother's and she told me if I should ever find myself in no condition to go home that I should just come here for the night." She smiled slightly. "Last night I must have had a little too much fun. My friends knew to bring me here."

"Why not go to a hotel?"

"My father notified all the decent hotels that he would not pay any bills that I should incur." She snorted. "My parents would think it a scandal if I were to stay in a hotel room anyway—they might suspect that I wasn't alone."

Rebecca was almost incapable of replying. She had never heard such an explanation before. And she was eager to speak with her sister to find out why she was offering Colden House as a place for drunk rich girls to avoid their parents.

"Now," said Robatin, "if you would be so kind as to bring me that washbasin, I'll clean up and telephone home for a carriage to pick me up." She smiled slyly. "I'll tell them I was doing volunteer work here, and they'll be proud that I was doing something charitable."

Rebecca had no trouble replying now. "We have no servants here, Miss Robatin. The girls who come to Colden House work hard to take care of themselves. I *will*, however, take you to the telephone because I would like you out of here as soon as possible."

"Well, that's rather ill mannered of you," said Robatin.

Stephanie Quilty quietly appeared, with a filled washbasin in hand and a towel draped over her arm. Rebecca hadn't even noticed that the girl had left to get it. She was mildly annoyed that Stephanie was doing the other girl's bidding, but she realized that it would at least get her out sooner.

Before Robatin dipped her hands in the water, Rebecca remembered what she'd seen last night. "Were you in some kind of a fight, last night?" she asked.

Robatin paused. "A *fight?*"

"There's blood under your nails," said Rebecca. "And skin. I noticed it when I put you to bed. I thought perhaps you'd been in a struggle."

Robatin stared at her fingertips blankly, as if she didn't recall a thing about how they'd gotten that way. Finally she said, "It doesn't matter. I need a manicure anyway." But she scrubbed her fingers for some time, until it appeared she was trying to erase a memory more than anything tangible.

CHAPTER 3

As it turned out, Marshall Webb hadn't had to break his dinner date with Rebecca. She had telephoned him first and asked to postpone the date, explaining that her assistant wouldn't be returning to Colden House until Saturday and she simply couldn't leave the place unattended. Marshall tried to sound sorry but understanding, and didn't mention that he would have had to change their plans anyway.

So on Friday night, half an hour before Joshua Thompson's scheduled speech, Webb arrived at Canarsee Hall on Joralemon Street, a stone's throw west of City Hall Park in downtown Brooklyn. Canarsee Hall, named for the tribe of Indians that once occupied the area and retaining the original spelling, was a boxy edifice of redbrick and white colonnades that could have passed for a government office or a bank. Webb barely gave the building a glance as he approached, however, because it was the crowd in front that attracted his attention.

Like most residents of Manhattan, Webb hadn't considered the issue of consolidation to be an emotional one; it was more a matter of whether combining into a Greater New York would improve government functions and municipal services. But here in Brooklyn, he could see, the issue was stirring strong feelings.

Leafleteers advocating both sides of the issue were aggressively pushing their literature on passersby while shouting, "Consolidation now!" or, "Keep Brooklyn independent!" Webb received handbills and urgent spiels from both the Brooklyn Consolidation League and the League for Brooklyn Independence. Newsboys also scurried about, offering their own papers, mostly the evening edition of the *Brooklyn Daily Eagle.*

Grouped on the edge of the political crowd were street toughs, probably from the nearby waterfront. Brooklyn had no shortage of such men; they could rival those of the Bowery or the Tenderloin when it came to fisticuffs. These were the types who are attracted to any large gathering—especially gatherings that might turn confrontational. And physical confrontation seemed imminent, Webb noticed. The summer heat had barely abated during the evening hours, and the steamy temperature had the already contentious crowd on edge.

Hansom cabs, coaches, and streetcars deposited their passengers at the curb in front of the hall where they were immediately accosted by partisans of the issue who proceeded to argue their cases loudly and emphatically. One elderly man with a bamboo cane was helped out of an elegant brougham by his coachman; the moment he stepped onto the sidewalk, pro- and anticonsolidation campaigners shoved their way in front of him, pushing handbills in front of his face. Neither of the campaigners was particularly large, but they both had the single-minded fervor of those religious zealots who preached the impending end of the world from street corner soapboxes. The two men jostled each other for position, then began grabbing at each other's leaflets, and soon punches were thrown. In the scuffle, the old man with the cane was knocked over and had to be pulled to his feet by his driver.

Helmeted police officers weren't helping matters much with their method of crowd control. They barked orders to "Keep it movin'!" and "Clear the sidewalk!" and randomly poked their nightsticks into the ribs of those who didn't move fast enough. Only those men who were well dressed—and therefore possibly of some importance—escaped the prods of the nightsticks.

Marshall Webb always dressed impeccably, and so he was able to linger outside the hall for a while unscathed, jotting down notes for his article. As more people arrived to hear Joshua Thompson's speech, the pro-consolidation forces dwindled to a small minority, and were openly shoved about and ridiculed by the overwhelming numbers who advocated independence. The sidewalk was soon covered by Brooklyn Consolidation League handbills that had been dropped by fleeing BCL leafleteers or thrown to the ground by their opponents.

As Webb began walking up the steps to the entrance of the hall, he noted that this was Friday, July 27. There were still more than three months to go before voters would have their say at the polls.

If tonight was any indication, the campaign was going to generate enough heat to extend summer all the way into November.

The atmosphere was somewhat cooler, and considerably calmer, inside Canarsee Hall. The building's tall side windows were open and ceiling fans circulated air that was as fresh as could be found on a summer night in Brooklyn. Webb estimated that three or four hundred people, almost all of them adult males, sat in hard-backed wood benches that had probably once served as church pews. There were no confrontations; apparently this audience was strictly a pro-independence crowd that had come to hear the city of Brooklyn's leading voice against merging with New York City.

Ten minutes after the scheduled start, a rotund man who was perspiring heavily stepped to the podium. He tugged nervously at his crooked bow tie and introduced himself as Stephen Brandt, one of the editors of the *Brooklyn Daily Eagle*. Brandt stammered something about the *Eagle*'s unswerving dedication to preserving the city's independent status, then began to deliver a rather uninspired account of Brooklyn's historical importance to the nation.

While Brandt droned on, Webb checked some of the notes he'd made earlier in the day on the consolidation issue. The primary impetus for the move to merge into a Greater New York was the need to share resources. Manhattan's leaders—both municipal and business—wanted access to Brooklyn's waterfront; shipping was vital to commerce, and Brooklyn had the shipping docks that Manhattan lacked. Brooklyn, in turn, needed water; nearly a million people now lived in the city of Brooklyn and suffered from a woefully inadequate water supply, which could be remedied by access to the New Croton Aqueduct in Manhattan. So the deal seemed simple: the cities would merge, providing Brooklyn with plentiful fresh water and Manhattan commercial interests with access to the waterfront.

Webb thought a merger would also remedy some other problems, such as transportation. This evening, Webb had been one of the quarter of a million people who crossed the Brooklyn Bridge every day—and just like the rest of them, he suffered through the slow, chaotic procedure involved in getting across. Streetcars from the Manhattan side would cross the East River with a load of passengers, let them off in Brooklyn, then return empty to pick up the next carload. Brooklyn streetcars traversed the bridge similarly, bringing their passengers over to Manhattan, and also returning empty. Currently, neither Brooklyn nor New York would permit the other city's cars to pick up passengers on its side of the East River. Simply allowing the railway companies to carry passengers in both directions would cut the congestion in half, and that alone should be sufficient reason for those who traveled the bridge daily to vote in favor of consolidation.

Webb was checking some other notes he'd made about the reasons for opposing consolidation when he noticed that Brandt's remarks were coming to a conclusion. After urging the crowd to support the newspaper that supported the city of Brooklyn—and mentioning that the *Daily Eagle* was still only two cents—Brandt said, "Now, it is my distinct privilege and honor to introduce the man you have all come to hear: one of Brooklyn's leading citizens, a man who has stepped forward to lead the fight for Brooklyn independence . . . Mr. Joshua Thompson."

At the mention of Thompson's name, half of the audience stood and applauded. They continued to cheer as Thompson rose from a seat at the end of the front row and took Brandt's place at the podium.

Webb remained seated and craned his neck to see past the men standing in front of him. Thompson, a tall lean man in his late sixties, looked like a Presbyterian minister. He was attired in a severe black suit and around his high stiff collar was a silver-gray necktie that nearly matched his thinning hair and thick walrus mustache. After a prolonged ovation, which Thompson acknowledged with a tight smile and slight nods of his head, the audience sat back down and let him speak.

"My fellow citizens of the *city* of *Brooklyn,*" Thompson began. He then had to pause as thunderous applause greeted his words. This could be a long night, Webb thought, if the audience was going to applaud every time the phrase "city of Brooklyn" was spoken.

Thompson waved a bony hand to quiet the crowd and went on. "I am most gratified by your presence here and by your loyalty to the *city* of *Brooklyn.*" There were more cheers and applause, and this time Thompson made no move to quell it.

"To hell with New York!" yelled a burly man in a patched old sack suit to Webb's right. From behind him came a high-pitched cry of "Let them keep their damned water! Give me *liberty!*" Webb jotted down the words in his notebook.

The noise gradually began to die down. Webb noticed that Thompson didn't appear particularly gratified. Although the mustache that draped his upper lip might have hidden it, Webb didn't think that Thompson had cracked so much as a smile since he first stood in front of the assembly. There was certainly no humor in the man's dark eyes, which were still visible despite the wiry eyebrows that sprouted wildly above them. Thompson was a man on a mission, Webb decided; he was serious about his cause, not merely someone who enjoyed publicity.

When the noise again died to the point where Thompson could go on, he resumed his speech. "Many of you know me," he said in an even voice. "Or at least you know of me. I was born in Brooklyn—in Brooklyn Heights. I've lived here all my life, and I've prospered here—and many of you have prospered along with me. The Thompson Manufacturing Company has provided good jobs to thousands of Brooklynites since I started my business in 1858. And I hope that if there is anything you know about me, it is this: you can trust my word."

After some murmurs of affirmation, Thompson gave a slight nod of his narrow head in acknowledgment and continued. "I want to tell you this: I have nothing to gain personally by opposing this evil consolidation scheme. I have just about lived my threescore and ten, and I am quite comfortable. But I do stand to lose something if consolidation passes—something more important than any material possession." He paused for effect, and his consistently dour expression grew slightly grimmer. "I would lose my identity as a son of the greatest city on earth." His voice dropped to little more than a raspy whisper. "I would lose my *liberty*."

There were cries of "No!" and "Never!" from the audience.

Thompson's voice rose again. "Ask yourselves: who is promoting this evil attempt to take over our beloved city? I'll tell you who. It is the greedy bankers and shady businessmen and Tammany-controlled politicians across the river. They want to take over *our city* because they have fouled their own nest! Just look over the bridge to see what they have wrought: rampant vice everywhere from the Bowery to the Tenderloin, squalid tenements teeming with bums and immigrants, corrupt politicians who take their orders from the bosses of Tammany Hall, a crooked police department that plunders its own citizenry." He drew a long breath. "I ask you: Is that what we want for the city of Brooklyn?"

The loud cries of response were almost identical, either "No!" or "Hell no!" and many of the shouts were punctuated by clenched fists punching the air.

Thompson's long face remained grim, showing how seriously he took the impending referendum. He allowed the cries to die down and a long, expectant silence to fall over the room before continuing.

"*Brooklyn,*" he finally went on, "is the city of churches. *New York* is the city of Tammany Hall.

"*Brooklyn* is the city of homes. *New York* is the city of tenements.

"*Brooklyn* is a city of honest working men. *New York* is a city of criminals and derelicts."

He paused again. "Tell me: in which city do *you* want to live?"

The shouts, the loudest yet, were unanimously for Brooklyn.

As Thompson went on with his speech, presenting Brooklyn as the epitome of all that was good in civilization and New York as a cross between Sodom and Babylon, Webb continued to record his words and note the reactions of the crowd.

Half an hour later, Webb's pencil was largely idle. Thompson had continued to speak, interrupted only by frequent bursts of applause and roars of support, but he was repeating the same points he'd already made several times before. Webb began to fidget in his seat, hoping Thompson would finish soon so that he could try to interview him about his campaign.

When Thompson did conclude, to a prolonged standing ovation, he was followed by Stephen Brandt, who made some complimentary remarks about Thompson and another sales pitch to follow all the latest news in the *Daily Eagle*. The crowd began to file out of the seats toward the door.

Webb kept an eye on Thompson, and briefly debated whether to approach him inside the hall or outside. Since the wealthy manufacturer was surrounded by well-wishers at the moment, Webb decided on the latter course. Webb also moved to the door, then lingered there, waiting for Thompson to reach the exit.

It was at least another fifteen minutes until Thompson worked his way through the supporters who remained and was within a few yards of the door.

"Mr. Thompson!" Webb called.

Thompson nodded in reply as if acknowledging another supporter, and continued to head for the door, placing a silk top hat on his head.

Webb called his name again and followed him outside Canarsee Hall. The sky was dark, except for a half-moon, but the street was well lit, and lanterns glowed from dozens of carriages and hansom cabs parked along the curb. Much of the crowd was on its way home, but some were gathered in small groups or arguing with a couple dozen pro-consolidation men who'd bravely returned. Police officers urged everyone to go home. Keeping step with Thompson, who was walking toward a waiting carriage, Webb said, "My name is Marshall Webb. I'm with *Harper's Weekly*."

Thompson drew up short and turned to face him. "Webb . . . you wrote that series on Tammany Hall."

"Yes, I did."

The glare of a nearby street lamp shone on Thompson's long, craggy face, and Webb thought he saw a few lines on that face twitch upward in approval. "We all owe you a debt of gratitude, Mr. Webb. You exposed the type of evils that we're seeking to keep out of Brooklyn."

"Thank you, sir. As a matter of fact, I'm reporting on your campaign. *Harper's* would like to make the public aware of your efforts to keep the Tammany influence out of 'the city of homes and churches.' I listened to your speech tonight, and I was hoping I could ask you a few questions for my article. My editor believes this is a tremendously important issue." Webb took his notebook from his pocket to indicate that he fully expected Thompson to agree to the interview.

Thompson gave a glance at the waiting brougham, then turned back to Webb. "Of course, I can spare you some time. Our campaign can use—"

Thompson's jaw suddenly shifted. And it kept shifting grotesquely as blood spurted from the side of his face. The skin was rent, exposing bare bone.

Webb was frozen, stunned at what was happening to Joshua Thompson's head. The old man's eyes rolled up and he began to fall.

Webb moved to catch him while his mind registered the fact that Thompson must have been shot. But he hadn't heard gunfire, only the crunch of a lead slug shattering into the man's jaw.

Before Webb could touch Thompson's coat, another shot tore into the old man's head just above the ear and his skull virtually exploded. Webb averted his gaze from the horrific wound. In shock, he let the man drop to the sidewalk. The fall could no longer harm him anyway. There wasn't enough left of Joshua Thompson's graying head for him to still be alive.

For the next few minutes, time lost its continuity. Webb noticed what was happening around him, but his senses didn't seem to function normally— he registered events in no particular order. After Thompson crumpled to the pavement, Webb imagined that he had heard the second shot.

Still numb, Webb turned to look around. Both bullets had struck Thompson on the side of his head facing the street, so Webb first glanced in that direction. He saw no one holding a gun, but he didn't expect to—if the shot had been from nearby, it would have been more audible.

Webb then looked at the nearby carriages and hansom cabs snarling traffic on Joralemon Street; most were still parked and double parked, while a few slowly ground their wheels over the uneven cobblestones. Angry drivers yelled and cursed about being blocked as they tried to get their passengers home; in their frustration they cracked their whips at horses who had no space to move, and some of the horses snorted in pain and protest. When a bit of space did appear between vehicles, often as not a pedestrian heading home would dart into it since the sidewalk was also crammed with groups of men arguing the consolidation issue. Street noise was something a New Yorker became accustomed to, and it hadn't dawned on Webb until this moment that there simply might have been so much of it that the gunshot couldn't be heard above the traffic and the crowd.

Webb glanced across the street to the Lantigua Hotel, a four-story redbrick structure with striped awnings over its windows. There were lights in fewer than half of those windows, and again Webb noticed nothing out of the ordinary.

An object suddenly cracked into Webb's ribs, and he grabbed his side while reprimanding himself for being so stupid as to continue standing at the spot where a gunman had been firing. He pulled his hand away from his side and glanced down at his open palm—no blood.

"Get the hell out of the way!" As a patrolman shoved Webb aside, he realized that the blow had been from the officer's nightstick.

"Thompson's shot!" cried the patrolman.

The news was repeated and transmitted through the crowd. Along with it were more cries—gasps of disbelief, accusations against the Brooklyn Consolidation League, and vows of revenge.

Two more police officers, including a burly sergeant with the face of a bulldog, soon stood over Thompson's body. "Old bastard's sure dead," pronounced the sergeant. To one of the officers, he commanded, "Lowther, go get the captain—and tell him to come fast!"

Onlookers were now circling the body. With dusk falling, and in the yellow glow of the streetlights, the blood that soiled Thompson's clothes and pooled on the sidewalk appeared brown rather than red. It didn't look quite as harsh, Webb thought, more like a sepia photograph.

"Get back!" the sergeant again commanded, this time as a general order to all the men and curious boys now crowding around for a look at the body. "I said everybody back, damn it!" The warning had no effect and he barked to another patrolman to call the precinct for reinforcements.

Those officers near the body fell to work with their nightsticks, ordering the onlookers to leave the area and driving home the point with jabs and blows of hard walnut.

Webb remained where he stood, successfully dodging the occasional nightstick jabs aimed in his direction. In the back of his mind, the journalist in him was determined to record and report what was happening.

The police finally had some success with the crowd around Thompson's body, but they soon had other problems. Thompson supporters turned their attention to the pro-consolidation men in the crowd and began to shove and punch them to retaliate for Thompson's death. The outnumbered consolidation men had little chance; the best they could do was try to ward off the blows. Webb saw one driver hop from the seat of his cab with an axe handle—a frequent tool for settling traffic disputes in New York—and used it on the head of one poor man who was so hemmed in by the angry crowd that he could not even lift his arm to protect himself.

Troy Soos

Extra police officers were soon on the scene, however, and they began breaking up the most violent groups.

The burly sergeant, maintaining his position near Thompson's body, screamed, "Clear the streets! Get everyone the hell out of here!"

Some patrolmen stepped into the street and ordered cabbies and coachmen to drive away. Others remained on the sidewalk outside Canarsee Hall, breaking up recurring fights and telling everyone to go home. Still more positioned themselves across the street and at the ends of the block to keep curious residents who'd come out of their homes and businesses from entering the area.

Order was slow to be restored, and the frustrated sergeant commanded his officers to take anyone who didn't leave the scene to jail. Departing carriages had left enough space for a couple of paddy wagons to park near the curb, and patrolmen began to load them with brawlers who refused to disperse.

The sergeant then noticed Webb still standing nearby. "What the hell are you doin' here? You want to be the first one to get locked up?"

"I'm Marshall Webb, a writer with *Harper's,*" he explained. "I'm writing about Thompson."

"That a fact?" The sergeant rapped the end of his nightstick against the badge on his chest. "*I'm* Trey Patterson, a sergeant with the Brooklyn Police Department. And if you don't get yer ass out of here, you're gonna be doin' yer writing in a jail cell." He then poked Webb in the chest.

Although it was a hard enough jab to move most men, Webb didn't budge. "I'm reporting—"

Patterson's next blow was a sharp rap to Webb's knee. Webb couldn't help but stumble as he tried to keep his balance. With a satisfied smirk on his pug face, Patterson ordered a patrolman, "Put this bastard in the wagon."

Buck Morehouse had only intended to rest his eyes for a few moments, but washing down four sausages with an equal number of beers for dinner had made him drowsier than he expected. So the sharp rap at his apartment door had to penetrate a sound sleep to wake him.

"Yeah, yeah! Comin'," he said as he shook the sleep from his head. It was dark in his apartment; night had fallen since he'd sat down to rest and he'd neglected to leave a light on. But he knew the tiny apartment well, and reached out to switch on an electric lamp. With another shake of his head, Morehouse hoisted his short round body out of the overstuffed chair in which he'd napped and walked the few steps to the door. His head was still a bit foggy, and he thought he should probably have a beer to clear it.

Just as another rap struck the door, Morehouse pulled it open to see George Rayser, who'd been on the force as long as Morehouse but had never risen above the rank of patrolman. Rayser's uniform was dirty, as usual, and the brass buttons hadn't been polished in years. "What the hell you want, George?" Morehouse demanded. "I was in the middle of something important."

"Ain't what *I* want, Buck—"

"Detective," corrected Morehouse.

Rayser appeared not to notice. "It's what the captain wants—and he wants you." Rayser cast a baleful glance around the shabby apartment and snorted with disdain. "Sure hope *I* make detective someday—then maybe I can afford a mansion like this," he said sarcastically.

"Sure, you'd make a great detective, George. You can't even find your pecker when you go to piss."

His old friend thought for a moment, but could come up with nothing better to reply than "Yes, I can."

"Say, I got beer in the icebox," said Morehouse. "We got time?"

Rayser licked his thick lips, obviously tempted. "Nah, the captain wants you right away. Been trouble at Canarsee Hall."

"What kind of trouble?"

"Joshua Thompson's been killed."

"Damn!" Morehouse grabbed his derby from where it hung on an unused light sconce. "Why the hell didn't you tell me?"

Rayser shrugged. "Don't see no reason to hurry. Thompson ain't gonna get any deader."

Morehouse rolled his eyes, thinking to himself that it was that kind of logic that kept Rayser a beat cop. He pushed past the bulky patrolman and led the way down the stairs to Myrtle Avenue. His second-floor apartment was over a bakery and the smell of baked bread hung in the stairway. It triggered a craving in his belly, and he hoped he wouldn't be tied up with the captain for long.

When they reached the sidewalk, both of them puffing from descending an entire flight of stairs, Rayser said, "Be faster to walk. The streets around the hall been closed to traffic."

"Damn!" It was a good eight blocks to Canarsee Hall from Morehouse's home, and he didn't care for exercise. He tugged up his drooping pants a notch. "Well, let's go then."

They didn't make good time, and by the time they reached Captain Oscar Sturup standing on the steps outside the hall, the senior officer was fuming. Sturup gave Morehouse a withering look. "Where the hell have you been?"

"I was—" Morehouse briefly considered telling him the truth, that he'd been home resting because he was going out late at night to meet with a couple of fences about the jewel thefts. "We . . ." He was about to say that despite hurrying, they were held up by the crowds of curious Brooklynites blockaded by a small army of police officers. When he glanced at Rayser, he saw that the patrolman had discreetly vanished, leaving Morehouse to accept the captain's wrath alone. "Sorry, sir," he finally said.

Sturup stood tall and straight; even his tight lips and trimmed beard appeared rigid. "We have a murder," he said. "Joshua Thompson has been shot and killed." In answer to Morehouse's glance at the pool of blood on the pavement, the captain added, "Already had the body taken away."

"Do you have the killer?"

Sturup scowled. "If we did, I wouldn't have sent for *you*. That's going to be your responsibility. You are in charge of the investigation."

Morehouse was stunned. The murder of such a prominent man should be investigated by a more senior officer. "But I—"

Sturup cut him off. "And solve it quickly. The consequences of failing to catch Thompson's killer could be terrible."

Morehouse wasn't sure if the captain meant

they would be bad for him or for the department or for the city. Then he understood: he was being assigned to the case because no one higher up was going to risk the political consequences of failure. "Yes, sir," he said with no enthusiasm or confidence.

"Very good." Sturup nodded sharply. "Get started then."

Morehouse looked around. "Were there witnesses?"

"Must have been," the captain answered. "There were a couple hundred men out here when he was shot."

"Where are they?"

"Some went home, some were taken to jail." Sturup explained, "We could have had a riot here. The most pressing matter was to clear the street and establish order." He conceded, "It might make your investigation a bit more difficult, but I'm confident that you're up to the task."

No witnesses, no suspects, the body taken away. Hoping that there might be something left to go on, Morehouse asked—almost pleaded—"Was the murder weapon found?"

"Finding it is part of your investigation, I should think," said Sturup. His final words were, "You're in charge. Do whatever you need to do to solve this crime."

"Yes, sir." Morehouse sighed. At the moment, he couldn't even think of what his first step should be.

CHAPTER 4

Rebecca Davies was discovering that, as she got older, she had a greater appreciation for traditions and continuity. Not in every respect, of course—there were many things in society that she believed needed to be changed—but there were some customs that she was beginning to find comforting.

As she sat in the elegant dining room of her parents' Fifth Avenue mansion, Rebecca found herself enjoying the simple fact that it was so unchanged. The old brownstone had been in the Davies family for years, and served almost like a fortress, insulating the wealthy clan from the outside world. Rebecca had been one of the few Davieses to shed that insulation when she'd moved into Colden House and assumed responsibility for running the shelter. Her primary contact with her family since then was Sunday dinner, which she was expected to attend if the family was going to continue its financial support of Colden House. Rebecca used to find the dinners an unwelcome interruption from important work at the shelter, but now they were starting to seem a welcome respite from the harsh reality that she encountered throughout the week.

Rebecca looked around the table. As always, the men wore formal dress suits and the ladies their finest gowns. And, as always, the servants made sure that the room itself was similarly well appointed—the mahogany table and carved chairs were polished to a high gloss, the silverware had a mirror finish, and the china sparkled almost as brightly as the crystal chandelier that hung from the ceiling.

Aunt Esther, a birdlike woman whose silver hair had been set in the same style for several decades, asked Rebecca from across the table, "Where is your young Mr. Webb today?" To Aunt Esther, everyone was "young."

"He was arrested Friday night," Rebecca answered brightly. As much as she was beginning to find the traditions of the family dinner table comforting, she still enjoyed taking an occasional jab at the stuffiness of the proceedings.

Her announcement caused only a brief pause in the dinner conversation, however. For one thing, the family members were much too well bred to display any kind of emotion. For another, they all knew that it wasn't the first time Marshall Webb had been in jail.

"Well, give him our regards, dear," said Aunt Esther before turning to Rebecca's mother to compliment her on the squab.

"Thank you, I shall." Rebecca thought to herself that she was fibbing a little by failing to mention that Marshall had only spent one night in the Brooklyn jail. He could have come to dinner today, but was quick to latch on to any excuse to avoid these Davies family occasions.

The conversations continued on the same topics that were discussed every Sunday. The men spoke about the latest news from the Union and Knickerbocker Clubs. The women talked about who wore what at the last society ball and what they would wear at the next one. Rebecca's aunts seemed to have internal clocks that ensured that they would go no more than ten minutes without dropping the name "Astor" or "Vanderbilt" into any conversation.

Rebecca's father rang a silver bell and two liveried servants promptly appeared at his side. "More claret," he ordered, and the servants quickly moved to comply with his request.

Rebecca looked at her father for a moment. The only change in him over the past few years was that his cottony hair was making a slow retreat from his forehead. Retired from active business, he simply spent his time enjoying good wine and games of chess that he won only when opponents graciously allowed him to do so.

She then looked at her brother-in-law, Jacob Updegraff, a Wall Street banker from a family even wealthier and more established than the Davieses. Updegraff, who had a strong brow, a thick neck, and a long sharp nose, *had* changed in the last year. Rebecca had found him to be an insufferably arrogant man, whose one redeeming quality was that he was loved by her sister Alice. Last year, beset with enormous losses in the failing economy, Updegraff proved incapable of dealing with the pressure; he'd become so angry and hostile that

Alice, fearing for her safety, left him and stayed with Rebecca in Colden House. Eventually, after he humbled himself and pleaded for her to return, Alice did go back to him. Ever since then, Jacob Updegraff was a changed man, slightly less arrogant and much kinder to his wife.

Alice, seated next to her husband, was changed, too. Her appearance, petite and pretty, was the same. And, as always, she was clothed in the finest fashion, today a peach-colored silk gown with delicate lace on the cuffs and collar. But there was a subtle difference in her demeanor; a shy girl, Alice had always hidden her own thoughts behind a veil of good manners and polite conversation. Now she had an air of confidence about her that Rebecca enjoyed seeing.

Rebecca hoped to speak with her sister today, but the Davies home was not conducive to important discussions. Servants were ordered about, polite inquiries were made as to health, and society gossip was freely bantered about. But no one ever really spoke to each other.

The dessert course, which consisted of an extraordinarily light chocolate soufflé with a hazelnut sauce, was almost over. According to family ritual, the ladies would then retire to the music room and the men to the library for cognac and cigars. Rebecca decided she would try to speak with Alice on the way to the music room, before they all settled inside for more predictable chitchat about balls and fashion and which families were considered acceptable society and which had slipped a rung or two on the social ladder.

Once Rebecca's father rang the bell for the servants to clear the table, the family rose from their

seats and slowly headed for either the library or
the music room, depending on their gender. Alice
made a detour for the restroom. Rebecca walked
after her and waited outside.

When Alice emerged, every blond hair perfectly
in place and the shine gone from her dainty nose,
she greeted Rebecca with an easy smile.

"Alice," Rebecca said. "There's something I need
to ask you." She then moved to the side of the hallway, indicating that she didn't want to ask it in front
of the rest of the family.

"Of course, Rebecca." Alice stepped closer to
her, so they could speak softly. "Anything."

Rebecca could smell the delicate scent of expensive French perfume. "There was a young lady
who came to Colden House a couple of nights ago.
She gave her name as Lucy Robatin. And . . ." Rebecca hesitated. "And she said that *you* told her
she could come to Colden House."

"Oh yes. Quite a nice girl." Alice frowned slightly.
"How is she?"

From her encounter with Miss Robatin, Rebecca
didn't think she could ever be described as "quite
a nice girl." "I assume she's fine now," she answered.
"But when she arrived at Colden House she was
thoroughly drunk. She'd even thrown up all over
herself."

"Well, thank you for taking care of her," Alice
said. "I'm sure her family will be most appreciative.
The Robatins are old friends of Mr. Updegraff—
quite prominent, you know."

Rebecca was hesitant to reprimand her sister.
When Alice returned to her husband last year, she
gave as one of her conditions that he provide on-
going support to help keep Colden House in op-

eration. And since her stay at the house, Alice came by once a week to help in running the place. "But, Alice," Rebecca said. "Why send her to *Colden House?* Miss Robatin could have gone home, or to a hotel."

"Oh no," Alice said. "Her father has warned her that the next time she came home in such a state she would be turned away from the door."

"So she's done this before?"

"Yes. I believe her friends have been a bad influence on her. She's been somewhat unruly lately. Difficult for her family to control."

"Her 'friends,'" Rebecca said, struggling to maintain her composure, "dumped her on the front steps of Colden House in the middle of the night. If Miss Robatin chooses to associate with friends like that, and drink herself sick, I see no reason why we should take her in. I have girls with *no* friends, *no* resources, and *no* place to go who need what little bed space we have." She realized her voice had been rising as she spoke, and she added in a softer tone, "Why would you tell her to come to Colden House?"

Alice was a bit taken aback by the rebuke. "Her family and ours are friends. I overheard her father warn her about being disowned if she didn't correct her behavior, and I felt bad for her. I told her that if she ever got into trouble, there would be a place for her at Colden House."

"But, Alice, Colden House is not a place for drunk rich girls to sleep it off. We're not running a flophouse."

"The *poor* girls you take in never had a drink?" Alice asked.

Rebecca knew that some had—and some had done much worse than that. "My point is that Miss

Robatin had the resources to stay some place else. Colden House is for those who have no place else to go."

Alice held firm. "Lucy Robatin did not have any place else to go." She then asked pointedly, "Do you mean to tell me that simply because a girl is born into privilege she does not deserve assistance or kindness?"

Rebecca considered that for a moment. "No, of course that's not what I mean." She thought that if Alice had seen the way Miss Robatin behaved as a guest of Colden House, she would have thrown her out herself though. "Shall we go to the music room?" she then offered.

Alice again adopted her shy, polite veneer in preparation of returning to the family routine. "Yes, let's."

Rebecca meanwhile wondered if, because her sister had lived her entire life in the rarified world of wealth and privilege, she would never truly be able to understand society's most unfortunate creatures. Or was it the other way around? Had Rebecca been working with the poor for so long that she no longer understood her own kind—her own family?

Finally! A break in the case.

Buck Morehouse hung up the receiver and almost ran out of the station house. It was Sunday afternoon, almost forty-eight hours since Joshua Thompson had been shot and killed, and there had been exactly zero progress toward finding his killer. Until now.

Out on the street, Morehouse hustled his bulk

as quickly as he could to Joralemon Street. The afternoon sun was brutal—it felt like a hundred degrees, Morehouse thought—and he was soon sweating profusely. Foot traffic was fairly light, but many of the ladies on the street held parasols to fend off the sunlight, and more than one of the parasols clipped his derby as he passed by.

By the time he reached the Lantigua Hotel, Morehouse was panting for breath and his collar was soaked with sweat. As he entered the lobby, he took off his derby and mopped his forehead, neck, and throat with a wadded handkerchief. Looking around, he saw that the lobby appeared clean but rather plainly furnished. There were spittoons but no plants, papered walls but no paintings, and plain carpeting with no ornamental throw rugs. Half a dozen well-used armchairs and a horsehair sofa were positioned about the room; there were several men seated in them, reading the Sunday newspapers. To the side of the lobby, many more men and a few women were clustered three deep around the hotel's small bar.

"Detective!"

The call came from near the elevator. Morehouse spotted a uniformed officer beckoning him and quickly approached him. He didn't recognize the young patrolman. "Son," he said, "don't shout to me like that. If I wanted the world to know I was a police officer, I'd wear a uniform."

The young officer flushed. "Yes, sir. Sorry, sir."

"No harm done," said Morehouse. "We've had half the police force around here the last couple of days anyway—won't be a surprise to anyone that there's another cop on the scene. Just remember for the future: detectives work best when they don't advertise themselves."

The patrolman nodded. "Yes, sir."

Morehouse liked this young fellow; hardly any officer called him "sir." "What's your name, son?"

"Kennedy, sir."

"Well, Kennedy, where's the rifle?" The telephone call he'd received from Sergeant Patterson, reporting that a rifle had been found in the Lantigua Hotel.

"Still in the room, sir."

"Then let's go."

Kennedy started toward the elevator door.

Morehouse eyed the old elevator and its ancient attendant warily and held back. "What room number?"

"Three-twelve," answered Kennedy.

Morehouse sighed and followed him into the elevator. He was still catching his breath from the trek to the hotel and didn't want to face two flights of stairs. Despite an uncomfortable upward lurch, the elevator safely arrived on the third floor.

"This way, sir." Kennedy led the way to room 312.

Inside the small room were Sergeant Trey Patterson, who had ordered the street cleared the night Thompson was shot, and two more patrolmen. Patterson and Morehouse exchanged curt nods of greeting.

There was little furniture in the plain room—an iron rail bed, a washstand, a small bureau, and a straight-backed chair. Lying lengthwise on top of the bed was a lever-action rifle. "Glad you finally found it," said Morehouse, with a touch of annoyance.

"Well . . . the fact is . . ." Patterson stammered. "It was the chambermaid who found it."

Morehouse struggled to keep from exploding. "Would you care to tell me how a chambermaid could succeed in a search that you failed at?" He gestured at the rifle. "Or was it just hidden too well for you?"

The sergeant pulled himself a little taller, clearly not happy at being chastised in front of the patrolmen. He ordered them out of the room to "stand guard" before answering Morehouse. "The fact is, we missed it. Friday night was a madhouse—you know that. I was trying to keep the streets from exploding into a riot."

"I know that. And you did a good job. *But we also have to find the killer.*" Morehouse paused, realizing that he could probably be heard through the door by the patrolmen. And they didn't need to hear their superiors arguing. Morehouse was just so frustrated; he had ordered a sweep of the area to see if a witness or a weapon could be found, and Patterson's men had managed to miss a rifle lying in plain view on a bed. He sighed. "All right, how was it missed?"

"What difference does it make?" Patterson grumbled. "We got it now."

"Because I'd like to know what else might have been missed—whoever it was that fired the rifle, for instance."

Patterson turned and looked out the window to Canarsee Hall. "Like I said, first thing I did was get the street cleared and secure"—he turned back to face Morehouse—"and Captain Sturup said I did the right thing."

"Like *I* said, you did. Now what about the search?"

"Well, I still had to keep a lot of men on the streets

to keep order. But when you ordered us to canvass the area Friday night, I sent as many men as I could spare. Told 'em to look for anything and anyone that might tell us something. I know they came through the hotel—they reported to me that they knocked on every door and talked to anyone who might have seen or heard anything. Didn't find anything suspicious though."

Again pointing at the rifle on the bed, Morehouse said, "They didn't find *this* suspicious?"

Patterson appeared sheepish. "I asked Lowther— he was one of the men I sent to search. Told me they were trying to talk to as many people as they could as soon as possible—so they skipped some of the rooms if nobody answered the door."

Morehouse almost felt sick to his stomach. How could a Brooklyn police officer be so inept?

"Now, I know that wasn't smart," Patterson admitted, as if reading the detective's thoughts. "But there still could have been a killer on the loose, so I can understand them concentratin' their search for people."

"Very well." Morehouse decided the only thing to do now was go forward with what they finally had found. "No one was registered to this room?"

"Yeah, there was. But nobody's seen 'im." Patterson shrugged. "Just disappeared, as far as the desk clerk knows."

"I'll speak with him," Morehouse muttered. First, he picked up the rifle from the bed and gave it a cursory examination. The weapon was a Winchester .44, a fairly old model, Morehouse thought, but in good condition.

Still holding the rifle, he walked to the open window, which allowed hot air from outside to mingle with the stifling air in the room. Patterson stepped aside for him. Morehouse looked out the open window, first to the sidewalk directly below, then across the street to the steps of Canarsee Hall. He raised the rifle and brought a newsboy into the sight. An easy shot with a weapon like this, he decided. Lowering it, lest he scare anyone who might glance up at the hotel, he asked, "No one heard the shot?"

"A couple people thought they might have, but they all thought it came from the street. There *was* a lot of noise out there."

True enough, thought Morehouse. And if the muzzle of the rifle was outside the window, perhaps it did sound as if the shot came from the street. "And nobody saw anyone leave this room after the shooting?"

"No. Not that we could find."

Morehouse pondered that for a moment. It made sense to him that the hotel guests would be looking out their own windows at the ruckus below, not in the hallway where the gunman was fleeing.

He turned to Patterson and handed him the rifle. "Bring this into the station house. I'm going to speak to the desk clerk."

Staffing the desk was the hotel manager, a gangly man of about thirty-five with unruly red hair and thick spectacles who appeared nervous at speaking with a police detective. "I will be most happy to be of any assistance," he promised, while blinking owlishly behind his glasses.

"Thank you, Mr. . . ."

"Elliott, sir."

"Here's what I need to know, Mr. Elliott: who was registered to room 312 on Friday night?"

Elliott tugged as his stiff collar. "Yes, sir. I checked on that as soon as we found the rifle. The room was registered to a Mr. J.C. Fullerton of Chicago." He grabbed the canvas-bound hotel register and slid it in front of Morehouse. "There," he said, pointing a shaky finger at the signature line.

Morehouse pulled his head back so that he could read the ledger more comfortably—for some reason, he had to hold reading materials farther away than he did a few years ago. The writing was a bit blurry, but he could read the signature that Elliott had noted. "When did he check in?"

"Friday, late morning, I should think."

"You remember him?"

"Not at all."

"Then how do you remember what time he registered?"

"I don't." Elliott waved a hand at the ledger. "His is one of the first names listed for that day."

I should have noticed that, thought Morehouse. "Yes, of course." He examined the page more closely. Probably half the guests gave their surnames as "Smith," with "John Smith" being the most popular, but there were several "James Smiths" and a "Donald Smith" as well. "This hotel appears to be quite popular with the Smith family," he remarked.

Elliott blinked rapidly. "Well, sir." He cleared his throat. "We are quite a respectable hotel—a fine place for families to stay."

Morehouse couldn't help but chuckle at the manager's bald-faced response. "Yes, I'm sure." He glanced over to the bar, where the tempting women gave every impression that they were willing to be "Mrs. Smith" for a day—or a night. Or perhaps for an hour or two. But prostitution wasn't Morehouse's department or concern. Looking directly at Elliott again, he said, "Tell me everything you know about J.C. Fullerton."

"I believe I already have, sir."

"Only that he checked in?"

"Yes, sir. Mr. J.C. Fullerton of Chicago registered sometime late Friday morning and . . ." He spread his hands. "And that's it."

"He never checked out?"

"No, sir."

"Did he pay in advance?"

"For one night."

"So he should have checked out Saturday morning."

"Yes, sir."

"Then why didn't you check his room? Why didn't your chambermaid find the rifle until today?"

"Normally, we would have. But, you see, with all the trouble Friday night—the fights in the street, the police blocking traffic, the fear of more violence—some of our guests were unable to return to the hotel Friday night. So on Saturday, we didn't try to rush any guests out of here." Elliott flashed an ingratiating smile. "We try to be considerate of our guests, you see."

"Wouldn't she have at least cleaned the room on Saturday?"

"Not necessarily, sir. You see, it is hotel policy to only clean the rooms when requested or when a guest checks out."

Of course, thought Morehouse. *They wouldn't want to interrupt one of the Smiths.* He was frustrated. So far, all he had was the rifle and a name that was likely as not fictitious. "Would Mr. Fullerton have

shown you a calling card or reference letter when
he checked in?"

"Oh, that wouldn't be required if he paid in advance. We respect our guests' privacy."

"I'm sure the Smith family appreciates that,"
Morehouse said wryly.

"Well—"

Morehouse cut him off. "Is there anybody here
who remembers seeing Fullerton when he checked
in? A bellboy, maybe, or a chambermaid?"

"Not that I know of, sir."

"Well, I appreciate your help, Mr. Elliott."

"Always a pleasure to help the police." Elliott
flashed another humorless smile.

"Glad to hear that, 'cause I tell you what I'm
going to do. It's a hot day, and I sweated about a
gallon getting over here. So I'm going to go over
to your bar and have a beer. And I'll ask some of
your guests there if they remember Fullerton. And
then I'll have a couple of patrolman stay in your
lobby and ask questions of anyone who comes in."

Elliott blanched. "I don't see any need for—"

"Now *you* go and talk to every single person on
your staff. Find me someone who remembers seeing Fullerton. Until then, either me or one of my
men is going to be standing at your bar."

For a moment, Elliott appeared to be in shock.
Then his hand shot out and hit the bell several
times to summon a bellboy.

Morehouse headed for the bar, confident that
Elliot would be making his inquiries quickly. He
was less confident that they would be fruitful.

CHAPTER 5

Keith Hopkins's droopy mustache fairly quivered with his excitement. "So you spent the entire night in jail? What was that like?"

"I can't say that it was pleasant," Marshall Webb answered honestly. "But it was only one night." He didn't mention that he'd been in jail before, and his brief stay in Brooklyn's Raymond Street Jail Friday night was actually not as bad as some of his other previous incarcerations.

"I can't believe they arrested you." Hopkins sneezed, spraying the papers on his desk.

"They did." Webb was happy that Hopkins was seated at his own desk so that he was out of the line of fire from any more sneezes.

"Damned hay fever." Hopkins mopped at his nose and mustache with a red handkerchief. "I can't wait for winter." He turned his watery eye to Webb. "They took you off in a paddy wagon?"

This was Monday morning and by now everyone in the *Harper's* office already knew the circumstances of Webb's arrest, but Hopkins seemed to enjoy hearing about it again and again. So Webb decided to repeat the basic sequence of events. "Yes. The police were trying to clear everyone off the street. I didn't go when they wanted me to, so I was handcuffed and tossed in a paddy wagon with about ten other men—and we were just one of the wagon loads they took in that night. Brought to the Raymond Street Jail, we were all charged with disorderly conduct and put into cells for the night. Next morning, charges were dropped and we were all released." It had been a long, difficult night, with so many prisoners packed so tightly into fetid cells that there was no room to lie down and sleep. From experience, Webb knew that those conditions could result in a night of violence, but most of those arrested were simply caught up in the sweep, not hardened criminals, so although there were a few scuffles over space in the cell there were no bloody fights.

Harry Hargis had entered the office meanwhile, looking dapper in an exquisitely tailored cashmere suit that must have cost at least twenty-five dollars. "I'd like you to know," he announced, "that *Harper's* has protested your arrest to the authorities." The editor puffed at his slim cigar. "Absolutely criminal of the police to arrest a member of the press for doing his job."

Hopkins, who hadn't noticed Hargis's entrance, lowered his head and fell to work writing furiously. Webb knew that what the financial writer had been working on was another mock obituary for a silk mill that had gone bankrupt; he hoped that Hargis wouldn't take the time to review Hopkins's work—the editor had little tolerance for wasting time during business hours, and he had no sense of humor that Webb had ever been able to discern.

"Thank you," Webb said to the editor. "But no harm done."

Hargis waved a manicured hand. "We can't allow them to get away with such scurrilous behavior. We *must* protect the integrity of the press." Hargis then pulled a swivel chair from an unoccupied desk and sat down next to Webb. "Tell me: where are you in the story?"

Webb leaned back in his own chair and tapped his pen on a thin sheaf of foolscap on his desk. "I've almost completed what I originally set out to do. I've written up some background information on the consolidation issue, and described who's for it and who's against it. I also have a detailed report of Joshua Thompson's speech. What I don't have—what I don't know how to describe—is the effect his death will have on the campaign."

"No one has the answer to that, do they?" said Hargis. "There's no way of knowing at this point."

"I suppose not. But I keep wondering *why* Thompson was killed. Everyone seems to assume that it was because he was against consolidation, but I'm a bit skeptical about that."

"Why? It's obvious, isn't it? Thompson was the leading opponent of consolidation; kill the leader and you kill his campaign."

"Or you make him a martyr and give his campaign more sympathy and more supporters."

"Perhaps." Hargis drew on his cigar and exhaled slowly. "You were the closest to him when he was shot, weren't you?"

Webb admitted that he was. He noticed Hopkins glance over at him with interest. Although Webb had told his editor that he had been standing right next to Thompson when he was killed, he hadn't mentioned it to anyone else. He didn't want to have to relive the gory details of what he had seen.

Hargis took the cigar from his mouth and brushed a finger along each of his waxed mustaches. "Well, here's what I want you to do, Webb: write two articles, one on the consolidation issue and another on Thompson's murder. Find out everything you can about his death."

Webb was unenthusiastic. "The daily newspapers have already been full of stories about the shooting," he said.

"Stories, but not information."

That was true, Webb had to concede. He'd read the *Brooklyn Eagle* this weekend, as well as the major New York papers, and was struck by the fact that there were so few details on the circumstances of Joshua Thomspon's death. There was outrage in the editorials, reactions from partisans of both sides in the consolidation debate, and speculation as to the effect his death would have on the vote in November. But there was no information on clues or suspects. "If there *are* developments," he said, "won't the daily papers beat us to publication anyway?" It was one of the problems inherent in a weekly publication—there was no chance to publish breaking news.

"They might," Hargis agreed. "But we have a resource they don't."

"What's that?"

"You." The editor smiled. "You made a reputation for yourself with the Tammany Hall series. The police know who you are and so do the politicians.

And they know they won't be able to ignore you. Make some inquiries. See if you can find out why Joshua Thompson was killed."

Webb was still leery. As for the police knowing him, he had identified himself to that Brooklyn sergeant and all it had gotten him was a cracked knee and a night in the Raymond Street Jail. "I thought you wanted me to focus on the *politics* of the consolidation issue," he said. "Now you want a crime story?"

Hargis leaned forward. "Consolidation is going to be the biggest change to New York since the Dutch came to this island. And Joshua Thompson's murder might affect whether or not consolidation passes. This 'crime story' *is* political—maybe the biggest political story of the century."

Although the latter statement was overblown, Webb thought, Hargis did have a point about the potential impact of Thompson's death. Webb again tapped a pen on the article he had already written, then pushed the papers aside. He had some more inquiries to make.

Buck Morehouse was slouched forward in his chair, his elbow resting on the scarred surface of his old oak desk and his head propped up on his palm. He stared at the Winchester .44 propped next to the battered file cabinet and scratched at his unshaven cheek.

"Hard at work, I see." Captain Sturup stood in the doorway of Morehouse's tiny office, contempt visible on his lips.

"I was thinking."

"Looks more like you're hiding in here."

If it appeared that way, Morehouse thought, it wasn't his fault. When he was promoted to detective, he'd been assigned to this cramped office, which Morehouse suspected had once been a janitor's closet. Its sparse furnishings were so shabby that a janitor would probably have thrown them in the trash though. The only positive feature of the office was that he didn't have to share it with anyone.

"Well?" prodded the captain. "Where are you on the Thompson shooting? You must have made some progress by now."

Morehouse looked past the captain, into the bustling squad room of the station house. The Second Precinct was housed at 49 Fulton Street, a stone's throw from the King's County Courthouse, in the heart of downtown Brooklyn. It was one of the busiest police stations in the city, and as he looked at the uniformed officers in the squad room, Morehouse almost wished he were one of them again, working on nice easy assaults and robberies. Anything but this damned Thompson case. "*Some* progress, yes," he finally answered.

"Good. Fill me in."

There was nothing that the captain didn't already know, but Morehouse sat up and gestured at the rifle. "We found the murder weapon yesterday."

"Did you?" snapped Sturup. "My understanding was that a chambermaid found it."

"Yes, that's true. But at least we have it now. And we believe it was indeed the weapon used to shoot Joshua Thompson." He chose not to mention that the belief was based primarily on where the weapon was found; the bullets that had slammed into Thompson's head had been so mangled in the impacts that it wasn't even possible to confirm that they were from a .44 rifle.

Sturup nodded. "The key, *Detective,* is to determine who fired it." His words dripped with scorn.

Morehouse ignored the tone in the captain's voice; he was feeling scornful of this entire investigation himself. First, the street had been cleared of all possible witnesses before they could be questioned. Then the police sweep of the area had failed to discover the rifle. By now, three days had gone by, and the case was feeling distinctly cool. Nevertheless, he continued his report to the captain, "The room was registered to a 'J.C. Fullerton' from Chicago, according to the register. I've sent a wire to the Chicago police asking if they know of him."

"Have you heard anything?"

"Not yet." Nor did he expect to. Morehouse felt certain that the name was a fictitious one—what kind of murderer would be so foolish as to sign in under his own name?

"And you intend to simply sit here until you get a reply from Chicago. Doesn't seem to me—"

"No." The interruption was insubordinate, and Sturup's quick scowl indicated that he took it as such, but Morehouse was physically tired from long hours of work, tired of trying to make sense of a case with so little to go on, and most definitely tired of being Sturup's whipping boy. "I do have plans for the investigation." He put his hand on a stack of arrest records on his desk. "I've collected a list of potential witnesses, and I'll be interviewing them myself."

"Well . . . very good, then." Sturup appeared somewhat mollified. You *will* keep me informed of progress."

"Of course, sir."

"It is *imperative* that this be solved soon. We've been getting phone calls from very important people on both sides of the river—there's a lot of concern over what effect this killing will have on consolidation."

"I understand, sir." What Morehouse understood was that, although the case might be growing cold as far as leads went, politically it was only heating up.

"I even had a telephone call from an editor of the *Daily Eagle*—Stephen Brandt, I believe his name was. Of course, the *Eagle* is absolutely incensed that one of their allies against consolidation has been killed." Sturup snorted. "According to their damned articles, Joshua Thompson was a hero and some kind of martyr for the cause of Brooklyn independence."

"Yes, I've read the stories."

"Well, you might find yourself *in* them."

Morehouse started. "Sir?"

"I told the editor that the investigation is entirely in your hands. So don't be surprised if Brandt starts bothering you for information on the case." Sturup raised a finger. "And I should warn you: he is going to expect progress."

If there was none, Morehouse gathered, it would not be Sturup to blame. The captain had made sure of that.

Sturup moved to go out the door, then turned back to Morehouse. "Oh, there was another jewelry store robbery last night. Diamonds, I believe.

Don't suppose you're getting anywhere with that case, are you?"

Morehouse admitted that he'd been focused solely on the Thompson murder the past few days. Although he thought it obvious that that should be the highest priority, he tried to sound apologetic about failing to crack the jewel heists.

The captain grunted with disapproval and left Morehouse's office.

As soon as he was alone, Morehouse put the robberies out of his mind and picked up the records of those who'd been arrested on Friday night during the street sweep. It had occurred to the detective that since the men had been rounded up for being on the scene of the crime, they were most likely to have witnessed something important. It was his plan to locate and interview them. And one name in particular caught his eye.

CHAPTER 6

Marshall Webb and Rebecca Davies had been seeing each other for more than two years. Although he had always found her to be an attractive woman, now as he gazed at her across the small table in Enzio's Restaurant, he decided that she was growing more beautiful the longer he knew her.

Soft light from a dripping candle stuck in a Chianti bottle danced about her face, caressing it with flickering shadows and highlights. Rebecca's honey-blond hair was in a chignon, with a few long unruly strands hanging all the way down to her lace-trimmed basque. Her fine features, sometimes a bit stern, were softened this evening with a relaxed smile that lifted her full red lips.

Webb knew that he was smiling, too. The two of them rarely had had a chance to be together lately, and a quiet dinner at one of New York's finest Italian restaurants was a treat for them.

Rebecca briefly pursed her lips as she made a final review of the menu. To the waiter, she said, "I'll have the chicken cacciatore." Then she looked to Webb. "I don't even know why I look at the menu; I always order the same thing here." She laughed lightly. "But it is *so* good."

"So is the veal," Webb said, also chuckling. Enzio's had become their favorite restaurant, and both of them by now had established favorite dishes. "Scaloppini," he said to the waiter.

"Very good, sir." The elderly waiter, who had an unfortunate demeanor that seemed to challenge diners to prove themselves worthy of dining in his restaurant, took the menus and slinked away to the kitchen.

"So how is everything at Colden House?" Webb asked.

"Better now that Miss Hummel is back." Rebecca's face darkened briefly. "But she did mention that she wasn't feeling all that well this evening. Do you mind terribly if we call it a night after dinner?"

Webb hesitated. For one thing, he did mind; he had hoped for a walk in the park or perhaps champagne in a roof garden afterward. For another, he didn't want her to think that it didn't matter to him that their evening out would have to be cut short.

Rebecca added, "There's a new young lady— Stephanie Quilty—who's been a tremendous help, but I know the house is going to be full tonight and I'd hate to leave Miss Hummel and Miss Quilty to handle it on their own."

"That's quite all right," Webb said. "I understand." So that she wouldn't feel too guilty, he added, "I have some work to do, too."

"It's not going to get you another night in jail, is it?" Rebecca teased.

Webb laughed. "I hope not. But I never can tell."

"What are you working on?"

Webb filled her in on Harry Hargis's idea that he investigate the Thompson shooting. The two of them discussed the matter, both the importance of the issue and the possible dangers for Webb, until dinner arrived.

As they started on their meals, Webb asked, "What does your father and brother-in-law think of consolidation?"

Rebecca's fork paused in midair. "I don't know." She thought a moment. "I don't recall them ever saying anything about it." With a smile, she added, "But you know our family—no one really says anything and no one really listens."

Webb was about to reply, "True," but didn't want to insult her family, so he uttered a noncommittal noise.

Rebecca smiled. "It's all right. I said it first, so you can agree." She swallowed a bite of chicken. "But you know, if you want to speak with them about consolidation, you can come to dinner Sunday. They did ask about you yesterday."

"Well . . . if I can . . . perhaps . . . I don't know what I'll be doing Sunday." He wasn't sure that enduring a Davies family dinner would be worth whatever information he might get out of it.

"Oh, it won't be so bad. You have to admit, the food is always good. My father does have an excellent chef."

"As long as you're there, the company will be good, too."

Rebecca blushed slightly and murmured, "Well, thank you."

Webb had meant it. In fact, he would like to spend more time with Rebecca—to the point of settling down together even. But the reality was that theirs was an unusual match. For one thing, both of them were rather old for traditional courting—he was over thirty, while she was approaching that age. Then there was the matter of Colden House. Rebecca was so wedded to the place and its mission that it didn't seem she could ever make a home with him. And, finally, his own job was so irregular, with unusual assignments that required odd hours.

"I hate to quarrel with her, but I just thought Alice was wrong about telling that girl to come to Colden House."

Webb realized that Rebecca had been telling him about some argument that she'd had with her sister. Since he hadn't been paying attention, he didn't know what response was required. Once again, he opted for a noncommittal murmur.

This time Rebecca didn't seem to notice, and she chatted blithely on.

After dessert, Rebecca again mentioned that she needed to get back to Colden House, and Webb reluctantly escorted her home.

On the way back to his own home afterward, he thought to himself that no, there didn't seem to be much chance of them settling down together.

Buck Morehouse sat on the steps of a well-kept brownstone on East Fourteenth Street, methodically chewing on gumdrops from the bag he kept in his pocket.

As much as he loved Brooklyn, he was glad to be out of it for a while, especially out of the station house. He'd come to feel like a one-man police force. Captain Sturup and the rest of the depart-

ment were keeping their distance from him lest
they be tainted by any failure of his to solve the
Thompson murder.

Sunlight was fading, but there was still plenty
for Morehouse to see. This area of Manhattan,
near Union Square, was crowded with a variety of
entertainment, commercial, and residential buildings. One of the busiest streets in the city, it was
also crowded with slow-moving vehicles and daring
pedestrians who risked darting through the snarled
traffic. The area had once been the heart of New
York City's entertainment district, and enough attractions remained to still give the neighborhood
a strong theatrical presence. The entertainment
venues ranged from Huber's Dime Museum and
Tony Pastor's Variety House to Steinway Hall and
the Academy of Music, and electric lights from
these places provided a colorful glow.

There were also numerous dining and drinking
establishments, and it was these that Morehouse
began thinking about. As fond as he was of licorice
gumdrops, they simply did not make for a satisfying supper. He pulled a watch from his vest pocket.
Another fifteen minutes, he decided; then he would
get himself a proper meal.

He'd waited twenty before standing up and brush-
ing off the seat of his pants. He'd only taken a few
steps west when he saw the man he'd been expecting, a lanky fellow a little over six feet tall dressed
in a charcoal-gray cutaway suit, with a black silk
Windsor tie knotted neatly against a high wing collar. What identified him were the impeccable brown
whiskers, with a thick mustache that swooped down
to merge smoothly into the side whiskers, leaving
his chin bare. To be sure, though, Morehouse pulled

the rogues' gallery photograph from his pocket. Yes, this was Marshall Webb, looking the same as when he'd been arrested Friday night.

Morehouse stepped into the man's path. "Mr. Webb?"

"Yes . . ." He frowned as if trying to place him.

"We haven't met." Morehouse pulled out a badge. "Detective Buck Morehouse, Brooklyn Police Department."

"Out of your jurisdiction, aren't you?"

Considering that Webb's last encounter with the Brooklyn police hadn't been exactly cordial, Morehouse wasn't expecting a warm welcome. "I'd only like to ask you a few questions, Mr. Webb. But if you prefer"—the detective jerked his chin toward a New York patrolman talking with an attractive young lady on the corner—"I could ask one of the local police to join us."

"That won't be necessary." Webb held a hand toward the front steps on which Morehouse had been sitting for more than an hour. "Would you prefer to talk inside, Detective?"

"Please."

They walked up a flight of stairs and into Webb's second-floor apartment.

Morehouse glanced about what appeared to be a combination parlor, library, and dining room, his experienced eyes trying to see if they could learn anything about Mr. Marshall Webb from his surroundings. The décor was rather spare; there were no paintings or tapestries on the walls, the mantel of the small fireplace had only an enameled iron clock upon it, and there wasn't a single photograph to be seen anywhere. The only images on the drab beige walls were a few framed Civil War woodcuts that might have been cut from the pages *Frank Leslie's Illustrated Newspaper*. A massive rolltop desk, stained dark, was the largest piece of furniture, with matching glass-door bookcases on either side of it. Near the single window that overlooked East Fourteenth Street was a small dining table and a pair of bent-back chairs.

Webb gestured to a spacious leather easy chair. "Please, make yourself comfortable."

After all that time on the hard stoop, the soft chair looked inviting, and Morehouse promptly lowered his posterior onto the seat. He placed his derby on the coffee table while Webb sat down across from him on a small sofa.

"I appreciate you speaking with me," Morehouse began. "I know you weren't well treated by my fellow officers the other night."

Webb shrugged slightly as if a night in jail had been but a minor inconvenience. "They had a difficult situation on their hands."

"Yes, very difficult. And I'm afraid that in the urgency of the situation, some things were forgotten."

"Such as?"

"Interviewing potential witnesses. Such as yourself."

"I'm not sure that I'm much of a witness," Webb replied. "I saw what happened to Joshua Thompson, of course, but didn't see who pulled the trigger."

"Could you tell me what you did see?" Morehouse took out a notebook and pencil. "Never know what might be useful."

Webb leaned back and look up at the ceiling for a moment. "I was in the hall for Mr. Thompson's speech, covering it for *Harper's*. When it was over, I

followed him outside and asked for an interview.
He agreed. Then . . ." Webb hesitated, and Morehouse sensed that he didn't like reliving what happened next. The writer went on, "Then a bullet hit
his head and he started to fall. I didn't know what
happened for a moment, but I tried to catch him.
When the second bullet hit him, his head almost
exploded and I saw right away that he must be
dead."

"You didn't see where the shot came from?"

"No. In fact, I'm not even sure I heard it." Webb
paused to think for a moment. "But I did wonder
about the direction. From the way Thompson was
standing, and where the shots struck him, I thought
it might have been fired from the hotel across the
street. Or perhaps from a passing carriage."

"It was from the hotel." Shortly after uttering the
words, Morehouse found himself regretting them.

Webb took out a notebook of his own. "From a
window or the roof?" he asked, shaking a pen to
get the ink flowing.

Reluctantly, Morehouse admitted that it was
from a third-floor window. "Did you see—"

Webb cut him off with a question of his own.
"Did you find the weapon? Or any witnesses at the
hotel?"

"Mr. Webb," Morehouse said slowly, "*I'm* the detective. Please let me investigate the case."

The writer smiled. "I wouldn't dream of inter-
fering. But my editor wants me to write a report on
the case, so I'm afraid I'll have to do some investigating of my own." His pen was poised again, and
he repeated the question about whether the murder weapon had been found.

Morehouse coughed, mostly to give himself a

moment to think. Then he coughed again. "Throat's a bit dry," he hinted.

"Forgive me," said Webb. "I've neglected to offer you something to drink. I believe I have beer in the icebox."

Morehouse had to give Webb credit—he had managed to deduce his favorite beverage. "Sounds good," he said.

While Webb went to get the beer, Morehouse considered that the two of them might be able to help each other. The Brooklyn Police Department was certainly proving to be of little help; the uniformed officers were inept, unable to find a rifle that wasn't even hidden, and his superiors were distancing themselves from the entire case, leaving Morehouse to succeed or fail on his own. This Marshall Webb, on the other hand, had a good reputation and was planning to do his own investigation anyway.

When Webb handed him a tall glass of dark beer, Morehouse gulped a couple of sips and uttered a satisfied sigh. "Ah, that hits the spot." He then rested the glass on his belly and said, "I have a proposition for you, Mr. Webb."

Webb nodded for him to go on.

"Ordinarily, the Brooklyn Police Department doesn't share information with civilians about active investigations. But this is a rather *extra*-ordinary situation. It happens that I read your series on Tammany Hall in *Harper's Weekly*, and you did a helluva job—a solid investigation without the nonsensical stuff that might appear in Pulitzer's newspaper. And your story is getting real results in Albany now. Who was that Manhattan captain that just lost his job?"

"David Start." Webb's mustache twitched in a smile. "But I didn't think a police officer would consider another one losing his job to be a good thing."

Morehouse shrugged. "He was a New York cop, not Brooklyn. And he was crooked."

"Yes, he was," said Webb.

"Anyway, what I suggest is that we work together—share information."

Webb considered the suggestion. "Well, we're basically after the same thing, so I think that, yes, we can help each other."

"There will be some things that might have to be kept confidential for a while," Morehouse warned. "I would have to ask you to hold back on publishing anything that might hurt the investigation."

"I believe you'll find me to be discreet when necessary."

The two of them then looked at each other in silence for a few moments. "So," Morehouse finally said, "what have you found so far?"

"Nothing at all," Webb answered matter-of-factly. "I was only given the assignment today. So far, all I have is general information on the consolidation campaign. And, of course, my own observations the night Thompson was killed." He leaned back in the sofa. "What do you have?"

This wasn't a poker game, Morehouse thought. If they were to cooperate with each other, one of them would have to start. He then told the writer what little information he did have, including the gun and the name of the man registered to room 312 at the Lantigua Hotel.

"Any witnesses?" Webb asked.

"No, I was hoping you might have seen something useful. But I will interview the others who were arrested Friday night." He had a sudden idea of how Webb could help. "Would you like to take half and I'll take half?"

Webb shook his head no. "I doubt that will lead anywhere."

"Why not?"

"If I, or anyone else, had seen anything useful, don't you think we'd have spoken up that night? I'd sure rather have been telling the police what I'd witnessed instead of being stuck in that cell."

Made sense, Morehouse thought, but he would still speak to those arrested if only because he had so few other avenues of investigation. "Where are *you* going to start?" he asked Webb.

The writer answered as if it was obvious, "I thought I would try to find out who would want Joshua Thomspson dead."

Morehouse thought the answer to that was obvious. "Since Thompson was one of the most prominent voices against consolidation, seems to me he was likely killed by somebody who disagreed with him—especially considering he was shot right after his speech." He downed the rest of his beer.

Webb took his glass and went back to the icebox to refill it, much to Morehouse's gratitude. From the kitchen area, he asked Morehouse, "You think it was just one madman, another Charles Guiteau?" He returned with the glass not quite full. "Sorry. I'm afraid that's all I have left."

"Quite all right, thank you." Morehouse took a sip before answering. He actually didn't think Thompson's killer was the same sort of assassin who had killed President Garfield. "I was thinking that Thompson's death was more likely ordered—maybe by Tammany Hall or one of the gangs. Some group who thought they had something to lose if consolidation was defeated."

Webb frowned slightly. "I believe Tammany is *opposed* to consolidation—the same as Thompson was."

"Maybe not Tammany, then," Morehouse conceded. "But we have our own political machines in Brooklyn—and our own crime bosses—so it could have been one of them if they thought Thompson's efforts were hurting them."

Webb still appeared skeptical. "I've been thinking about that today. And I'm starting to believe that his murder might not have anything to do with the consolidation campaign."

"But obviously—"

Webb held up a hand and continued, "The circumstances make it appear obvious. But what *isn't* obvious is what the ramifications of his murder will be. It's as likely as not that there will *more* sympathy to Thompson's cause. Killing him might end up killing the idea of consolidation."

"You think so?"

"I don't know. But I don't believe anyone can foresee what the consequences will be." Webb leaned forward. "One thing I do know is that Tammany rarely takes any action if they're uncertain of the outcome—that's why they rig elections and pay off politicians. Why would they have Joshua Thompson killed unless they were certain that it would have the effect they wanted?"

Morehouse considered that, and thought Webb might have a point. But he wasn't convinced. "You said you would start by trying to find out who would want Joshua Thompson dead. Where *exactly* would you start, if not with his political opponents?"

"The same place as with any other man who was murdered: who had a motive to kill him? Did someone have a grudge against him? I don't expect you could make a fortune as he did without harming some people along the way. Or is there someone who stands to benefit financially from his death?"

"If the motive for killing Thompson had nothing to do with his politics, why kill him out in the street with hundreds of people around like that? Why not do it some place private with less chance of getting caught?"

"Perhaps because shooting him at Canarsee Hall would lead the police to jump to the conclusion that the motive was political and they would fail to look for other motives."

Morehouse stared at Webb in silence for a few moments. This writer seemed smart and capable. But Morehouse wasn't sure that he was going to find working with him particularly enjoyable.

CHAPTER 7

Although most of *Harper's Weekly*'s contributors would have relished office space at the publication, Marshall Webb found that working from the office was more of a hindrance than a help. For one thing, there was only one telephone in the office, shared by four writers, and the nature of some of Webb's calls necessitated privacy. The matters about which he wrote also required that he venture outside the office in order to uncover information—he couldn't very well invite Bowery thugs or crooked police officials or Tammany Hall henchmen into the office in order to be interviewed about their illicit activities.

So, Webb stayed home for a while Tuesday morning, making some telephone calls that he wanted to keep confidential. When he did arrive at *Harper's*, an hour later than his usual time, he went directly to the office of Harry M. Hargis. He was kept waiting for just a minute while Hargis's personal secre-

tary checked to see that the editor would grant
Webb an audience.

Hargis's office was a far cry from the plain, sparsely furnished one that Webb shared with Keith
Hopkins and the other writers. Harry Hargis liked
his surroundings to be as elegant as his attire, which
today consisted of a pale blue suit with a checked
silk vest. The cravat tied around his crisp white collar, and the carnation pinned to his lapel, were the
identical shade of red; he'd probably had the florist
go through dozens of flowers before he found a
perfect match.

As always, Webb had the sense that he'd entered
a museum rather than a place of business. Hargis
decorated his office with acquisitions from his many
trips abroad. Much of the floor was covered by a
huge oriental rug that he'd purchased on a visit to
Persia, from the walls hung several oil paintings from
France and Holland, and there were reproductions
of Michaelangelo's *David* and a couple of Greek
bronzes. The only indication of the office's true purpose was a gilt-lettered plaque that read HARPER'S
WEEKLY, with the publication's immodest motto, A
JOURNAL OF CIVILIZATION, below the title.

"Congratulations are once again in order, Mr.
Webb," Hargis began, with a satisfied smile.

"Thank you. For . . . ?" Webb didn't know what
Hargis was referring to.

"I received a telephone call from Albany this
morning. Captain Patrick Topps of the New York
City Police Department is about to be a prisoner of
the New York Department of Corrections for taking
graft from the gambling houses on Twenty-eighth
Street. And the evidence was developed largely because of your series last year." He reached across

his carved mahogany desk, to shake hands with Webb. "Good work."

Webb thanked him again.

Hargis then idly wiped the hand that had shaken Webb's with his pocket handkerchief. "I stopped by your office a little while ago to give you the news, but you weren't in yet."

Webb was neither offended that Hargis seemed to be trying to erase the touch of his hand nor chastised by Hargis's implied rebuke about being late. "No, that's why I wanted to speak with you. I will be working on the Thompson murder—as you suggested—and I will have to be out of the office much of the time in order to do that." At Hargis's slight frown, he added, "I will, of course, provide you with regular progress reports."

"I suppose being out of the office is warranted under the circumstances," the editor acknowledged.

"In fact, I need to be out most of today."

Hargis proceeded to fold and refold the handkerchief until he had it exactly to his liking before returning it to his pocket. "Well, what about the first piece—the one on consolidation? Can you finish that this morning? We can run that in the next issue and then wait for more developments on the Thompson case."

Webb thought for a moment. Yes, he decided, he should be able to get a final draft of that story done before noon and still be able to make his appointment. "I'll have it to you by twelve," he said.

Hargis appeared pleased with Webb's answer, and offered him free reign to investigate the Thompson matter as he saw fit.

* * *

Webb barely made the self-imposed deadline of noon for submitting his consolation story. Keith Hopkins had insisted on reading him two new business obituaries as well as a rather dreadful limerick about a girl from Nantucket. Between Hopkins's distractions and his own compulsion to revise his writing until every sentence was just right, Webb was running so late when he left the *Harper's* office that he feared he might miss his meeting.

The crowded Ninth Avenue el, which ran particularly slow at lunchtime, made him even later. By the time it screeched to a halt at Seventy-seventh Street, Webb had almost resigned himself to disappointment. Nevertheless he went into the American Museum of Natural History, a colossal building that reminded Webb of a castle, and made his way up four flights of stairs to its library.

With relief, he spotted a familiar figure seated at one of the tables looking at an illustrated book about dogs. There were only a couple of other patrons in the hushed room, both of them of a professorial appearance, and they were absorbed in their own reading material.

Webb quickly passed one of the dark wood shelves that lined the walls of the room and pulled a volume at random. Without looking directly at the man he'd come to see, he took a seat across from him at the reading table.

The man whispered, "Time is money, Webb."

"Couldn't be helped." He did glance up at Danny Macklin, a man built like a fireplug and with a face nearly as red. Although they were indoors, Macklin kept his cloth cap on, tilted low over his forehead, and the collar of his overcoat was turned up. Almost all that was visible was his pug nose and a wide mouth full of bad teeth. "Thanks for meeting me," Webb added.

Macklin shrugged. "There'll be a payoff for me one way or another."

That payoff wouldn't be money—at least not from Webb. He knew that what Macklin wanted was power. The forty-five-year-old product of Five Points had already achieved some degree of it; he was one of the thirteen Sachems who ran the Tammany Society and well as one of Tammany's ward bosses. But he wanted a bigger piece of the pie—more influence, more clout, more money. Macklin had provided Webb with information when he was writing his series on Tammany's role in New York political corruption. Doing so was a danger for him—a certain death sentence if he was found out—so they met in the library of the museum. There wasn't a saloon or theater or office that didn't have someone who might spot them, but Tammany henchmen were as likely to patronize a library as they were to become ballet dancers. Also, Seventy-seventh Street was so far from the heart of the city that it was almost on the frontier; hardly any New Yorkers ventured this far north unless they were intending to visit the museum.

"Whaddaya want to know?" Macklin asked directly, still keeping his eyes on his book and his voice low.

"Is Tammany fighting against consolidation?"

"Well, there ain't exactly an easy answer to that one. Boss Croker's against it, and so are most of the other Sachems, so Tammany as a whole is against it. Me, I like the idea of merging."

Webb was well aware of Macklin's motive in speaking with him. Since he wanted to move up in the power circles, Macklin was willing to reveal anything that might harm his rivals and leave him an opening to enhance his own influence. What the ambitious Sachem didn't seem to grasp, and what Webb didn't intend to point out, was that if Webb and other reformers succeeded the entire corrupt system would collapse—there would be no role for Macklin to move into and no illicit profits to be skimmed from city coffers or extorted from the city's vice businesses.

"Say, would you look at the size of this mutt?" Macklin swiveled his book so that Webb could see a color plate of a Great Dane. "I oughta get me a couple of these—be good protection, I bet."

If Macklin wanted to protect himself, Webb thought, he should remember that the two of them shouldn't appear to be communicating with each other. "Why is Croker against consolidation?"

"Because we got New York all wrapped up nice and neat. We own this city and we can take what we want from who we want. Ain't a judge or a cop or a goddamn street sweeper gets a job without our say-so—and they got to pay us to get that say-so. But if the city changes—Brooklyn and Queens and Staten Island—come into it, then we don't got control as tight as we do now. Leastways, that Croker's thinking." He turned a page in his book. "Me, I think different."

"How do you see it?" Webb prodded.

"Makes sense to me that if the city gets bigger, we got a bigger pie. You think Brooklyn don't got whorehouses that'll pay us for protection? Or Queens don't got unlicensed saloons? Course they do. And think of all the political positions to be filled—we could really make a killing on selling those appointments." He nodded to himself. "Yeah, if Croker wasn't turning yellow in his old age, he'd see it, too." He then turned his head and spat on the floor, to the horror of the others using the library. "But then Croker proved himself yellow when he went to Ireland. Things get a little hot here and he leaves the country for half a year." He spat again, and one of the older patrons nearby coughed in disapproval.

Webb, whose Tammany Hall articles had helped generate the heat that drove Croker to the safety of Ireland, asked, "What do you hear about Joshua Thompson?"

Macklin shrugged. "Only that he's dead."

"Who *wanted* him dead?"

"Damned if I know." He looked up slowly, and tugged his cap higher so that he had a clear view of Webb. "Hey . . . what you tryin' to say? You think we had somethin' to do with that? Ye're goddamn crazy if you do."

"I'm just asking," said Webb. "Tell me, Danny. You know politics like hardly anybody else in this city. What's the effect of Thompson's death going to have on the vote in November?"

Macklin appeared flattered, and paused to think. His ruddy face contorted this way and that for a while, then it seemed to sag. He answered softly, "Tell you the truth, Webb: I dunno. Could be his side gets sympathy. But it could also turn out that with him out of the picture, his side loses steam." He hunched his shoulders. "Just can't say."

Webb always gave careful consideration to whatever Danny Macklin told him. Macklin was out to hurt his rivals and bolster himself, so Webb knew his statements would probably be slanted to have that effect. But Macklin had proven himself to be a reliable source last year, and what he said now jibed with Webb's own opinion of the Thompson killing: without being able to predict the political fallout from their action, it was unlikely that Tammany was behind Joshua Thompson's murder.

Buck Morehouse was far from convinced that Marshall Webb was correct. The detective in him still thought that there had to be a connection between the circumstances under which Joshua Thompson had been killed and the reason for his murder. It was a political motive, Morehouse believed.

Nevertheless, the *Harper's* writer did have a point: It was worth investigating all possible motives, and speaking with those close to Thompson. Besides, he'd already spoken with half a dozen of the men who'd been arrested along with Webb Friday night, and not one of them admitted to witnessing anything that might provide a clue to Thompson's killer.

Late Tuesday afternoon, Morehouse took the short walk to Brooklyn Heights, specifically to a stately double brownstone on Pierrepont, just west of fashionable Clinton Street. Thompson had certainly prospered in business to afford a mansion such as this, Morehouse thought.

Almost immediately after his rapping on the brass knocker, the carved front door was opened by an ancient, rigid butler in a black suit. He gave Morehouse the once-over as contemptuously as if he were a door-to-door salesman.

Morehouse took out his badge. "Detective More-house, Brooklyn Police Department."

The butler's demeanor didn't improve much at hearing Morehouse's true profession. "Yes, Detective?" he asked in a quavery voice.

"Could I speak with Mr. Thompson please?"

"Mr. Thompson is dead, sir." The butler cleared his throat. "I should think that the Brooklyn Police Department would be aware of that unfortunate fact." His wrinkled face made a most unpleasant scowl.

"Mr. *Eugene* Thompson," Morehouse elaborated. He almost added, "You old fool," but kept the thought to himself.

"Oh, *young* Mr. Thompson." Judging by the butler's expression, it hadn't occurred to him that Morehouse could have meant Joshua Thompson's son. "I'm afraid young Mr. Thompson is not available."

"Not here, or not available?"

"He is not here, Detective."

Morehouse had checked, and knew that Joshua Thompson was survived by his widow, a bachelor son, Eugene, and a married daughter named Catherine McCutcheon. He'd have preferred to speak to the son, assuming that the women would be too emotional after Thompson's death. "Do you expect him back soon?"

"I am sorry, Detective, but I am not privy to young Mr. Thompson's schedule. He might be back at any moment, or not until next week."

"Is there another family member I can speak with?"

"Mrs. Thompson is receiving no one, but I shall

see if Mrs. McCutcheon is available." He opened
the door and stepped aside to allow Morehouse
into the wide tiled foyer.

While Morehouse waited, derby in hand, the detective thought to himself that he should have come
to see the family sooner. True, he'd been busy as
the sole investigator on the case, trying to make
sense of the immediate aftermath of the killing.
But the real reason he'd held off coming to see
Thompson's survivors was that he felt uneasy about
the prospect. He didn't mind interrogating the
toughest criminals or shaking down snitches for
information or even being harangued by the captain for failure to make sufficient progress, but had
never grown comfortable with speaking to those
unfortunate families who were grieving the loss of
a loved one.

Evenly paced footsteps clacked on the curving
staircase, and then a trim woman in mourning black
came into the foyer. "Mr. Morehouse?"

The detective nodded.

"I am Catherine McCutcheon. I understand you
wish to speak with me." Mrs. McCutchean had
chestnut-brown hair pulled high in a tight bun.
Her delicate facial features were equally tight, with
her lips appearing as taut as guitar strings. The
black gown had little shape to it, but Morehouse
could tell that she was of slender build and medium
stature. He pegged her age at forty-five, but conceded to himself that the severe mourning attire
might be causing him to err on the high side.

"First, please accept my condolences on the loss
of your father," the detective ventured.

"Thank you." Thompson's daughter accepted
the sentiments with as little emotion as Morehouse

had expressed them. "Now what would you like to speak with me about? Have you found my father's assassin?"

"No, I'm afraid we haven't. But we are investigating every possibility—and that's why have I have to trouble you with some questions."

She nodded. "Very well." With a pale hand, she gestured down the hallway. "Shall we go into the drawing room?" Mrs. McCutcheon spoke the words as if issuing a royal command.

Morehouse obediently followed her into a spacious drawing room that had a masculine feel. There was a wide brick fireplace with marble figurines on its oak mantel, and an ebony grand piano. The furnishings were dark and heavy, including ponderous Turkish chairs with velvet upholstery, drab colored tapestries on the paneled walls, and a brown bearskin rug with the head attached and snarling.

Mrs. McCutcheon picked up a silver bell from a marble-topped side table and rang it. "Would you care for a refreshment, Mr. Morehouse?"

As much as he craved a beer, the detective thought it might be an inappropriate choice under the circumstances, and opted for lemonade instead. Thompson's daughter relayed the request to the butler who'd promptly answered the bell, and requested a sherry for herself. At hearing her selection, Morehouse was tempted to say, "Make that two," but decided he would just have to make do with the lemonade.

While they waited for the drinks, they sat down in facing armchairs that could have seated men twice his size. Mrs. McCutcheon commented on how terribly hot the summer had been. Morehouse sensed that she was putting off any serious discussion until they'd been served their beverages.

That turned out to be the case. As soon as the butler had delivered their drinks and departed the drawing room, Thompson's daughter said, "You may ask your questions now, Mr. Morehouse."

Actually, Morehouse had to wait a minute. The lemonade had no sugar in it, and one swallow caused his mouth to pucker and his tongue to stiffen. When he recovered, he said, "This is largely routine, Mrs. McCutcheon. We are doing a thorough investigation into your father's murder—"

"Assassination," she corrected.

Morehouse didn't particularly care what word was used—Thompson would remain just as dead. "Assassination," he repeated, hoping she would appreciate him adopting her term. "Anyway, we must review all possible motives for his . . . being shot." He then worked his mouth trying to generate some moisture in it.

"There was one motive: my father was killed because he was fighting for Brooklyn's independence, and there are some who want to cede our city to that one across the river."

"To be honest," Morehouse replied, "I believe you are probably right. However, we cannot ignore other possibilities. We must do everything in our power to get justice for your father."

Mrs. McCutcheon took a sip of her sherry. "I appreciate that. So, how can I help you?"

"Do you know if your father had received any threats?"

She hesitated. "I don't know of any specific threats, no. Of course, some people would shout the vilest slurs at him when he spoke in public.

And editorial writers—from the *New York* newspapers—seemed to delight in castigating him for
his devotion to Brooklyn."

"But no threats of violence?"

Mrs. McCutcheon shook her head no. "None
that I'm award of."

"What about his life outside the consolidation
campaign? Was there anything out of the ordinary
there? Any enemies?"

She frowned. "My father, Mr. Morehouse, was a
pillar of the community. His business provided
employment to hundreds even through the silver
panic and this depression. He was a generous supporter of our church—Plymouth Church. And"—
she seemed to make an effort at sniffling, but no
tears were produced—"and he was loved by his
family."

That all may have been true, but Morehouse
wasn't going to let her off with such a general en-
dorsement of her father's character. "Did he have
any business rivals, Mrs. McCutcheon?"

After another sip of sherry, Thompson's daughter answered. "My father spent forty years building
his company. He started with a small shoe factory
in Williamsburg, then bought a machine shop next
door to it that had gone out of business. By the time
the war came, Thompson Manufacturing turned
all its efforts to helping save the Union—anything
the army needed, my father helped provide, from
boots to canteens to firearms. And after the war,
he kept building until he had established the largest manufacturing concern in Brooklyn." She smiled
a tight smile. "Other businesses may envy us, Mr.
Morehouse, but we have no 'rivals.' Thompson
Manufacturing is peerless."

"Could any of the other business owners have been so jealous of your father that they would want to harm him?"

"At this point? After forty years?" She shook her head. "No, I don't believe so. I don't see whom it could possibly benefit."

Perhaps not a rival, then, Morehouse thought. But maybe someone was eager to take over the fine business that Joshua Thompson had spent so long building. "Will your brother be running the company now?" he asked.

She started slightly. "Why should you assume that?"

"Isn't he the only son?"

"My brother Eugene is a fine man," she said. "I love him dearly. But even he would be the first to admit that business matters are of no interest to him." For the first time she gave a smile that indicated genuine amusement, apparently as she imagined her brother trying to run the company. "No, Mr. Morehouse, my brother has few interests outside of tennis and golf."

"Then who . . . ?"

"I am currently managing the family business," she answered. "I have been closely involved in it for almost a year now. When my father began spending so much of his time fighting against that terrible consolidation scheme, he began teaching me about the company's operations. In recent months, he had entrusted me with many of the major decisions."

"Will you continue to run the company?"

"I hadn't considered that. Perhaps after we recover from the shock of my father's death, we will be able to give some attention to business matters again."

The detective doubted that she hadn't thought about who would run Thompson Manufacturing.

Catherine McCutcheon rang for the butler and ordered another sherry.

Morehouse declined the offer of another lemonade, again expressed his condolences on her loss, and thanked her for her time.

CHAPTER 8

So far, every letter that had come in the morning mail reported discouraging news. Rebecca Davies was so disheartened by what she read that she was tempted to leave the rest of the mail unopened, so that she could at least pretend for a while that one of them might turn out to be positive.

She was working at her corner desk in the small, plainly furnished sitting room of Colden House. For years, she had corresponded with a growing network of contacts throughout the eastern half of the United States, finding jobs, and sometimes housing, for her girls. Many of the young women who sought shelter at Colden House were fleeing from abusive husbands, fathers, or sweatshop bosses, so at first Rebecca had tried to find safe havens outside the city for those girls. Then, as jobs became more difficult to find in New York, she expanded her search to find employment for girls willing to relocate to a new area. The jobs were seldom easy ones, but she did make sure that the mills or factories where she placed her girls provided decent working conditions and livable wages.

Rebecca opened another letter and read that Matthis Textiles, one of the better mills in Lowell, Massachusetts, where she had sent dozens of girls in recent years, had just closed its doors—a loss of fifteen hundred jobs.

It was one of the conditions for staying at Colden House that the residents who were physically capable of doing so had to help with chores in the shelter and be actively seeking employment. But how could a girl find a job when there simply were none to be had?

Rebecca reread the letter about Matthis Textiles. *Fifteen hundred* workers had just lost their livelihoods. Many of them would no doubt end up on the streets, like the girls who came to Colden House. No one—certainly not the politicians or the bankers—seemed to truly understand what it meant to have nothing—not even the prospect of another meal, never mind hope of a decent future.

The newspapers had been full of reports about financial losses during the past year or so as the national depression had taken hold. Headlines announced factory closings and railroad bankruptcies, and they would tally the number of workers who had lost employments—thousands every week—but they never provided a picture of what the impact of a job loss was to an *individual* worker. Rebecca Davies, unfortunately, saw the result vividly every day.

A feeling of hopelessness began to take hold in Rebecca's heart. It struck now and then, but she had learned over the years to fend it off. The emotion was understandable, considering what she saw and heard about the wretched lives of the girls who came to Colden House, but if she allowed herself to be too affected by it she wouldn't be able to do the work that was necessary to help them.

The hallway telephone jolted Rebecca with its insistent ring. She hopped up from her seat, grateful for the interruption.

By the time she picked up the receiver, she had almost entirely shaken off the feeling of despair. "Hello?"

"Rebecca?" The soft voice was her sister's.

"Yes, Alice."

"How are you?"

Rebecca could tell from the tone that this wasn't a social call, but her sister had retained too many of the social graces that had been ingrained in them to omit basic courtesies. "Fine, Alice. And you?"

"I'm well, thank you." She paused. "As is Mr. Updegraff."

Rebecca understood from the way Alice said it that she was being mildly rebuked for having failed to ask about her brother-in-law's well-being. But the fact was that Rebecca didn't particularly care about the arrogant Updegraff's welfare and rarely thought to inquire about him. She decided to get to the point. "Is there anything the matter, Alice?"

"There might be. Do you remember Lucy Robatin? We had a, uh, discussion about her on Sunday."

"Yes, of course." Both the discussion and the memory of the unpleasant Miss Robatin were vivid in Rebecca's memory.

"Did she come to Colden House last night?"

"No." If she had, Rebecca would have thrown the young woman out on her expensively attired fanny. "Why?"

"She's missing. She never came home last night, so I thought she might have come there."

From what little she'd seen of Lucy Robatin, Rebecca didn't think being out all night was unusual for her. But it was now late afternoon. "Her parents haven't heard from her?"

"No, and her mother is awfully worried about her."

"The night she did come here, there were some young friends of hers in the carriage. Has her family contacted her friends?"

Alice didn't answer immediately. "Her family is rather torn about this. Mr. Robatin says it's time they washed their hands of her—he says she's been nothing but trouble and a discredit to the family. Her mother, though . . . well, she's a *mother*, and she wants her daughter safe at home."

"I'm sorry, but I haven't seen her." Rebecca wondered, however, if she might have simply missed seeing Miss Robatin; perhaps the young woman *had* come to Colden House while Rebecca was out or otherwise occupied. "I will check, though," she offered. "Perhaps someone else here has seen her."

"Thank you. Do let me know if you learn anything. Her mother is really quite distraught and I would like to be of help if I can."

"I will."

"And, Rebecca . . ."

"Yes?"

"I know you didn't like her, but if she does come

to Colden House, *please* don't turn her away. Just
let her in and telephone me."

As satisfying as it might have been to turn Miss
Robatin away, Rebecca couldn't deny her sister's
request and promised that she would do as she
asked.

After hanging up the telephone, Rebecca sought
out Miss Hummel. She found her in the hot kitchen,
chopping vegetables for supper while several girls
cleaned the pots and pans that had been used to
cook lunch.

Miss Hummel, a short gray-haired woman,
dressed as usual in a starched dress and apron that
made her look like a combination nurse and maid,
was the only full-time employee of Colden House.
She had been Rebecca's assistant for years, and
she worked with a quiet efficiency that was invalu-
able in keeping the operations of the shelter going
smoothly.

"Miss Hummel," Rebecca called from the kitchen
doorway.

The older woman looked up. "Yes, Miss Davies?"
She caught on that Rebecca wanted to speak with
her away from the other girls. She quickly wiped
her hands on her apron and joined Rebecca in the
hallway.

"A week ago," Rebecca began in a hushed voice,
"a young woman came to Colden House. You were
in Boston at the time, so you didn't see her."
Rebecca then gave Miss Hummel a description of
Lucy Robatin. "Has she come back to the house in
the last twenty-four hours?" she asked.

"No, ma'am," answered the assistant. Her mouth
twisted slightly in an expression of distaste—a rare

display of emotion from the steely Miss Hummel. "And from what you've just told me about her, I can't say that I'm looking forward to making her acquaintance."

Rebecca restrained a smile. Her description must have been accurate to elicit such a response. "If she does come, you'll tell me immediately, won't you—please?"

Miss Hummel assured her that she would.

Rebecca turned to leave, then asked, "Do you know where Miss Quilty is this afternoon?"

"I believe she said she was going out front with her book. But she might be in her room."

Since "out front" meant across the street in Battery Park, Rebecca tried the upstairs rooms first. Miss Quilty wasn't there.

Rebecca then pinned a straw bonnet to her hair and went out the front door. She crossed directly across State Street and received a piercing whistle from the driver of a coal wagon. Like most New York women, she was well practiced at showing no response to such crude attentions. But she was tempted to whistle back sometime just to see what the reaction would be.

Stephanie Quilty was in a fairly quiet area of Battery Park, away from both the traffic of State Street and the chaotic area near the Barge Office where immigrants were ferried over from Ellis Island. Quilty was seated on a bench, poring over a *McGuffy Reader*.

The wispy girl looked so childlike, Rebecca thought. Not only was her tiny figure dressed in a gingham frock more suitable for a twelve-year-old, but she read like a child, her lips moving and her finger tracing the words of the reading primer. At age seventeen, the girl could do little more than write her own name.

Rebecca knew about the girl's tragic past. At an early age, she'd been left in the care of a hard-drinking uncle who every month "loaned" her to a tenement landlord in lieu of making the rent payment. When her uncle died, she was left alone and put out on the street by the landlord who had tired of her in favor of newer, younger girls. Quilty scratched out a living, doing whatever it took to stay alive, but also picked up a morphine habit to numb herself against the harshness of her existence. On her own, she'd given up the morphine and come to Colden House to try to start a new better life. She was one of the hardest workers in the shelter, always volunteering to help with any chore.

The young woman was so absorbed in her book that she didn't notice Rebecca until she spoke her name. Quilty then looked up, her perpetually sad brown eyes widening with fear. "I'm sorry, Miss Davies. I was just reading. Is there something you want me to do at the house?"

"No, no. That's quite all right." Rebecca sat down beside her. "I'm glad you're spending some time with this book—reading is one of the most important skills a person can have." She laid a hand gently on the girl's thin forearm. "In fact, I wish you'd spend more time like this. Sometimes I think you do too much work around the house."

"I only want to help."

"And you do. But promise me to take a little more time for yourself. It will do you good."

Quilty bit her lip and nodded.

"Now, do you remember the girl who came to

Colden House a week ago? Her name was Lucy Robatin and you saw her in the morning—you brought her the washbasin."

"Yes, I remember her." A flicker of fear was in her eyes again. "Has she come back?"

"That's what I came to ask you." Rebecca tried to keep a soft tone in her voice. "Have you seen her again?"

Quilty shook her head no.

"You're sure?"

"I'd remember her, ma'am. Especially the way she smelled—I haven't smelled opium for a long time."

"*Opium?*" Rebecca recalled that Lucy Robatin had reeked of alcohol and vomit, but opium? "Are you sure?"

"Yes, ma'am. It was on her clothes." Quilty looked suddenly embarrassed. "I know what it smells like."

Rebecca muttered in disbelief. "She smoked opium?"

"Maybe not, ma'am. Maybe she was only in a place where somebody else was smoking it."

Either way, that was something her family probably didn't know. Rebecca thought about it, and recalled the blood and skin she'd found under Lucy Robatin's fingernails.

For the first time, she considered that the young woman's disappearance might be more serious than merely a late night out with her friends.

After a few moments of thought, Rebecca decided to call Alice with the new information and let her sister decide what to tell the Robatin family.

CHAPTER 9

It was now one week since Joshua Thompson had been gunned down in the street in front of Canarsee Hall. And in front of at least a hundred people, not one of whom saw a thing.

Buck Morehouse stared at the stacks of papers on his desk. One of them consisted of the arrest papers of those who'd been taken to jail that night. Morehouse had by now contacted more than half of them and gleaned not a single piece of useful information for his trouble.

The other papers were newspapers, from both Brooklyn and New York. A week after the event, the New York papers were no longer reporting anything about Thompson—no surprise since they didn't seem to believe that anything that transpired outside the island of Manhattan could be of much consequence.

The *Brooklyn Daily Eagle*, on the other hand, was another matter. The consolidation debate was still a front-page story every day, and the topic of almost every letter and opinion in the editorial section. Three main threads were addressed in every issue of the *Eagle*.

The first—and the one that caused Morehouse the most distress—was that the Brooklyn Police Department should be taken to task for its failure to protect one of the city's most illustrious citizens and for its subsequent failure to find the killer. Thanks to Captain Sturup, the *Eagle* even named Morehouse as the detective in charge of the investigation.

The second angle of consolidation was a call for civic pride. Readers were exhorted to keep Thompson's fight for Brooklyn independence alive and redouble their efforts to defeat consolidation.

Finally, the newspaper kept readers abreast of the findings of the Lexow Committee in Albany. Another Manhattan police captain had recently been dismissed for accepting bribes and the *Eagle* was thorough in listing every charge and allegation against Tammany Hall and the New York City Police Department. It all made for an ugly picture of what kind of rampant corruption could take over Brooklyn if voters supported consolidation in November's referendum.

Morehouse hadn't been reviewing the newspapers just to read about how inept an investigator he was, however. This case, he'd decided, couldn't be separated from the politics that surrounded it and he needed to try to learn all that he could about the political angles involved. He was a street cop—and a good one—but not a politician. If he did have any political savvy, he thought sourly, it wouldn't have taken him twenty years to work his way up from patrolman.

"Do you do *any* work? Or have you given up?"

Morehouse looked up at Oscar Sturup, looking particularly officious today in his medal-encrusted blue uniform, and resisted the temptation to ask the captain the same question. Other than popping into his doorway several times a day, Sturup had totally divorced himself from all cases that might make him damage his reputation—and harm his chances of getting a favorable position should the Brooklyn and New York Police Departments end up merging.

Receiving no answer, the captain then said, "We got a call from Loesser's. Their jewelry department was hit again last night—gold, mostly. You getting anywhere on *that* case?"

"I've been on the Thompson case almost every minute. I thought that would be a higher priority than robbery."

"You need to clear *both* cases." Sturup was exasperated. "Look, just arrest somebody—anybody. Then we got something we can tell the papers."

"Yes, sir." Morehouse didn't intend to arrest just an unfortunate "anybody," but a simple "yes, sir" was the easiest way of getting rid of the captain.

It had the desired effect. Sturup grunted and nodded, then strode off toward the booking area.

Morehouse looked again at the papers on his desk. He had to admit to himself that he might be in over his head on the Thompson case. But the rash of robberies of Brooklyn stores was something that he should be able to solve. He knew the streets and he knew most of the precinct's criminal element. Besides, if he succeeded in solving this case, maybe his future with the department wouldn't be looking quite so bleak.

He was refreshing himself on the details of the earlier robberies when his phone rang. "Yeah?"

"Detective Morehouse?"

"Yeah, that's me."

"Marshall Webb. At *Harper's*. I was just calling to see if there's anything new on the Thompson murder."

Morehouse had the urge to hang up on him. First Sturup and now this writer reminding him that he was getting nowhere. But they had agreed to cooperate, and if Morehouse was to have any chance of solving the Thompson case, he might need Webb's help. "There might be," he answered. "Can you come to the station house so we can talk about it?"

Webb answered that he would be there within the hour.

The last time Marshall Webb had been a guest of the Brooklyn Police Department, he'd been confined to a crowded cell in the notorious Raymond Street Jail. So he wasn't particularly looking forward to spending time in the Second Precinct station house, other than to learn what Buck Morehouse might have uncovered in the Thompson murder investigation.

Once he arrived at the police station and was escorted by a uniformed officer to the detective's office, Webb discovered that he wouldn't be there long.

Morehouse was seated at a small desk, his back to the door. He swiveled around when the officer announced a visitor. "Webb," Morehouse greeted him. "Good of you to come."

It appeared that the short round detective had just finished lunch. Crumbs of black bread dotted his wrinkled brown sack suit and there was a smear of mustard on his jacket cuff. It was the same suit that he'd been wearing when he came to Webb's apartment and looked like he'd had it on ever since then.

"Glad to," said Webb. "I'm eager to hear what you've learned about Joshua Thompson." Although in seeing the detective, he was less than optimistic that the man could have made any progress. Buck Morehouse had a rubbery face that seemed to have been partially melted in the heat of the summer. He had no beard or mustache, but the man wasn't proficient enough with a razor to be called clean-shaven, either. The detective's eyes were small and appeared deep-set by the puffy flesh that surrounded them. Webb hoped that there was more intelligence behind them than appearances indicated.

Morehouse stood and tugged at the lapels of his jacket in a futile attempt to straighten it out some; he didn't bother to brush off the crumbs. "You mind if we talk while I work? I'm in the middle of another investigation, too."

"Not at all," Webb agreed.

"Good." From the top of a chipped file cabinet, Morehouse took a derby that was frayed on the brim, and put it over short-cropped hair that looked like it had been trimmed by a blind barber. "We're going to a ball game."

It took more then half an hour for them to travel the mile or so down to Eastern Park, home of Brooklyn's National League baseball team, recently dubbed the Trolley Dodgers.

Webb wasn't much of a baseball fan, but he was curious to see what kind of investigation Buck Morehouse could be involved in that required that he go to a ballpark. Besides, the detective still hadn't said a word about the Thompson case, and Webb needed to get some information for his next *Harper's* piece.

To get to the park entrance, the two men first had to tread their way over the maze of streetcar tracks that inspired the team's peculiar nickname and avoid the trolleys that seemed to come and go from every direction. It was especially chaotic in this area of the city, half a dozen blocks west of Prospect Park, because it was home to the Brooklyn Rapid Transit Yard where so many of the city's trolley lines terminated.

Morehouse flashed his badge at the gate and both men were ushered in without having to pay the two-bits admission. After a stop at the concession stand, where Morehouse's badge allowed them to stock up on beer, sausages, and peanuts—again at no charge—Webb followed the detective to a couple of choice seats near the railing on the first base side of the park. Webb wondered if Morehouse even needed to be paid a salary since he appeared to use his police credentials as a form of currency.

They sat down and Morehouse quaffed a good portion of his beer. He belched and rested the bottle on his protruding belly. "You a baseball fan, Webb?"

"I haven't really followed the game," the writer admitted.

"Well, at least you're not a Giants fan then." He

pointed toward a dozen men warming up near the third base bench. "You see the fellows in the gray uniforms over there?"

"Yes . . ."

"Best team in baseball: the Baltimore Orioles. Hate to say it, being a Brooklyn man myself, but they got it all over the other teams in the league." Morehouse then pointed out some of Baltimore's most noted players—John McGraw, Willie Keeler, Hughie Jennings, Wilbert Robinson, Dan Brouthers—and provided Webb with details about their batting averages, fielding abilities, and base running skills.

Webb had heard some of the names before, but saw no reason to pay as close attention to the players' achievements as Buck Morehouse apparently did. It was his plan to leave the game as soon as he and the detective compared notes on the Thompson murder. Several times he tried to interrupt Morehouse's baseball monologues, but without success.

He then concentrated on drinking his own beer and looked about the ballpark. It was an unusual structure to find in a modern city; the park's double-decked grandstand was topped by conical spires, and from the tall spires brightly colored standards rippled in the breeze. To Webb, it looked like the grounds of a medieval jousting tournament. And the stands were almost full, with at least two thousand spectators waiting for the action to begin.

Once the game started, with the Trolley Dodger's Brickyard Kennedy pitching to the Orioles' lineup, Morehouse settled back in his seat and quieted down somewhat. That was partly due to his absorption in the game, but also because his mouth was almost continually occupied by drink and food.

Webb noticed that the detective frequently took his eyes off the diamond to glance about the stands.

Webb ate his sausage and allowed the detective one inning without interruption before bringing up the name of Joshua Thompson again.

"Yeah, guess we should talk about that," said Morehouse with a sigh. He looked at Webb and tapped himself on the chin. "Mustard."

"Oh." Webb dabbed at the same spot on his own chin and removed the smudge. "Thanks." He thought it odd that Morehouse had noticed a drop of mustard on his chin but was oblivious of all the crumbs and stains that had accumulated on his person; from his jowls to his shoes, Morehouse looked like a cafeteria floor after lunch hour.

"Let's move." Morehouse stood and grabbed his bag of peanuts, all that was left of his provisions.

Webb assumed that Morehouse wanted to go to a more remote spot to speak, but instead they made another trip to the concession stand and then took a couple of seats on the third base side of the park.

With Morehouse devoted to his fresh bottle of lager, Webb decided to begin. He leaned toward the detective slightly and said in a low voice. "I checked with a source I have in Tammany. He tells me Boss Croker is as opposed to consolidation as Joshua Thompson was. And he swears that Tammany had nothing to do with Thompson's death."

"You believe him?"

"Yes. Primarily because he insists that Tammany wouldn't take such an action unless they could predict the consequences."

Morehouse had the good sense not to even ask the name of the source, something Webb wouldn't have revealed. "We got our own bosses in Brooklyn.

Hugh McLaughlin's the important one, and he—" The detective suddenly bellowed at the hometown batter, Tommy Corcoran, "What the hell ya swingin' at, ya bum, ya!" Having been struck out by the Orioles' Kid Gleason, Corcoran trudged back to the Brooklyn bench. Morehouse wasn't the only one hooting at him; Brooklyn fans were extraordinarily vocal in expressing themselves—some of them must have had lungs of leather, from the sound of them, Webb thought.

When Morehouse calmed down, Webb prodded him, "You were saying something about Hugh McLaughlin."

"Oh yeah. He runs the political show in Brooklyn. But he's against consolidation too." He turned his eyes to Webb. "So you don't think there was any political involvement in Thompson getting killed?"

"Well, that's good enough for me." He took a sip of beer and added thoughtfully. "Tell you the truth, I don't follow politics much. I'm just a beat cop in a suit. I know most every low-life crook in Brooklyn—but almost nothing about the men with real power, the ones who plan their crimes in company boardrooms or bank offices or even City Hall." He turned again to Webb. "That's where I'm hoping *you* can . . ." As his voice trailed off, so did his eyes, now looking past Webb. "There he is."

"There *who* is?"

"Silk Bercini." Morehouse slowly stood. "Come with me. He might try to run, and I'm not as fast as I used to be."

Webb couldn't fathom Morehouse's way of doing things, but he also got up and followed the detective. The Trolley Dodgers had made their third out, and a number of fans were walking about on their way to the lavatories and food vendors. It made it easier to approach a banty rooster of a man in a loose gray suit who was standing next to one of the entrances through which the crowd passed.

"There he is," said Morehouse. "That's Bercini."

Webb had already caught on that this man, who had oily black hair topped by a derby in even worse condition than Morehouse's, was the detective's prey. "What does he—"

Before Webb could finish the question, Morehouse sprang at the man, grabbing him by the forearm.

"What the hell?" Bercini squawked. He tried to wriggle his way out of the detective's grasp, while Webb moved around and grabbed his other arm. It was a skinny arm, but Webb could feel muscles like steel cables under the jacket sleeve. Then the muscles relaxed slightly as a look of recognition came over Bercini's face. "Hey, Bucky, I didn't know it was you." An unctuous smile spread on his angular face. "What's with the strong-arm approach?"

"Come with me, Silk." Morehouse didn't loosen his grip as he pulled Bercini toward the exit.

"Not so rough!" Bercini protested. "I gotta sensitive touch, you know."

"I know," said the detective. "If you didn't, you wouldn't be the best pickpocket in Brooklyn."

"Come on now, Buck." Bercini smiled more broadly. "Give me some credit—I'm the best in all of New York."

"I don't care about New York. All I care about is Brooklyn."

The pickpocket suddenly tried to wrench his arm free from Webb's grasp, but the writer's grip was tight. "Who's your friend, Buck?"

"He's new," the detective answered, without further elaboration.

Bercini whined, "No fair, comin' at me two on one."

"Tough."

Once they were under the grandstand, near the men's room, Morehouse drew to a halt and pushed Bercini against a pillar that supported the upper deck. "Figured I'd find you here, Silk. This ball game's got to have the biggest crowd in Brooklyn today, and I know how much you like crowds—all those pockets for you to dig into."

"Hey, I'm just a baseball fan. Honest!"

Webb could tell that Bercini's protest of innocence was merely pro forma; there was no conviction in the words.

Morehouse took off his derby and held it out as if he were taking up a collection. "Everything out of your pockets and in here," he ordered.

"All I got is my own. I'm tellin' ya the truth."

Morehouse jerked his head toward Webb. "You got ten seconds or I turn him loose on you. And I've seen him do a search—he'll pull the teeth right out of your mouth."

Webb tried to look intimidating. Since he stood a foot taller than Bercini, it wasn't difficult.

"All right," said the pickpocket. "I might have found a couple of things on the ground." He moved for an inside pocket of his jacket.

Webb and Morehouse both relaxed their grips to allow him enough freedom to move, but stay close enough that he couldn't escape past them.

Bercini made a show of emptying every inner and outer pocket of his jacket. Morehouse's derby was soon half full with watches and billfolds. At one point, a middle-aged man came out of the men's room and looked at them with some concern. Webb realized it must have appeared that they were robbing Bercini, but the man simply walked away—either because he didn't want to miss the ball game or didn't think a mugging was any of his business.

Morehouse poked Bercini in the chest. "Now the vest."

The pickpocket hesitated, but another poke from Morehouse caused him to dig inside his vest where he'd stored another half dozen watches. "I gotta live, ya know, Buck," he grumbled.

"Hell," said Morehouse, looking down at the glittering gold in his hat, "you could live a year on this haul, Silk. And the game ain't even half over."

"Can I help it if I'm good at my job?"

"Well, here's the thing." Morehouse put his rubbery face directly in front of the pickpocket's. "As of this moment, you're out of business."

"Hey, you can't—" The protest died in Bercini's throat when the detective suddenly punched him hard in the belly.

"Don't interrupt." Morehouse grabbed Bercini's jaw and held it so that the pickpocket had to look him in the eyes. "There've been some jewelry heists, lately—Loesser's got hit last night. And I want it stopped."

"You know I don't—" He was stopped with another punch.

"What did I say about interruptin'?"

Bercini wisely didn't answer.

Morehouse went on, "I know you don't pull those kinds of jobs. But somebody does know who's been hitting the stores and I want you to find out."

Bercini opened his mouth to protest, then promptly shut it again.

The detective looked down in his derby. "Now, I know you're not planning to open a watch store with all this. You got a fence—and your fence gets goods like these from more crooks than just you. So you go to him. Tell him I'll be cracking down on every burglar and pickpocket and mugger in Brooklyn until I find out who's been hitting the stores. You got that?"

Bercini nodded but still said nothing.

"Good. Once I get that bastard behind bars, then the rest of you can go about your lives." Morehouse dug his fingers through the contents of his hat. "But don't get greedy like you did today. I'm gonna take this to the ticket booth in case anybody wants to claim their possessions."

Morehouse took a step back and Webb followed suit.

Bercini asked in a small voice, "What if nobody knows who's been doin' the jewel heists?"

"Somebody knows," answered the detective. "What do you think—the thief is *eatin'* the jewelry? No, it's being fenced." He turned to go, then turned back again. "Oh, and if I don't find out who did it, you really will have to find another line of work—'cause I'll break every bone in your hands."

Webb had the distinct impression that Silk Bercini would do his utmost to get Morehouse the information that he wanted.

After dropping the stolen property at the ticket booth, and once again loading up on beer and sausages, the two men returned to watch the ball game. While they'd been occupied with Bercini, the Orioles had scored twice to take a 2–0 lead and had the bases loaded with only one out.

They watched to see what would happen on the field before resuming their earlier conversation. Even Webb found himself getting interested. A day at a ballpark, in the sunshine and the open air, was a welcome change from life in downtown Manhattan. Not even the faints odors wafting over from the nearby Gowanus Canal put a damper on the afternoon.

To the cheers of the Brooklyn partisans, the Baltimore runners were stranded on base without scoring. Webb then turned to Morehouse. "You were saying you hoped I could help with the Thompson case."

Morehouse swallowed the enormous chunk of sausage he'd been chewing. "Oh yes. Like I said, I know how to deal with common crooks like Silk Bercini. But folks like the Thompsons . . ." He shook his head. "I just don't understand 'em."

Webb respected the fact that the detective not only was aware of his limitations but admitted them. "What can I do?"

"I met with Catherine McCutcheon—she's Thompson's daughter and she's taken over runnin' the family business now that he's dead."

"Did she have anything useful to say?"

"She talked," Morehouse answered thoughtfully, "but I'm not sure that it was useful. Tell you the truth, I got a funny feeling about her—I thought she was holding something back. But then"—he shrugged—"maybe I just don't know how rich people talk. Maybe they keep things to themselves more than regular people do."

It was Webb's experience that Morehouse's conjecture was correct. "Anything in particular she said—or didn't say—that caught your attention?"

"I asked if her father had any enemies, either business or personal. According to her, Joshua Thompson was a saint." Morehouse frowned slightly. "Now, I don't know any millionaires personally, but from what I hear, not a lot of men get rich without making some enemies on the way."

"I believe that's true," said Webb. "Did she say anything about their family? Any problems there?" It also wasn't unusual, Webb knew, that wealthy families often had differences about how to manage their money.

"Thompson left a widow—I didn't meet her. And a son, Eugene. I didn't speak with him, either. According to the sister, he doesn't get involved with business. Tennis and golf were all she said he was interested in." Morehouse snorted. "Golf! Can you imagine? *That's* not a sport. *Baseball* is a sport." His attention was back to the field, where the Trolley Dodgers had managed to get their first two runners on base.

"What do you want me to do?" Webb prompted.

"Talk to the sister again. And the brother too. See what you can learn from them."

"The sister might be suspicious at being questioned twice."

"I thought about that. You could tell her you're writing some nice article about her father for *Harper's*. You don't have to say anything about investigating his death."

That sounded sensible to Webb, who was beginning to think that Buck Morehouse was more capable than he first appeared. "I'll see what I can find out," he said.

Morehouse checked his pocket watch. "I should get back to the station house." Then the next batter walked to load the bases. "And as soon as the game's over, that's right where I'm gonna go."

Webb decided that he would stay, too, and ordered a couple more beers from a passing vendor.

CHAPTER 10

There was little left of the splendid *bombe de glace* that the Davies chef had concocted for Sunday dessert when Mr. Davies rang the bell signaling that the servants were to clear the table. Since it also signaled the commencement of the post-dinner ritual, one that specified that the sexes be separate, Rebecca gave Marshall Webb a warm smile before rising from the table.

Although she knew that Webb hadn't come because he enjoyed socializing with her family, Rebecca was happy to have him by her side for any reason. They didn't have many chances to spend time together lately, and she missed his company. There were few people of either gender with whom Rebecca enjoyed sharing intelligent conversation as much as she did with Webb. And the fact that he was such a handsome man was a bonus; he looked especially so today, she thought, in formal dinner clothes that fit his tall frame so well. She did have to talk him into something about his whiskers,

though; the Franz Josef style, with a carefully culti-
vated mustache over a clean-shaven chin, was a bit
too old-fashioned—and patches of gray were starting to sprout in the neatly groomed brown whiskers.

Webb rose and held the back of her chair as she
got up. Although Rebecca was far from a stickler
for etiquette—in fact she thought many social ritu-
als were annoyances that should be dispensed with—
she appreciated Webb's gentlemanly gestures.

After one more look and a shared smile, Webb
went toward the library door accompanied by her
father and Jacob Updegraff, while Rebecca turned
in the direction of the music room.

Alice, who was a vision of loveliness in a shimmering green gown that brought out the gold in
her elegantly coiffed hair, sidled up to Rebecca before they got to the music room. "Oh, Rebecca,"
she said, "have you seen the ferns lately? They are
simply thriving this summer!"

"No, I haven't."

Alice took Rebecca by the arm. "Let me show
you. I'm sure the other ladies will excuse us for a
minute."

Rebecca had little interest in plants, but she
could tell that horticulture wasn't the reason Alice
had pulled her aside. So she quietly followed her
sister to the conservatory, a spacious room on the
west side of the mansion.

They stepped into a scene that was utterly at
odds with its Fifth Avenue setting. Several years
ago, Rebecca's mother had decided to create a
tropical setting within the walls of their home. The
conservatory was like a jungle, lush with ferns and
palms. Creeping vines grew up a trellis and crawled
along the ceiling. The outside wall of the room was

set with large windows that allowed the afternoon sun to stream through freely, bringing in plentiful light and generating an oppressive heat. It was like having a jungle right in the heart of Manhattan.

"Lucy Robatin is still missing," Alice said.

Rebecca was sorry to hear that; she knew that once a girl had been missing for several days, it could mean that she was in serious trouble. "Her family hasn't heard anything from her?"

"No, not a word." Alice's voice was small, but it echoed in the strangely appointed room.

"Did you tell her family about the opium?"

Alice walked toward an ornate birdbath in the center of the room. It was large enough to accommodate a condor, and continually replenished by fresh water, but no bird would ever have a chance to make use of it. The room had once been stocked with several free-flying parakeets and cockatoos, but once Rebecca's mother discovered that the birds messed the floor she ordered them confined to cages. And, once she decided that their chirping disrupted the serenity of the room, she had them expelled from the premises completely.

"How could I say such a thing to the Robatins?" Alice asked. "To suggest that their daughter"—her voice dropped to a whisper—"smokes *opium* . . . that would be a terrible thing to say."

"How could you *not?*" Rebecca didn't understand why her sister wouldn't have shared the information with the Robatins. "It might have something to do with why she's missing."

"I just—" Alice bit her lower lip. "You don't understand, Rebecca. Perhaps you used to, but not anymore. There are certain things that simply are not discussed in polite society."

"You're concerned about being *polite?*" What Alice had said was true; Rebecca no longer understood the rationale for such stifling rules of behavior. "A young woman's well-being, perhaps even her life, might be at stake, and you're not willing to discuss it with her family? You said you were friends with the Robatins. What kind of friendship is that?"

Alice looked as if she'd been slapped, and Rebecca regretted her harsh tone. After taking a moment to compose herself, Alice answered calmly, "It is not the sort of friendship where we would meddle in each other's personal lives." She reached out and ran a finger along the browning leaf of a potted palm. Keeping her eyes on the plant instead of Rebecca, she went on, "The relationship between our families was based on business. Victor Robatin and Mr. Updegraff have done business together for years—Mr. Robatin has extensive real estate holdings in Manhattan and my husband's bank has financed many of his acquisitions. As a result of the financial association, our families became acquainted socially as well. But we maintain a respectful distance." She looked at Rebecca. "Mr. Updegraff is adamant that a proper balance be maintained with those he does business with—relations must be kept cordial, but they shouldn't get so close that complications could result that might hinder future business transactions. I'm certain that telling the Robatins that their daughter might be an opium smoker would be the kind of 'complication' Mr. Updegraff prefers to avoid."

Rebecca knew her brother-in-law well enough to know that Alice was right: To him, business came first—even, perhaps, before the life of a young woman. "What about *you,* Alice?" She touched her sister's elbow and motioned to a wicker window seat, where the two of them sat down. "You've been coming to Colden House once a week for almost a year now, helping the girls and getting to know them. And you know what can happen to them. Aren't you worried about Lucy Robatin?"

"Of course I am."

"Don't you—"

The door to the conservatory opened, and Aunt Esther poked her wrinkled face into the room. "*There* you two are. We were wondering where you went. Aren't you coming to the music room? It appears that the Vanderbilts are actually going to"— her voice dropped— "*divorce.*" Her bony shoulders shuddered to show how horrid she considered such an event. "We were just about to discuss it."

Rebecca had no interest in the Vanderbilts' marital problems, but she feigned enthusiasm for the subject, and promised her aunt that she and Alice would be along shortly.

When Aunt Esther had left them alone again, Alice said, "I *am* worried about Lucy Robatin, but her situation might not be as bad as you think."

"What do you mean?"

"We don't *know* that she's been using opium, do we?"

"No, we don't," Rebecca conceded.

"You said someone smelled it on her clothes— perhaps she was simply in a room where someone else was smoking it."

"That could be." Rebecca thought a moment. "Maybe she didn't smoke opium. But she did have a violent encounter with someone. I saw the blood and skin under her fingernails." She turned to her sister. "There is enough cause for concern to speak with her parents—whatever effect that might have on Mr. Updegraff's business."

"It's not only because of Mr. Updegraff that I'm loathe to say anything to them," Alice said. "Remember, I told you that Mr. Robatin had told Lucy that the next time she came home intoxicated, he would turn her away?"

"Yes, I remember." That was why Alice had told her to go to Colden House if she was in such a condition.

"Now that she hasn't come home at all, Mr. Robatin says that she is no longer a member of the family. He has forbidden anyone to mention her in his presence. She is basically disowned."

"And what does *Mrs.* Robatin say about that?" Rebecca doubted that the girl's mother could discard her child as readily as her father apparently had.

"I don't know," said Alice. "We haven't discussed it."

"You might have to, Alice. Lucy Robatin has been missing for days. You know how much danger a girl alone in New York can face—even a girl from a prominent family."

"Yes, I realize that. But her father—"

"Her father is willing to give up on her—to throw her away." Rebecca laid a hand on Alice's forearm. "Are you?"

Alice was quiet for sometime, clearly debating with herself, probably torn between family duty and personal conscience. She finally answered in a whisper, "No. No, I'm not."

* * *

The Davies library was plush with dark wood, rich leather, heavy drapes, and oriental rugs. On the shelves were leather-bound books and illustrated folios, many of them brittle with age. But Marshall Webb knew that reading wasn't the primary activity that took place in the room.

The walls were adorned with English hunting prints and an eclectic collection of medieval broadswords, Italian daggers, and flintlock firearms. Over the mantel was a set of antique French dueling pistols. But the sporting images and dangerous trappings were all purely decorative; the Davies men knew nothing of the outdoors or how to use such weapons.

No, the main focus of the Davies library was the mahogany sideboard that held crystal decanters of fine ports and well-aged brandies and cedar boxes of expensive Cuban cigars.

Jacob Updegraff did the honors, first providing his father-in-law with a glass of port and a dark cigar that smelled to Webb like burning tar. Thus provisioned, Mr. Davies then sat down in a corner easy chair and contented himself with blowing smoke rings that nearly matched his wooly white hair. He would soon be "resting his eyes," Webb knew, which meant he would have to be watched so that his burning cigar wouldn't fall and start a fire.

After Webb and Updegraff also had snifters of brandy and lit cigars, they settled into a pair of leather wing chairs on the other side of the library.

The two men weren't on the friendliest of terms, so, as usual, they eyed each other cautiously for a while before speaking. Jacob Updegraff had a strong brow, a prominent chin, and a short, thick neck; in

different clothes, he could easily fit in with any
street gang in the Bowery, and Webb knew that
when it came to business the banker was every bit
as ruthless as one of the Bowery thugs.

After a few pointless observations about the
weather, which served only to break the stultifying
silence, Webb brought up the subject that he'd
come to discuss. "You have a shrewd sense of business, Updegraff," he began, knowing that flatter-
ing his sense of self-importance was the surest way
to get him to speak. "What do you think of this
consolidation matter? Are you in favor?"

Updegraff exhaled a long stream of smoke and
his nose tilted up at an arrogant angle. "Of course
I'm in favor of consolidation. *Everyone* who under-
stands anything about finance and commerce sup-
ports it."

"Everyone in New York," Webb said.

"Of course." From his tone, Updegraff didn't
seem to believe there was anyone of consequence
outside of Manhattan.

"What do *you* see as the advantage of merging?"
Webb knew the arguments, but wanted to hear directly from someone with Updegraff's fiscal experience and business connections.

"Commerce," Updegraff answered promptly.
"It's the lifeblood of New York, and we must ensure that it be sustained." He poked the air with
his cigar to stress his point. "The city is growing,
but the island isn't, of course—the waterfront is as
big as it's going to get. If we want to increase shipping—which we must—we have to take over the
Brooklyn docks." He planted his cigar back between

his teeth and mumbled, "Too bad we have to take the rest of that shabby city along with it, but that's the price we have to pay, I suppose."

"Is that why Brooklyn's upper class is opposed to consolidation? Because New Yorkers consider it a takeover instead of a merger?"

Updegraff snorted. "Brooklyn doesn't *have* an 'upper class.'"

"Not even the Pratts or the Lows or the Pierreponts?" Webb mentioned a few of that city's most prominent families.

"Oh, a few of them have done *moderately* well for themselves." He eyed Webb. "Do you have a particular interest in the issue?"

"I'm covering it for *Harper's.*"

Updegraff grunted and took a sip of his cognac.

Although Webb's series on Tammany Hall might have been viewed as important by some, he knew that people like the Davieses and Updegraffs considered it unseemly to write about unpleasant matters for public consumption. Corruption and vice were to be ignored and covered up, not exposed in the newspapers; it was terribly impolite to do so.

From his corner chair, Mr. Davies cleared his throat for attention. He was holding his empty port glass. Usually he was asleep by now, but Jacob Updegraff got up and poured him another port.

When the banker returned to his seat, Webb asked, "Did you know Joshua Thompson?"

"No. I heard of him, of course. But I've never met him, and never had any business dealings with him. He was of a rather humble family, I believe."

If so, thought Webb, it would have been refreshing. Humility was something that never plagued the Updegraffs or the Davieses. "Perhaps originally," he said. "But he made himself a millionaire."

"Oh, every now and then one of those merchants across the river gets lucky in business—hardly makes him a man of any consequence." Updegraff downed a good part of his brandy. "I tell you, Brooklyn isn't even a fourth-rate city. All those Irish around the Navy Yard, and the Italians in Red Hook; and Fort Greene is full of darkies. How can a proper city grow without good families to run it?"

Webb decided not to enumerate all the different ethnic groups that populated the island of Manhattan. He simply said, "All of those Brooklynites will be New Yorkers if consolidation passes."

Updegraff scowled slightly. "What I'm hoping—and I'm not alone in thinking this way—is that once we've annexed Brooklyn we can clear out our own tenements and problem areas and move the riffraff across the river." He then held up a warning forefinger. "What I say is not for publication, you understand."

Webb said that he did understand. He also understood now why Joshua Thompson and others in Brooklyn would fight so hard to keep their city independent of the likes of Jacob Updegraff.

CHAPTER 11

Monday morning had been a busy one for Buck Morehouse. Unfortunately, although he felt he'd done a lot of work, he wasn't sure that he'd accomplished anything of importance.

He'd come to the station house early, before Captain Sturup arrived, to do some paperwork. It was Morehouse's intent to stay out of the police station as much as possible when the captain was in. The detective planned to do his office work when the captain was off duty and do interviews and investigations outside the station house when Sturup was in; Morehouse didn't see how he could be productive otherwise with the captain's frequent interruptions.

Over a breakfast of black coffee and dark bread smeared thick with butter, Morehouse had gone over files, splitting his time between the department store break-ins and the Thompson murder. First, he'd reviewed the records of known burglars and made a list of possible suspects in the jewel robberies. Then, he'd again gone over the arrest records of those hauled in the night Thompson was killed, and made a few mental notes that he would follow up on.

Shortly before Captain Sturup was due to go on duty, Morehouse left for the courthouse, where he was able to review a copy of Joshua Thompson's will. Although he still believed that the motive for the businessman's murder was political, Marshall Webb did have a point about investigating Thompson's personal life. And one very personal reason for killing a millionaire was if the killer stood to inherit some of the wealth. Morehouse noticed nothing out of the ordinary in the list of family members and charities who were Joshua Thompson's beneficiaries, but he methodically noted every bequest in the will.

So, by eleven-thirty, Morehouse felt as if he'd already put in a full day's work. But he still had more to do.

There was a break in the oppressive heat that had gripped Brooklyn for most of the summer. This morning, light, swirling clouds filtered the sun so that its light was soft and its heat mild. Morehouse decided to enjoy the weather by walking to his next destination instead of commandeering a hansom cab or having a uniformed officer drive him in a department wagon.

Street traffic grew thicker as the lunch hour neared, and the sidewalks were increasingly crowded, but Morehouse was in no particular hurry as he headed north to Flushing Avenue. Din from the Navy Yard filled the air and a few cranes used in working on the ships poked above the Brooklyn skyline. Smokestacks from the adjacent foundry spewed brown smoke into the air. At Flushing, Morehouse turned east, past the U.S. Marine Barracks to Washington Avenue. Beyond the barracks, the Dutch gables and spires of Wallabout Market, where tons of produce were sold, were visible.

In the shadows of the market, Morehouse found the tavern he was seeking. No sign advertised the place, because new customers weren't especially wanted, but locals knew of the saloon as "Duffy's."

Morehouse walked into the low-ceilinged barroom, and gave his eyes a little time to get acclimated to the dim light. He could see the long bar, which was actually only five or six feet long and of rough construction; a shelf behind it held several brands of whiskey and rum. There were several tables and a dozen chairs, only a few of which matched. A couple of men were playing cards near the bar, and several more were seated near the back of the small room. The only decorations on the bare walls were stains—of what, Morehouse didn't want to venture a guess—and the smell of stale cigar smoke was the predominant odor.

The bartender, who looked like something that had escaped from the monkey house at the zoo, was putting out the free lunch spread on a side table. Morehouse was reminded that he hadn't stopped to eat and he stepped over to survey the food; he and the glowering bartender exchanged grunts of greeting. There was a fatty chunk of ham, a jar of pickled eggs, some pickles, and a wedge of cheese that was so moldy it could almost count as a vegetable.

Morehouse opted for a pickle. Chewing a bite of it, he went to the back of the bar. The two younger men sitting there stood up and crossed their arms like sentries presenting their rifles. The third man at the table, about fifty years old, wearing a cloth cap at an angle and an Irish sweater, told them, "Have yourselves a beer at the bar, boys." Looking up at Morehouse through bloodshot eyes, he said, "Haven't seen you in some time, Buck. Thought maybe you forgot about me." He nodded at a chair that had been vacated by one of the young men.

The detective sat down. "Couldn't forget you, Ian." He looked around. "Your beer any better than your food, Duffy?"

"It is." He called to the bartender and told him to bring a beer for Morehouse and a whiskey for himself. "And make it quick," he added.

The bartender almost jumped to comply, which came as no surprise to Morehouse. Ian Duffy ran one of the toughest gangs in Brooklyn, and he ran it with an iron hand. It was a notorious gang that specialized not in robbery or gambling, but in providing muscle for hire. There was even a price list, Morehouse knew, that specified the gang's fees; they would blacken eyes for only two dollars per eye, break a nose for ten, tear off an ear for fifteen, shoot a man in the leg for twenty-five dollars, and do "the big job" for a hundred.

When the drinks arrived, Duffy shifted the chaw of tobacco in his cheek and downed half his whiskey in a gulp. Part of it dripped down his chin and Duffy wiped it off with the back of a hand that had misshapen fingers. The broken fingers were only one remnant of the fights Duffy had survived; he had a jagged scar on his fleshy cheek and he was missing part of his left year. "This official?" asked Duffy. "Or you just lookin' for free beer?"

"Official," answered Morehouse. He hoisted his

beer glass. "But I *am* hoping you'll keep this full just to be hospitable." Then the detective sampled the dark brew, and found it to be quite satisfactory.

Duffy laughed. "There ain't a bar in Brooklyn has enough beer to keep *you* full, Buck!"

"You know me well." Morehouse chuckled, then tipped the glass back and drained it empty. He put it on the table and emitted a satisfied belch.

Duffy motioned for the bartender to bring a fresh beer. "But we'll do our best," he said. "Never know when I might need to depend on *your* hospitality." He grinned, exposing crooked teeth stained brown from tobacco.

"Considering your line of business, that could be any time." After Morehouse had the second beer in front of him, he added, "A few of your boys enjoyed our hospitality about ten days ago—in the Raymond Street Jail."

"That a fact?" Duffy spat a stream of tobacco juice into the half-full cuspidor next to the table.

"Yup. Jimmy Rishell, Mark Sackett, and Chad Phelps. They work for you, don't they?"

"From time to time."

Morehouse folded his arms on the sticky table and leaned forward. "Were they working for you the night Joshua Thompson got killed?"

"I didn't have nothin' to do with that," said Duffy.

"Seems curious to me that three men who work for you—and we all know what kind of work they do—should all be on the scene that night."

Duffy spat again and took a sip of whiskey. "Maybe they was just curious about what was going on. That occur to you?"

It had, actually. The three men had only been

brought in as a result of the sweep, not because they'd committed a crime. "Could be," answered Morehouse. "But it's a coincidence, and I don't like coincidences. They make me keep digging until I find something."

Ian Duffy eyed Morehouse for a long moment. "No need to waste your time lookin' into my business, Buck. The boys had nothing to do with Thompson getting shot. You got my word on it."

"Why *were* they there?"

Duffy called for another whiskey. "It was a small job—nothing, really. They were there to help out if there was any rough stuff between the two sides arguing about consolidation."

"Which side were they supposed to help out?" Morehouse knew that Duffy's gang had no allegiance except to the highest bidder; if they were involved in a political fight, the side they were on depended on who paid them.

"The independence side."

"Who hired you?"

Duffy hesitated. "Let's keep this between ourselves, okay, Buck? Could be bad for business if customers found out I give you a name."

The detective agreed, but didn't feel particularly obligated to keep the promise. It all depended on where the information led.

"Hugh McLaughlin, the boss."

McLaughlin, the power in Brooklyn politics, was known to oppose consolidation. Morehouse thought aloud, "McLaughlin supported Thompson; I don't expect he wanted him harmed."

"No. Like I said, we were just hired to be there in case the Brooklyn Consolidation League came out in force to oppose Thompson. There were only a few, so my boys hardly even got the chance to throw a punch."

Knowing the kind of men Duffy employed, that must have come as a disappointment to them. Morehouse sipped his beer and glanced over to the lunch counter; his belly was starting to growl and the ham was starting to look appealing. He looked back at Duffy. "Give me your professional opinion: who do you think would want to kill Joshua Thompson?"

The gang leader appeared to think it over. "Somebody who didn't like him, would be my guess."

Morehouse rolled his eyes.

"What I mean," Duffy went on, "is that I don't know it's to anyone's advantage to kill him over politics." He shrugged. "Can't tell what effect it'll have on the campaign."

So far, that seemed to be the prevailing opinion. "You haven't heard *anything* about who might have been behind the Thompson shooting?"

"Not a word. And if it was for hire, I would have—in fact, I'd have probably gotten the job." There was a note of pride in Duffy's voice.

Morehouse pushed his chair back. He decided it was time to find a saloon with a more substantial lunch spread.

Duffy rubbed his scarred cheek. "By the way, you sure it was *Thompson* who was supposed to be shot?"

The fact that Joshua Thompson *was* shot had been enough for Morehouse. "What do you mean?"

"I hear that writer who wrote those stories about Tammany Hall was standing right next to Thompson—maybe the shooter missed."

Morehouse slumped in his chair. That possibility hadn't occurred to him, but he had to concede that it was indeed a possibility. The shots had been fired from across the street; it was easy to miss by a foot from that distance. "You heard something about Tammany wanting Marshall Webb dead?"

"Nothing specific. And nothing lately. But when those articles came out, there was sure some people calling for his scalp."

That put a whole new slant on things, and Morehouse wasn't sure what to make of it. "Let me know if you do hear something, won't you? I'll owe you."

"You do already," Duffy reminded him. "But I'll let you know."

Morehouse stood. "Thanks."

Duffy nodded magnanimously. "There's something to remember, though."

"Yeah, I know, I know. I owe you."

"Yes, but what I mean is: I may not hear anything if Tammany is after Webb. Tammany doesn't have to hire anyone to take care of its business. They have enough people on their payroll to handle a simple shooting."

Morehouse mulled that over for a moment. As far as he could tell the Thompson shooting was turning out to be anything but "simple."

Marshall Webb took the slow-moving Grand Street Ferry across the equally sluggish East River. Grand Street in Manhattan and Grand Street in Brooklyn didn't align, so the ferry actually traveled half a mile north along the river before landing on the Brooklyn side of the river.

He then hopped a streetcar, which took him along

Grand through Williamsburg, which had once been a separate city itself before being annexed by Brooklyn, its neighbor to the south. Webb wondered how Joshua Thompson had reconciled being so opposed to Brooklyn's merger with New York, when Brooklyn itself had added so many surrounding cities and towns to its borders over the years—including Williamsburg, home of Thompson Manufacturing.

Near Bushwick Avenue, Webb found the headquarters of the late Joshua Thompson's business. It was indistinguishable from almost any other factory in the northeast, a three-story structure of redbrick, with small narrow windows. A modest sign over the front door read:

THOMPSON MANUFACTURING
FINE SHOES AND BOOTS

There was a small reception area inside, where Webb was greeted by a young male clerk who inquired what his business was.

"Marshall Webb, with *Harper's Weekly*," he answered, handing the clerk his card. "Mr. Floegel is expecting me."

"Yes, sir. I believe Mr. Floegel is in the shop right now. I'll see if I can find him for you."

The reception area was clean and open, furnished with varnished oak desks and chairs that were in good repair. A couple of potted plants were near the doorway, a braided oval rug covered much of the floor, and an oil portrait of the company's founder hung in a prominent position on the beige wall. The simple décor was appealing, a far cry from the ostentatious style that so many industrialists flaunted.

While he waited, Webb looked at some of the old photographs arrayed on the hallway wall. Some were sepia, some black-and-white; some were clear, sharp images, while others were faded and blurred. All showed various companies that over the years became part of the Thompson empire, and in most of them Joshua Thompson was posed next to the front door of whatever building was being photographed. Among them were a ramshackle blacksmith's shop, a hulking foundry, and a brick pencil factory with a huge pole painted to look like a sharpened pencil mounted above the door.

Webb could see Thompson age over the years as he scanned his changing image in the photographs. In some, there was a young boy, presumably Eugene Thompson. Thompson's son didn't age as much, however; he was only pictured from the ages of about five to twelve.

"Mr. Webb!"

He turned around to see the clerk accompanied by a thick-necked man of about fifty in a pin-striped suit with a matching vest. "Yes?"

The man stuck out a meaty hand. "Sam Floegel, general manager of Thompson Manufacturing. You're right on time."

"I know you're a busy man, Mr. Floegel." Webb shook his hand and quickly sized him up. Sam Floegel looked the part of a factory manager. His eyes were haggard and his jowls drooped; it was the look that Webb had often seen in his own brother, who as a shop manager had too much responsibility and too little reward. Floegel even matched his brother in his hairstyle, with a full black beard on his jaw but little hair above his ears; a patch of white at the chin appeared to cleave the whiskers in two. A thick, shimmering gold chain was draped across Floegel's prominent belly, but it was one of the few signs of affluence; his suit showed signs that Floegel often had to do some manual labor in addition to managing others.

"Happy to make time for the press." Floegel's smile indicated that what he said was true. "Especially *Harper's*—it's quite an honor." He motioned to the pictures on the wall. "I see you're interested in our history."

"Yes, indeed," said Webb. He pointed to the most faded photograph, of a relatively young Joshua Thompson standing stiffly in front of a small shoe repair shop. "Is this how it all started?"

Floegel nodded. "Hard to believe, but that was the beginning of Thompson Manufacturing. That picture was taken before the war. There weren't a lot of pictures taken back then, except studio portraits, so Mr. Thompson must have known in his bones that this little shoe shop was going to grow into something very important. It cost him quite a penny—and he didn't have many pennies back then—to get a photographer to come and snap this shot."

Webb took his notebook out and jotted down a few sentences. He had made this appointment with Sam Floegel because he thought the manager might be more forthcoming with information than Catherine McCutcheon. According to Buck Morehouse, Thompson's daughter had been very controlled in what she'd told him, and the detective thought she might be hiding something. So Webb had decided to start with the general manager, and see what he could learn from him first; Floegel might even reveal something about Catherine McCutcheon since he hadn't worked for her long enough to have an allegiance to her. So far, it appeared that the garrulous Floegel might turn out to be a font of information. But Webb had to maintain the pretext that he had established on the telephone—that he was writing an extensive story on Joshua Thompson and his company for *Harper's*.

Sam Floegel then took Webb on a trip through history, pointing out photographs and providing details on Thompson's expanding empire.

"When did you start working for Mr. Thompson?" Webb asked.

Floegel smoothed down the fringe of hair over his ears as if expecting to be photographed. "I began with the company in sixty-two. It was a busy time, during the war." He nodded, clearly enjoying the memory. "We made *everything* then—mostly to support the war effort, of course. When the army needed boots, they got boots made right here in Brooklyn, by Thompson employees. Same when they needed blankets, canteens, cartridges, bayonets . . . Like I said, everything."

Webb jotted a few notes. "That was the first big expansion of the company? Manufacturing all those goods for the war?"

Floegel nodded. "Government contracts—can't beat 'em." He pointed to a photograph of a machine shop. "Mr. Thompson bought this place and a few others before the war, so was already starting to grow the company, but yes, war contracts gave us our period of greatest growth."

Webb looked about the reception area. "You appear to have a nice facility here—but to be honest, I expected it to be larger."

"This is only one building," Floegel quickly explained. "Would you care for a tour? I'm sure you'll find it to be a most impressive operation."

"I'd be delighted."

Floegel led Webb toward a swinging door at the end of the hall. On the way, he said, "All we do in this particular factory is make footwear. There are plants all over Brooklyn where we manufacture many other goods. But this is also our headquarters—where we keep our business offices." He smiled. "Every now and then someone would suggest to Mr. Thompson that we run the business from some nice office building downtown, but I suppose since he started with a shoemaking shop he always wanted to stay close to the business he began with."

Through the door, they entered an expansive workroom that occupied the entire ground floor. At least a hundred men and women were hard at work at their benches hammering, cutting, and sewing to assemble a variety of footwear. But Webb's eyes were slow to take in the scene; it was his ears and nose that responded first. His ears were assaulted by the constant hammering, from both handheld hammers and even louder punch presses. The steady rattle of sewing machines punching their needles through leather added to the din. And the overwhelming smell of tanning chemicals and treated hides made Webb want to hold his breath. The dusty side windows were all levered open, but failed to provide adequate ventilation; Webb would have hated to be here in the winter when the windows were closed.

He followed Sam Floegel, though, as the manager led him around the room, explaining the process. They passed by old men cutting leather pieces to size, younger men hammering heels onto soles, and women stitching rows of buttons on high ladies' shoes.

Other than the overpowering smell, which probably nothing could eliminate, Webb noted that conditions were fairly good. The workshop was far from cramped; leather hides were neatly stacked along the walls, and boxes of completed shoes were piled at the ends of the benches. Workers had enough room to move easily, and most appeared content with their work; several of the women smiled at Webb as he passed by. Although the work wasn't easy, Webb was sure, Thompson Manufacturing was by no means a sweatshop.

"We make more than a dozen styles of ladies' shoes," Floegel boasted, "along with half a dozen men's shoes and eight kinds of boots." He looked at Webb. "What's your size? We just started making a men's model in kangaroo—feels wonderful on the feet. I'd be happy to give you a pair."

"Very kind of you," said Webb. But before he could state his size, Floegel was already expounding on the marvelous new system they had for gluing cork soles.

As they reached the end of the workbenches, Webb noticed there were some empty areas on the floor; from the wear around them, it appeared that there used to be equipment there. "Have you moved some things around?" he asked.

For the first time, Floegel's cheerful demeanor faltered. "Moved them out." He picked up a razor-toe balmoral and looked at it rather sadly. "It's this damn depression we're in. People are making their old shoes do for as long as they can, and so our sales are down this year." He eyed Webb. "That is not something we would want to publicize, of course."

"Oh, I see no reason to mention that in my article. The entire country is suffering from the depression. There's no need to remind our readers of that fact." Webb smiled agreeably and Floegel appeared relieved.

"We are taking steps to bolster the business," the manager said. He waved at the empty spaces. "We cleared out some of the shoemaking equipment to bring in a new line. We're going to start assembling harnesses—and we're hoping to get city contracts to outfit horses for the sanitation department and the fire brigades." He hesitated. "But that isn't official yet—I'd hate to jinx the deal by having it publicized prematurely. I hope you understand."

Webb made a show of crossing a line through some of his notes. "Easy enough to take care of."

"Thank you. We do want to keep the business thriving and our employees able to afford food and shelter. As you can see, our factory provides one of the best work environments in the city."

"It is one of the cleanest factories I've seen," Webb agreed. Of course, it might have been cleaned to make a good impression for the profile in *Harper's*.

"That's one of the things that got Mr. Thompson started in his campaign for Brooklyn independence."

"Working conditions?"

"Yes. Mr. Thompson went to every one of our shops and addressed the workers—even the women so that they could tell their husbands what he said. He told them that if consolidation passed, Brooklyn would be flooded with outcasts from Manhattan—workers who were used to living in tenements and slaving in sweatshops. If they came here, we wouldn't be able to compete—wages would drop, work conditions would become unbearable. Our employees could find themselves out on the streets."

"Mr. Thompson painted a rather bleak picture."

"But one that is all too likely." Sam Floegel then suggested, "Shall we go to my office to continue the discussion, Mr. Webb? It's much quieter and I can offer you some refreshment there."

Webb readily agreed and they had soon left the sound and smell of the factory for the relative comfort of Floegel's office. He took a straight-backed chair in front of Floegel's desk, while the manager settled into a swivel chair.

The second-floor office overlooked the street, so the sounds of traffic came unfiltered through the open windows. Webb's ears were still ringing from the noise of downstairs, though, so it sounded merely like a dull rumble. A large floor fan stirred the air, clearing out most of the smell of tanned leather that permeated the work areas of the building.

Floegel opened the door of a cabinet behind his desk. "I don't make it a habit of drinking during business hours, Mr. Webb, but I'd be happy to join you if you'd care for a little something. Let's see . . . rye, bourbon, rum, port . . . I could send out for beer if you'd like."

"Rye would be fine," Webb said, and Floegel poured a couple of shots.

The office was similar in style to the reception area, simple and utilitarian. Webb suspected that Floegel didn't get to spend much time sitting in his office.

"Here you go," said Floegel, placing the filled

glass on the desk in front of Webb. He offered a toast "to the memory of Joshua Thompson" and the two men each took a drink.

Webb noticed a photograph of a rather plump woman in an oval frame on the wall next to Floegel's desk. Next to it were two smaller ones of young men. He gestured toward them. "Your family?"

Floegel looked at the images with fondness. "Yes. I've been married thirty years come October."

"Congratulations!"

"Thank you." He shook his head. "Hard to believe it's been that many years—seems we've only spent about five of those together. But I do have business to tend to. I put one son through college—Yale—and then dental school and I have another finishing his senior year at Columbia." He sighed. "Well, someday I'll retire and maybe the missus and I can go on a second honeymoon or something."

"It must be hard to think of retirement now," said Webb, trying to sound sympathetic. "You must have a lot more responsibility having to take over Mr. Thompson's duties."

"I do, but at least we were prepared."

"How so?"

"Well, Mr. Thompson was a responsible man. He always wanted the company to continue operations with a minimum of disruption. So when he began spending so much time working against the consolidation referendum, he took steps to ensure that Thompson Manufacturing would still function smoothly."

"By delegating more responsibility to you?"

"Oh, I had a few more things that I needed to tend to—but I've handled most of the day-to-day operations for years now anyway. The biggest change was that he brought in his daughter Catherine; she has effectively been the president for half a year now—the big decisions are made by her. So she was all ready to take over when her father was so cruelly taken from us."

"Must be strange for you to be answering to his daughter. Wouldn't you have been better suited for the job?"

Floegel smiled. "I don't resent Mrs. McCutcheon, if that's what you're hinting at. Thompson Manufacturing is a family business and I've always known it would be taken over by one of Mr. Thompson's heirs. And, I must say, I have found Mrs. McCutcheon to be an intelligent and capable woman. The company is in good hands with her, and that's good for all of us."

"I'm delighted to hear that it is working out so well." Webb scribbled a few more notes. "Still, it is unusual for a woman to be running such an important company. Especially since Mr. Thompson also left a son. Eugene, isn't it?"

Floegel made an effort to keep a cheerful face. "Yes. Eugene Thompson. A fine young man."

"But not capable of stepping into his father's shoes?"

The manager struggled to find an appropriate response. "Eugene Thompson is a fine young man. Catherine McCutcheon is a fine lady with a good head for business."

Webb stood to shake Floegel's hand. "Thank you so much for your time. It's clear to me that *you're* the essential part of Thompson Manufacturing, no matter who sits in the president's chair."

Floegel also stood and returned his grip. "That's very kind of you to say, Mr. Webb."

"But do you think Mrs. McCutcheon would consent to an interview, too? I'm sure our readers would be interested in her perspective on the company."

"I don't know," Floegel answered. "I would be happy to give you an introduction though."

Webb thanked him again. He left the office wondering who might introduce him to Eugene Thompson. Or who would explain why there were no pictures of Eugene with his father after the age of about twelve.

CHAPTER 12

He'd developed a lead late Tuesday night, so Buck Morehouse had intended to spend Wednesday working on the jewel robberies, but when Marshall Webb telephoned wanting to meet and discuss the Thompson case he'd agreed, anticipating no difficulty in doing both at the same time.

Wednesday afternoon, Morehouse arrived at Ambrose Park in south Brooklyn. Damp summer heat was again smothering the city, and Morehouse yearned for some shade. While he waited on the sidewalk for Webb, Morehouse drank three cold lemonades from a street cart—and was so grateful for the relief that he even paid for one of them. He checked his watch with increasing frequency as he waited with decreasing patience. Webb was more than half an hour late.

Morehouse's annoyance with the writer gave way to concern as he remembered his encounter with Ian Duffy in the saloon. The gang leader had suggested that Webb might have been the intended

target of the gunman who killed Joshua Thompson.
If so, Webb could still be a target. And it was a possibility that Morehouse would have to warn him
about.

Webb finally appeared, his longs legs propelling
him quickly. The writer was, as usual, nattily attired; *Harper's* must pay him a handsome salary to
afford such fine tailoring, thought Morehouse. He
was perfectly garbed for a Fifth Avenue salon, but
overdressed for a Wild West show.

"Sorry I'm late," said Webb, huffing somewhat.
"The trolley I was on ran into a milk horse on
Pearl Street—stupid driver thought he could make
it across the tracks and now his poor animal is
dead. The driver's unharmed, of course."

Morehouse shook his head. "Ain't that always
the case?"

"Seems so. Anyway, I missed the ferry and had
to wait for the next one."

"That's all right." Morehouse jerked his head at
the banner that heralded BUFFALO BILL'S WILD WEST.
"The show's going on all day."

Much of Ambrose Park was under a series of vast
canvas tents erected by Buffalo Bill Cody's popular
traveling show. The appearance was of particular
interest in Brooklyn, where cowboys and Indians
were usually limited to the pages of lurid dime
novels.

"The tickets are on me this time," said Webb.

"Already got 'em. But thanks for the offer." Morehouse could see no reason for the writer to shell
out fifty cents each for the show. Not when the show
proprietors should be grateful to have a police officer on their grounds. This was Morehouse's view
no matter where he went; granting him free ad-

mission was a bargain considering the sense of security his presence surely provided.

They walked through the turnstiles of the main entrance, receiving copies of the program, and into the tent. The canvas canopy actually made a perimeter around a broad expanse of grass where the main attractions were staged. At one end of the grassy field was a cluster of teepees with colorfully dressed Indians lounging near a campfire; this was the "authentic Indian village" advertised in the program.

The crowd sat in bleacher seats and pressed along ropes from all directions for a good view of the proceedings. At the moment elk, buffalo, and wild horses were being paraded around the grounds while a leather-lunged announcer in a fringed suit of the same material described the habits of the animals.

"You mind if we walk around first?" asked Morehouse. "I'm looking for somebody and I'm sure he's around here some place."

"Not at all. Another pickpocket?"

"Close. Burglar." Morehouse began edging his way along the rear of the crowd, keeping an eye out for his prey.

Webb kept pace by his side. "You expect someone to break into a tent show?"

"No. He's working for them." Morehouse concentrated on scanning the people they passed and didn't explain further.

After circling the entire crowd with no success, the two of them took a couple of bleacher seats. They were provisioned with lemonade and peanuts that Webb had insisted on wasting his money on.

The writer reminded him, "On the phone you

said you had something new on the Thompson case."

"Yes, I read his will." Morehouse's attention was still distracted.

The wild animals were being led off the field while a crew of men in work clothes trotted around the grass shoveling and sweeping away their droppings. Morehouse didn't recognize any of the men.

"Anything of interest?" Webb prompted.

Morehouse fished in his pocket and pulled out the list of beneficiaries. "Not that I can tell." He handed it to Webb, who began to peruse it.

A roar went up from the enthusiastic crowd as Buffalo Bill Cody himself strode to the center of the field. His distinctive attire and trademark flowing white hair with a mustache and goatee were the only introduction he needed. Cody then spoke a few words about the importance of horsemanship throughout the world as a prelude to a presentation by the "Congress of Rough Riders," expert riders from around the world, including Russian Cossacks, Mexican Vaqueros, German Cuirassiers, and of course American cavalrymen.

As a contingent of ornately attired Vaqueros rode out, Webb said, "Nothing appears unusual—bequests to family and a number of charities."

"But those sums are enormous," said Morehouse. "The money alone adds up to more than a million dollars. And then there's the houses, businesses, land. Hell, I'm used to thugs who'll kill a man for his shoes. With what Thompson was leaving to people, any one of them might have killed him for an early inheritance."

"Hmm. Not just the people," Webb replied. "Even the charities might have been eager for his demise.

With the economy so bad, a lot of them are cash poor right now and some are folding." He looked again at the list. "Can I keep this for a while? I want to see if I can learn a little more."

"Keep it. I have another copy at the station house." Morehouse then considered again whether to tell Webb about Ian Duffy's suggestion. He had to tell him, he knew, but found himself reluctant to relay such a frightening possibility.

Webb put the paper in an inside pocket of his jacket. "I also plan to see a couple of Joshua Thompson's main beneficiaries, his son and daughter."

"You haven't spoken with them yet?"

"No, I met with Sam Floegel first—he's the general manager of Thompson's company. I wanted to know how the company operated first, and see if I could learn anything about the Thompson family from him."

"Did you?"

"I'm not sure. According to Floegel, Catherine McCutcheon is a very capable woman, groomed by her father to take over while he was occupied with the consolidation issue. He didn't have much to say about the son, Eugene, though; in fact, Floegel appeared decidedly uncomfortable when I pressed him for an opinion on Eugene." Webb turned to Morehouse. "You said he's something of a sportsman."

"That's what his sister told me."

"A gambler?"

"I don't know. She didn't mention that." Morehouse caught on to what Webb was driving at. "You think—"

"That if he was a gambler, Eugene Thompson might have needed money to pay his debts."

"If he *had* losses."

"Do you know any gamblers who *win* over the long term?"

"Yes." Morehouse smiled. "But they cheat."

Webb laughed. "I believe in that case they should be categorized as 'thieves,' not 'gamblers.' "

Morehouse's attention was again drawn to the arena. The cavalrymen were departing the field and a dozen or so laborers began dragging a log cabin to its center. They set up the set for what the program billed as "Attack on a Burning Cabin." The detective again focused on the workmen. And then he saw him, putting a small porch in place in front of the cabin.

"Would you excuse me?" he said to Webb. "There's somebody I got to go see."

"Your burglar?"

Morehouse stood. "Yes."

"Need help?" Webb offered, also starting to rise.

"No, I can handle this fellow." He thought it was good of the writer to offer, though.

Morehouse worked his way around the arena toward the section that the workmen had come from. He hoped they would return to the same place when they'd finished their labor.

Pushing his way past spectators, and ignoring their complaints, he made it barely ahead of the workmen. They had quickly put together the set for the next scene in the Wild West extravaganza.

A rope barricade separated the audience from the performers and stagehands; Morehouse showed his badge to a nearby usher in order to pass under it freely. The detective approached the group of workmen, who were sweating and panting from their intense efforts. One of them, in ragged denim overalls, had his head down, and appeared on the verge of throwing up.

"Well, if it isn't Frankie Lew," he said.

The man looked up. "Buck Morehouse, you son of a bitch. What the hell are you doin' here?" His eyes were narrow slits and his clean-shaven face was hard.

"Came to see you, Frankie. I heard you were working here."

Lew straightened. "Only as long as the show's in town. I got a family to feed and it's hard to get honest work these days."

Morehouse chortled. "Leave it to you to wait for a depression before you decide to try making an *honest* living!"

"Leave it to *you* to get a laugh at another man's misfortune." The wiry man's muscles tensed.

The other workers had stepped closer to them, and Morehouse had no doubt that they were on Lew's side if it came to a fight. He almost regretted turning down Marshall Webb's offer to come along—especially since the detective had fully intended to antagonize Lew almost to the man's breaking point.

"Let's take a walk," said Morehouse.

Lew continued to eye him with anger. To his coworkers, he said, "I'll be fine, boys."

There was no quiet place to be found, especially since the log cabin had by now been torched and whooping Indians on horseback were circling the family of settlers—the actors portraying settlers, that is—inside. While the crowd shrieked—some in horror at the "family's" danger, some in delight at the spectacle—Morehouse at least found a spot near a tent pole where they could speak in relative privacy.

"Looks like you forgot how to do honest labor, the way you were huffing and puffing there," observed Morehouse. "Thought you'd be in better shape after two years of busting rocks at Sing Sing."

Lew rolled up his shirtsleeve, revealing a sinewy arm. "You want to take me on?" he challenged. Although muscular, the skin color was still a sickly pale hue from his incarceration.

Morehouse answered, "And send you back for another five years for assaulting a police officer? Nah, I wouldn't do that to you, Frankie—especially seeing as I came here friendly like to ask for your help."

"*My* help?" Lew spat. "Like hell."

"Look, we both know you're going to go back to your old line of work. And if you help me now, maybe I can help you when you get nabbed again."

"I'm goin' straight." Lew was now spitting the words at Morehouse. "You think I'd be bustin' my ass like this for a dollar a day if I wasn't?"

Morehouse would have liked to believe him— and Lew might have believed it himself. But a forty-one-year-old career burglar was unlikely to change his ways for any length of time. "Here's my problem," he said. "The last few months, there've been almost a dozen jewel heists downtown. And this crook is good—not a lock or a door or a window can stop him. Goes in easy and leaves the place clean. You know, if I had to just make a guess as to who was doing the crimes I'd have to say it was Frankie Lew. You're the only one I know who's that talented."

If Lew was flattered at the compliment, he didn't

show it. "Helluva detective you are. How do you figure I'm stealing jewels in Brooklyn when I'm behind bars in Sing Sing? I didn't get out till two weeks ago."

"I know. I've been checking the records. I even called the prison to make sure you hadn't escaped."

"Then I can't be your man, can I, Mr. Detective?"

"No. But I figure you know who is."

"I don't—"

Morehouse cut him off. "I don't expect you to give me any names. But I figure maybe there was another prisoner in Sing Sing that you taught your tricks of the trade. Or maybe one of your former, uh, 'associates' here is taking up where you left off."

"I always worked alone."

"Doesn't matter. Here's what I want you to do: when you talk to your old friends—or your new ones—you let them know that these heists have got to stop. And you better spread the word fast; Namm's is getting a shipment of gold jewelry at the end of this week to replace what was stolen from them last month." He waved a finger. "And *nothing* is to happen to it."

"Nothing's gonna happen to it, far as I'm concerned," said Lew. "I'm out of that business."

"All right," said Morehouse. "But you do what I told you. Spread the word: no more robberies at any stores—at least not in Brooklyn. If there is, you can be sure you'll be back in Sing Sing."

"You're a rotten son of a bitch, Morehouse," Lew growled.

The detective shrugged. It wasn't his intent to make Lew like him.

When Morehouse returned to Marshall Webb,

the cavalry had already driven off the Indians and rescued the settlers from their burning cabin. The fire was extinguished and what remained of the structure was cleared from the field. Morehouse noticed that Frankie Lew was not among the other workers moving it off.

"How did it go?" Webb asked.

"I won't know for a few days, maybe not for a week or two." Morehouse thought that he'd done the best he could with Lew, though.

He continued to think about Lew and the robberies while Custer's Last Stand was reenacted in the arena. It was staged with the approval of Mrs. Custer, according to the program note.

The next act was one of the Wild West show's star attractions: Annie Oakley, billed as "Little Sure Shot." She demonstrated an entertaining program of trick shots, firing from the ground and from horseback at a variety of targets.

"She's incredible," said Webb.

"Hardly ever misses," observed Morehouse. That reminded him; he still had something to talk to Webb about. He turned to the writer. "You ever get any threats when you wrote those stories about Tammany Hall?"

"Almost every day."

"You take 'em serious?"

Webb ran a finger over his mustache. "Not usually. Tammany was just used to getting its way; it controlled the police, the courts, and the politicians. But it couldn't control the press. So when my articles were published, I think they just had to lash out somehow. They threatened everything from getting me fired to drowning me in the East River. Why?"

"Oh, I was talking with a plug-ugly I know; he runs one of the roughest gangs in Brooklyn. And he doesn't know this for a fact, but he's guessing that the bullets that killed Joshua Thompson might have been meant for you." He looked to see how Webb would react. "Puts things in a different light, doesn't it?"

Webb kept his eyes straight ahead. His jaw barely moved as he answered softly, "Yes, I suppose it does."

Since his discussion with Buck Morehouse earlier in the day, Marshall Webb had a persistent urge to look over his shoulder. He had to make a conscious effort to resist that urge; giving in to it would only make him a nervous wreck.

Webb had thought it over as he traveled back to Manhattan, and was almost entirely convinced that he had nothing to worry about. Killing him would achieve nothing for Tammany Hall; it was the state legislature, and the Lexow Committee, and the courts that were bringing the organization's crooked dealings to public attention now. All that killing Webb could accomplish now would be revenge. He didn't think that Tammany would risk so much just for that. Still, his neck kept twitching.

When the ferry docked in Lower Manhattan, Webb checked his pocket watch: ten past three. There was still quite a bit of time left in the work-day—hopefully, even for a banker.

The New Amsterdam Trust Company was on Exchange Place, a short block from Wall Street. Its granite bulk exuded a sense of financial security.

Inside, Webb spoke with a young man at a teller's

window. The teller made a telephone call, then unlocked a door to allow Webb into the bank's offices.

The main floor of the New Amsterdam Trust Company was where the lower-level accountants and bookkeepers labored. Several dozen high oak desks, all illuminated by identical green-shaded brass lamps, were staffed by serious young men in somber dark suits.

Not one of the junior bankers looked up from his columns of numbers as Webb walked across the tiles to the rear of the building. There, he stepped into a small elevator decorated with intricately engraved brasswork; it was operated by a uniformed old man who successfully navigated the cage up to the second floor. This was where the senior bank officials had their private offices. Their names were painted in gold on the frosted glass of the doors. Webb stopped at the one that read JACOB R. UPDEGRAFF, PRESIDENT and knocked.

He was let in by a tall male secretary, who escorted him to a plush leather armchair in front of Jacob Updegraff's desk. The gesture was simply for the sake of formality, since Updegraff was seated behind the desk and could have simply asked Webb to sit down.

Webb had met Rebecca's brother-in-law a number of times—many more than he would have liked—but had seldom seen him in his work environment. It surprised Webb that the furnishings were so spare—even plainer than at the Thompson offices. The desk and chairs were of dark-stained oak, and several file cabinets and bookcases of the same wood and color were along the walls. Not a single photograph or painting adorned the walls, and the one rug was a solid dark green. On a pedestal behind Updegraff's swivel chair was a glass-domed stock ticker that chattered intermittently. One of the few luxuries was a cigar box on his desk.

"Thank you for agreeing to see me," said Webb. "I won't take more than a few minutes."

Updegraff shifted the lit cigar in his mouth and nodded. Webb couldn't tell if the movement was intended to say, "You're welcome" or "You're right about only getting a few minutes."

Webb reached into his jacket pocket and withdrew the paper Buck Morehouse had given him. "I mentioned on Sunday that I'm writing about the consolidation issue. That led me to Joshua Thompson and his murder of course." He glanced at the paper. "I have here a list of his beneficiaries and the amounts they will be inheriting. I was hoping you could look at it and tell me if it seems, well, normal."

"How could I determine that? I don't know the Thompson family." Updegraff scowled. He appeared to think that his time was being wasted.

"Joshua Thompson left quite a bit of his money—some rather substantial sums—to a number of charities. Perhaps you could tell me something about those."

Updegraff motioned impatiently for Webb to give him the paper. The banker's expression began to change as he read it. "Joshua Thompson did well for himself—for a Brooklyn man." He continued to read. "His family is being provided for very nicely indeed."

"Are the amounts standard for people . . . of af-

fluence?" Webb mentally finished the sentence
with *as rich as you*.

"There *is* no standard will. But after various do-
nations, and some small bequests, Thompson's
widow gets fifty percent of his estate, and his son
and daughter each get twenty-five. That's reasonable."

"And the charities?"

Updegraff tapped at the paper. "I've heard of a
few of them, and I understand them to be quite
reputable. But some of them are unknown to me—
it appears most of them operate in Brooklyn, judging by their names." He slid the paper back across
the desk. "I'm sorry I can't be of much help." He
then glanced back at the stock ticker, which was
sputtering with activity.

Webb didn't touch the paper. "This might be
important. How would I go about investigating
these charities?"

Updegraff clearly wanted to get back to his business. "Nantz!" he barked.

His secretary, who'd been quietly working at his
own small desk in a windowless corner, almost
jumped. "Yes, Mr. Updegraff?"

"I have a job for you." When Nantz came over to
his desk, Updegraff handed him the sheet of paper.
"Look into the charities on this list. Give me a report by the end of the day tomorrow." To Webb,
he asked, "Will that be soon enough?"

Webb said that it certainly would be and expressed his thanks. He didn't know if Updegraff
spoke so brusquely to his secretary all the time, or
if he was simply making a show of his authority, but
he did know that Jacob Updegraff was eager for
Webb to leave his office.

CHAPTER 13

Rebecca Davies didn't have to wait for the afternoon mail to read the bad news. It was in bold letters in a two-column headline on the front page of the Thursday morning *Herald:*

FINANCIAL FAILURE IN FALL RIVER
68 FACTORIES CLOSE—20,000 JOBLESS!

Twenty thousand. Rebecca could hardly fathom the number. All those families suddenly with no means of putting food on their tables, clothes on their backs, or keeping themselves sheltered. And they had few prospects of finding other employment in these desperate times.

Rebecca glanced at the small stack of envelopes on her writing desk. She almost dreaded opening the mail lately. Rarely did she receive a letter agreeing to take on a girl from Colden House. But on the off chance that there might be a job offer among the discouraging letters, Rebecca promptly read through the mail after every delivery. Doing so, she noted that conditions were getting worse all over the county; many of her correspondents were now asking Rebecca if they could send girls to New York to stay with her at the shelter.

Again reading the headline in the *Herald,* Rebecca wondered how many of those twenty thousand newly unemployed would end up in Manhattan. It was inevitable that some would, she knew. There weren't enough other jobs in Fall River, Massachusetts, to make up for those that had been lost—not even in a good economy. So families would end up relocating to larger cities—Boston, Providence, Hartford, and New York—in the desperate hope that a job might be available to them there. What they would find would be others like them, from small towns and other cities and countries, all looking for work that didn't exist. Even the most awful Hester Street sweatshops had all the workers they needed.

Stephanie Quilty cautiously stepped into the sitting room. "Miss Davies, ma'am. Mrs. Updegraff is here." There was concern etched on the girl's face; by now, though, Rebecca had gotten used to the fact that her young charge rarely showed happiness or pleasure. Miss Quilty always had a sad expression.

"Thank you. I'll—"

Before she could ask for her sister to be shown in, Alice was standing next to Miss Quilty.

Now Rebecca *was* worried. Although Alice had been coming to Colden House about once a week, and was willing to help with any chore that needed to be done in the place, she still stood on social ceremony when she arrived, waiting to be announced and shown in. The fact that Alice had deviated from that ritual was a good indication that something might be amiss.

Rebecca stood. "Alice. So good to see you." As always, Alice did look splendid, in a summer suit of pale green with black velvet trim and finely coiffed. She made quite a contrast with Miss Quilty, in her simple gingham frock, who seemed to fade away in comparison.

"I hope I haven't come at a bad time," said Alice.

"Not at all." Rebecca caught on that her sister hadn't come to help in the shelter today, but still couldn't guess the real purpose of her visit. "Please," she said, gesturing to the sofa. She then saw that Stephanie Quilty had faded away completely; the girl had silently left the room.

Once the sisters had moved to the sofa, Alice said, "Lucy Robatin still hasn't come home. There has been no word from her."

"Have you spoken with her family?"

"I tried. Even her mother is reluctant to say anything, however." Alice rested her gloved hands over the beaded purse on her lap. "The Robatins believe that Lucy disgraced the family with her wild behavior. They are *very* conscious of their social status and want nothing to diminish their place in New York society."

Rebecca restrained a smile. That evaluation of the Robatins could apply to almost any family with whom the Updegraffs and Davieses associated— including the Updegraff and Davies families themselves. "The family isn't concerned with what might have become of their daughter?"

"If so, they are not expressing that concern. Mr.

Robatin seems to feel that the worst already happened to his daughter some time ago. Now he insists that he has no daughter." Alice shook her head with disapproval. "Mr. Robatin is a hard man; I never did like him." She idly ran a finger over the tiny beads stitched to the purse. "I did learn some things, even though the Robatin family wasn't willing to speak."

"How?"

"Even though Mr. Robatin has made a fortune in real estate, he is penurious with the servants— pays the lowest wages of anyone I know." Alice smiled tightly. "I provided a few of the Robatin servants with a much-needed 'bonus' and in turn they were happy to answer all my questions."

Rebecca smiled herself; she never imagined that her sister, trained since childhood to be a proper young lady thoroughly versed in the social graces, would resort to bribing another family's servants for information. "What did you learn?"

"About a year ago, Lucy Robatin began to socialize with some other young people who were rather, um, high-spirited. They were of good families also, but a bit wild—quite fond of dancing, champagne, and the theater. None of which is bad, of course, but they were excessive in their entertainments and often improper in their behavior. According to one of the maids, Lucy Robatin sometimes didn't come home until dawn, and then in a drunk and disheveled condition. Her father began threatening that she had better change her ways. Several months ago, the two of them had a particularly unpleasant quarrel—the maid wasn't able to hear their words, but the tone was vicious, she said, and there was a lot of yelling." Alice sighed.

"After that quarrel, Lucy would go out more often and behave more wildly judging by her condition when she'd come home. Some nights she didn't come home at all."

"Miss Davies?" Stephanie Quilty stood just inside the sitting room door, holding a tray with a blue porcelain teapot and two cups. "I thought Mrs. Updegraff would like some tea."

"Why, yes, thank you," said Alice, smiling at the young woman.

Miss Quilty placed the tray on the coffee table and quietly withdrew from the room.

While Rebecca poured the tea, Alice commented, "What a nice girl she is. How is she doing here?"

"Very well." Rebecca added two spoonfuls of sugar to Alice's cup. "It seems she anticipates whatever might need to be done around the house and then quietly proceeds to do it. I don't know about her prospects, though," she added sadly. "She doesn't have a skill—in fact, she's only recently been learning how to read. And even if she did have a trade, there are no jobs to be had these days."

"Why don't you hire her to work here?" Alice took a sip of her tea.

"In Colden House?" Besides Rebecca, the shelter's only employee was Miss Hummel.

"Certainly. You could use the help, couldn't you? The young lady needs a job and you need someone reliable." Alice smiled slightly. "If you had her working here, you might even be able to take more time off to see your Mr. Webb."

It was Rebecca's turn to smile. "Yes, that would be nice." And Stephanie Quilty would certainly be an asset at Colden House. But that was something to consider later. "So what else did you learn about Lucy Robatin?" she asked.

"Well, there might be something to your belief that she was smoking opium. According to the servants, it has become quite fashionable for some wealthy young people to go on outings to Chinatown and visit the opium dens." She shook her head. "I can't imagine what the attraction is, but it seems to be the thing to do these days among the younger set."

This was something Rebecca hadn't heard of before. Affluent young men of Lucy Robatin's age often frequented sordid places such as brothels in the Tenderloin or gambling dens in the Lower East Side. But she didn't realize that they had added drugs to the vices they were exploring, or that they were taking young society women with them on their outings. "Did the Robatin servants say where Lucy went in Chinatown or who she went with?"

"No. I don't think they knew exactly where she went, and they might not have wanted to mention the names of any of Lucy Robatin's friends—I suspect some of the servants are looking for better positions elsewhere, and it would hurt their prospects to give the names of prospective employers." Alice reached into her purse. "I did get these, though."

She took out two photographs and handed them to Rebecca.

One was a sepia studio portrait. Lucy Robatin had been painstakingly prepared for the photograph. Not a hair was out of place, her gown was pristine, and she held a bouquet of flowers. Rebecca stared at the image for some moments, trying to reconcile it with the drunk, disheveled, ill-mannered young woman who had arrived at Colden House almost two weeks ago. Although the general features were the same, there was a kind of sweetness to the expression in the photograph. Rebecca thought Lucy Robatin's wide eyes had an innocence in them.

The second photograph was a family portrait; Lucy Robatin was standing next to an older couple. "Her parents?" Rebecca asked.

"Yes. These were the only photographs the maid could, um, acquire for me. I'm hoping they'll do."

They were good likenesses of the girl, Rebecca thought, but she wasn't quite sure why Alice had obtained them. "Do for what?"

"For showing to people who might have seen her."

"Where would we—"

"I thought it would make sense to go to some of those places in Chinatown and see if anyone could remember seeing her."

Rebecca almost dropped the photographs and looked at her sister. Alice could be quite naïve sometimes. "If they did, do you think they would tell us?"

"I don't know. But if we don't ask, then we might never know where she is—and how she is."

That was true, Rebecca had to agree. "But I don't know anyone in Chinatown. Do they even speak English there?"

Alice lifted her hands. "I don't know. I assumed you would."

Rebecca did know most of the poorer sections of New York—areas of which her sister was totally unfamiliar—but Chinatown was a world that was alien to even her. "No," she answered. "But I might know somebody who does."

The men looked ridiculous. Their attire was even sillier than that worn by baseball players, Marshall Webb thought. Dressed in crisp white flannel trousers and shirts, with puffy white cloth caps on their heads and checked canvas shoes on their feet, they didn't look like anything one would see on the streets of Manhattan.

But this wasn't Manhattan. The Knickerbocker Field Club was in Flatbush, on East Eighteenth Street, between Albemarle Road and Church Avenue. It was an area of Brooklyn that was still largely farmland. And here, some of the city's wealthy sportsmen had built this country club, a rustic place for them to play their games and socialize over fine food and drink.

Webb sat in a reed-backed lawn chair on the veranda of the clubhouse overlooking the courts. Two courts were occupied by men who pranced about and swatted at a little white ball with wooden tennis racquets. They didn't run very fast in their efforts, although Webb didn't know if that was due to the intense sun or because maintaining "good form" was at least as important as winning.

The man Webb watched mostly was Eugene Thompson. The son of the late Joshua Thompson was probably in his early thirties, tall and slender. He moved with ease over the grass court, more gracefully than the other men. Thompson also seemed to enjoy the game more than the others, smiling both at his own successes and good shots made by his opponent.

Webb told himself that he should enjoy this time in the outdoors, and the genteel entertainment. Rebecca had telephoned earlier in the day with some peculiar idea of traipsing through Chinatown to look for a missing girl. Failing to dissuade her, he had agreed to join her tonight. Compared to the prospect of searching through opium dens, it was a pleasure to spend some of the afternoon at a country club.

Eugene Thompson won his match, shook hands with his opponent, then came over to Webb. "Mr. Webb?" he asked. Thompson took off his cap, revealing thick, wavy black hair.

"Yes." Webb rose and the two men shook hands.

"Sorry," said Thompson, realizing that his hand was sweaty. "Had a bit of a workout there. I thought I'd finish old Polley in straight sets—I usually do. Am I late for our appointment?"

"Just a bit. But it gave me a chance to see part of the match."

Thompson smiled. "What did you think of the game?"

"I quite enjoyed it," Webb lied.

"Tennis is a fine game for gentlemen—and for the ladies, too. Some of them are taking up the sport." Thompson wiped his sweating brow. "What do you say we go inside where it's cooler and have a drink?"

Webb said yes and they went into the wood-frame clubhouse.

A great deal of money had been spent to give the place a look of rustic simplicity. There was dark wood paneling and exposed oak beams. Furnishings were spare but expensive. The decorations consisted primarily of sporting equipment hung about the walls and behind the bar; there were rowing oars, golf clubs, tennis racquets, and boxing gloves, some with dates, schools, or scores painted on them.

The two sat at a small, polished round table and a colored waiter in a white jacket promptly came to take their orders.

"Ever have a gin rickey?" Thompson asked.

Webb admitted that he hadn't even heard of the drink.

"It's the latest concoction—quite refreshing." Thompson then ordered a pair of the drinks.

Once the waiter left to get their drinks, Webb said, "I appreciate you seeing me, Mr. Thompson."

"My pleasure. You said you're with *Harper's?*"

"Yes." Webb took out his notebook. "I'm writing a story on your father. His death was a such a tragedy, but his life was quite a success story."

"*Harper's* has always done a good job covering gentlemen's sports," Thompson said. "Did you write the piece on the regatta last month?"

Webb was taken aback. "No, I write about politics. That's how I came to meet your father."

Thompson's only response was a noncommittal nod. Then he brightened when the gin rickeys arrived.

After trying his drink, which wasn't bad, Webb ventured, "Can I ask you about your father?"

"I'm not sure what I can tell you," Thompson answered. "To be honest with you, I didn't actually know him that well." He took a swallow of his drink. "We were very different."

They didn't look different, Webb thought. Eugene Thompson looked very much like the young Joshua Thompson who appeared in the photographs on the office wall of Thompson Manufacturing. He had the same long face with chiseled features; the main difference was that the son's were softened by a ready smile. "How often did you see your father?" Webb asked.

"Not often at all—major holidays and his birthday. I have my own apartment at the Hotel Margaret in Columbia Heights. And"—he lifted his glass again—"I have my own life."

"You weren't involved with the family business at all?"

"No." Having spotted his empty glass, the waiter reappeared and Thompson ordered another drink. He then directed his attention back to Webb. "You see, Mr. Webb, my father tried to bring me up in the business, and when I was young I thought I would follow in his footsteps." He shrugged. "But it takes a certain, uh, ruthless streak to succeed at business. And I simply do not have the kind of killer instinct that my father had."

"But you're competitive on the tennis court."

Thompson smiled again. "On the golf course, too. Yes, I can compete, Mr. Webb. I am a sportsman. I appreciate competition and a well-played game. But I always play fair and I never try to harm my opponent."

"So your father was 'ruthless' in his business dealings?"

Thompson hesitated, then answered simply, "Yes."

Webb remembered the photographs in the reception area of Thompson Manufacturing. He wondered when Eugene Thompson discovered that business wasn't for him—was that what resulted in his absence from any recent pictures?

The waiter returned and placed the fresh drink in front of Thompson. Webb's glass was still half-full and he declined the offer to freshen it.

Eugene Thompson looked down at his drink for a moment. Pushing the glass aside, he leaned forward. "May I speak freely, Mr. Webb? Without having my words appear in publication?"

"Certainly." Webb put his notebook away; he hadn't written anything in it yet, anyway.

Thompson nodded his thanks. "The reason I agreed to speak with you is that I wanted to see you face-to-face and ask that I not appear in your article at all."

"Why not?"

"My father was in the press quite a bit, especially after he took on the consolidation issue. And I have been mentioned in many of the stories—most often described as 'a profligate son' or a 'ne'er-do-well.' " Thompson shook his head. "I readily admit that I was a disappointment to my father and my family. But I am not a profligate—I find joy in sport, not gambling or vice. My wants are actually quite few, and my family provides me an adequate income to lead a comfortable life and pursue my games." He smiled. "Although not a productive member of society, I am not truly a ne'er-do-well, either, since what I do I do very well. I happen to be one of the best golfers in all New York, and my tennis game is coming along quite nicely."

"And you have no involvement at all in the family business?"

"None." Thompson picked up his glass and

rubbed a thumb along its side. "Of course, I benefit from the company in that I receive an annual allowance to support myself. But I have nothing to
do with the operations."

"I will respect your wishes," Webb said. "You won't
be mentioned in my article at all."

"Thank you."

"Your sister, though—Catherine McCutcheon. I
don't see how I can leave her out of it."

Thompson shrugged.

"She has assumed the responsibility of running
the business, so I suppose I will have to mention
that."

"Yes, I suppose that's true."

Webb thought for a moment. "Do you feel she is
capable of taking on such a task? It's rather unusual for a woman to be in charge of a major cor-
poration."

Thompson hesitated.

"This is still just between us," Webb promised.

"My answer is the same whether between us or
for publication: Catherine will do an excellent job
as president of Thompson Manufacturing. She is a
smart woman and most capable."

"Does she have the necessary ruthless streak you
spoke of earlier?"

Eugene Thompson was slow to answer that question. He first drank some of his gin rickey. Finally,
still looking at the glass, he said, "My sister is her
father's daughter." Then he glanced up at Webb.
"You would have to ask her any other questions
you might have."

Webb intended to do just that.

* * *

Rebecca Davies was in a part of New York City that was foreign to her—almost literally foreign. The corner of Mott and Pell Streets, where the hansom cab had let them off was only a mile from Colden House and a short distance northeast of City Hall Park. But it didn't seem like part of the United States at all.

The streets, sidewalks, and buildings were impeccably maintained by the local residents, far cleaner than even the stretch of Fifth Avenue where her parents lived. They were also sterile, though. There were few decorations and little color amidst the plain brick buildings. A few shops and laundries had signs lettered in Chinese characters, and telegraph poles were plastered with notices, also in Chinese.

"Do you have any idea where we are?" she asked Marshall Webb.

"Chinatown," he answered with a sly smile.

"I know *that!*" She gave him a playful poke to his chest.

Stephanie Quilty spoke up in a small voice. "I know where to go, Miss Davies." The young girl took a step north on Mott Street.

"Very well, you'll be our guide." Rebecca sighed. She wasn't eager to bring one of her charges along on an outing that might be dangerous, but there was little choice.

When she'd spoken with Marshall on the telephone, he had told her that Chinatown was a part of the city as alien to him as it was to most outsiders. Stephanie Quilty, always nearby lately, had heard the conversation and offered to go along to show them where to find the opium dens. Rebecca had agreed in part because the young woman was so eager to be of help that she didn't want to reject the offer. Now here the three of them were, at dusk on a sultry summer night.

"I can't get over how *clean* the street is," said Rebecca as she and Marshall followed the girl. "And hardly any people out at all." Few pedestrians were walking on the street, and there were no beggars or ruffians to be seen.

"It's safe, too," said Webb. "You don't have to fear walking the streets here at any time of day or night."

"I thought you didn't know anything about the area."

He chuckled. "I don't know how to find an opium den, but I do know what the police say about the area."

"And what's that?"

"That they don't even have to patrol Chinatown because the tongs—Chinese gangs—do it for them. It's the safest neighborhood in the Sixth Ward." He added wryly, "Not surprising, when you consider the ward also includes Mulberry Bend and the Bowery."

"*Gangs* keep it safe?" It was having Marshall with them that made Rebecca feel more secure.

"Yes. Their crimes take place behind closed doors. So if they keep the streets safe, the police stay away and the gangs' gambling and prostitution operations can go on without interference."

"And drugs," added Stephanie Quilty. She stopped before a small shop with Chinese characters on the window. "This is a tea shop. But you can get anything from opium to morphine."

"Looks closed," said Webb.

"The lights are out, but it's open all day and all

night. You just have to knock and ask for what you want."

To Rebecca, Webb asked, "And what *do* we ask for?"

She dug into her purse and pulled out the photographs of Lucy Robatin that Alice had given her. "We ask if Miss Robatin has been here."

Webb's eyebrows lifted and he pursed his lips. Clearly he thought little of the idea, but he had the good sense not to express his doubts verbally. In turn, Rebecca chose to ignore his cynical expression.

Clutching the photographs, Rebecca knocked on the tea-shop door. She tried to peer through the glass pane but could see nothing but darkness inside.

After a second knock, a voice so high pitched that Rebecca couldn't tell if it was male or female called, "What you want?"

She yelled back through the door, "We're looking for someone!"

"Go way! Nobody here!"

Rebecca turned to Stephanie. "How do I get in?"

"I'm not sure if you can now," the girl answered. "You don't look or sound like a customer."

"But they never even opened the door."

Webb answered, "They're in the dark." He pointed to a nearby street lamp. "You're lit up perfectly. They can see you but you can't see them."

"We can try again later," said Stephanie, starting up the street again. "There's another one a couple doors down."

This time they stopped in front of an herb shop.

Before knocking, Rebecca asked, "How do I sound like a customer?"

Instead of answering, Stephanie stepped to the door and knocked herself. When a questioning call came from inside, she answered, "Pen yen."

In moments the door opened, and they were let in by a small Oriental man of indeterminate age holding a burning candle. His hair was in a long black braid and he wore a loose blouse with wide sleeves. "Come," he said.

Rebecca almost gagged on the pungent smoke that filled the place. The smell got worse as they entered a dimly lit back room. She saw a row of bunks along the walls, where men and women reclined and smoked long pipes. Most of them were white and relatively young. Some appeared to be sleeping; Rebecca thought they all looked half dead.

In the center of the room, laid out like a buffet on a low table, were trays and boxes and needles and bowls, all the implements necessary for a well-equipped opium den. Several Oriental men squatted around the paraphernalia ready to provide users with whatever they wanted—if they had the cash.

The man who greeted them at the door held out his palm to Stephanie. "Two bit," he demanded.

Webb dug a quarter out of his pocket and gave it to him.

The man went over to one of the trays on the table and came back holding what looked like several pills. He handed one to Stephanie, then waved the others in front of Webb and Rebecca. "Two bit," he said again, apparently believing all three of them to be customers.

Rebecca took out the photographs again along with another twenty-five cents. She gave the man the money, but handed him back the pill. "All I want is to know if you've seen her." She pointed to the images on the photographs.

The response was a blank look. Eventually, he said again, "Two bit."

Rebecca gave him another quarter, hoping it would lead to information. All it got her was the proffer of another pill, which she again declined. She then pointed to the other men around the table and signaled that she wanted them to come over.

When the other men did, it was clear that communication was not going to be improved. Rebecca had to use hand motions to try to get across that she wanted them to look at the photographs. They did, and said a few words to each other in their own language. Their final reply to Rebecca was "No."

After Stephanie returned the pill she'd been given, the three of them left the herb shop. Rebecca's head was reeling from the opium smoke she'd inhaled.

After a few deep breaths of night air, Rebecca asked Stephanie, "What was it you asked for?"

"Pen yen. A small opium pill." As they continued down the street, Stephanie described the different types of opium available, the process of preparing and smoking it, and gave the Chinese names for most of the tools used in an opium "layout." Even the ashes left over were saved and sold to those who couldn't afford anything but the lowest grade of "dope."

Rebecca was sorry to realize that the young woman had such a familiarity with the vice.

As the night went on, Rebecca learned that Stephanie Quilty knew even more than how to smoke opium. Stephanie led them to a dozen basement and back-room dens along Mott and Pell Streets. Along the way, she pointed out apartments where women who'd become addicted to the drugs worked as prostitutes to pay for their opium and morphine.

Unfortunately, the only information Rebecca got during the entire excursion was from Miss Quilty. No one at any of the opium dens gave any indication of recognizing Lucy Robatin.

The only positive note to the evening was that Marshall never once expressed what she knew was in his mind: that the effort had been a hopeless one from the outset.

CHAPTER 14

Buck Morehouse had to admit to himself that he was getting nowhere in trying to find out who had shot Joshua Thompson. By now, he would be happy if he could simply determine whether or not Thompson was the intended target.

Ian Duffy, who had first suggested that the bullets might have been meant for Marshall Webb, was only a hired gun. The Irish gangster didn't decide who lived and who died; he only carried out the contracts other men hired him to execute. If Morehouse wanted to learn something about those who did make such decisions he would have to go elsewhere.

The place he went was City Hall.

Brooklyn's City Hall, located a few blocks from where Joshua Thompson had been killed, was a magnificent, towering stone structure crowned by a cupola with a bell and clock. The interior was equally splendid, with broad tiled hallways and high ceilings. Oil portraits of historic figures in Brooklyn politics adorned the walls. Every office that More-house had been in before was smartly furnished and had an air of municipal authority permeating it. But he wasn't going into any offices today.

On a leather bench in one of the hallways, across from the city clerk's office, sat Paul Epperly, in the same spot that he spent every business day. It was rumored that Epperly had come over the Atlantic Ocean with the first Dutch settlers, and he appeared almost that old. Epperly looked like a skeleton, pale, thin, and with only a few white strands of hair on his scalp. His skin hung loose under his jaw and his bony knees put a sharp angle in his trouser legs.

"You're looking good, Mr. Epperly," Morehouse said loudly when he was in range of the old man's ears. It was a true statement as far his Epperly's attire went. His suit was finer than anything the mayor wore, his high stiff color glaring white, and his silk cravat impeccable. His clawlike hands were clasped over the silver head of a Malacca walking stick.

Epperly looked up at him with eyes that seemed on the verge of falling out from the sagging lids around them. "Wish I could say the same about you, Buck."

Morehouse patted his belly. "I suppose I have put on a pound or two since I saw you last."

"Nothing wrong with a belly," said Epperly, "as long as you got a decent jacket over it. You need a new suit, Detective."

Morehouse looked down at his stained and wrinkled sack suit. "Yeah, well, I been thinking of getting another one."

"And a tie that you haven't used as a napkin."

With a chuckle, Morehouse promised that he would. Then he asked, "Can you spare me a few minutes, Mr. Epperly?" He knew that Epperly had plenty of time; the man spent his days seated on this bench while the machinery of Brooklyn government ground on around him.

Those who worked in City Hall, from the mayor to the councilmen and down to the secretaries, all knew Paul Epperly as a longtime fixture in the place, and treated him with token respect. But most of them, especially the younger ones, viewed him as an eccentric old man who was just waiting to die. Morehouse knew better; Epperly had provided him with information in the past—rarely specific information, such as names and places—but usually enough to send Morehouse in the right direction. Sometimes, Epperly knew of trouble brewing that he wanted Morehouse to head off; other times, as now, the detective initiated the contact.

Epperly patted the leather seat. "Step into my office."

Morehouse sat down next to the old man. "I'm not sure that it's a matter to be discussed with all these people around."

"Well, I don't leave from here until six." Epperly smiled. "Besides, do you see anyone paying attention to us?"

No one was; they were all absorbed in their own business. Still Morehouse kept his voice low, leaning toward Epperly's ear, as he asked, "What do you hear about the Joshua Thompson shooting?"

"I hear that it was a success: Thompson is dead."

"But do you know who was behind it?"

"How would I?"

"Because hardly anything happens in this city without you knowing the who, why, and how." Morehouse knew that in his younger days Epperly was active in Brooklyn gangs before switching to politics. Actually, it was more of an expansion into politics, since Epperly still remained privy to gangland activity. Now, officially retired, he still was aware of much more than most people gave him credit for.

"That may be," Epperly replied, "but one thing that I do *not* know is who killed Joshua Thompson."

"All right. What about Marshall Webb?"

"Who?"

"He's a writer with *Harper's Weekly*. He did that series on Tammany Hall last year."

"Oh yes." Epperly cackled. "*That* certainly ruffled some feathers." He turned his watery eyes to Morehouse. "You think *Webb* killed Thompson?"

"No, no." For a moment Morehouse wondered if Epperly's mental faculties were indeed slipping. "I mean do you think Webb might have been the target—and Thompson was hit accidentally? The two of them were standing within a foot of each other at the time of the shooting."

Epperly pondered that. "I've heard nothing about any plans to kill Mr. Webb. I'm sure Tammany would have no objections to Webb being killed, but I don't believe they ordered it. I would have heard something if they had."

"What about Thompson? Who benefits from his death, the independence side or the consolidation side?"

The old man thought for a moment and relaced his bony fingers over the head of his cane. "Well, it seems pretty clear that the independence side has been gaining support lately. The ward bosses have been canvassing their neighborhoods, and a lot of citizens are going to be voting to keep Brooklyn a separate city. But I can't say that the growing independence sentiment has anything to do with Joshua Thompson—either what he said when he was alive or the fact that he was killed—perhaps assassinated—while campaigning on the issue."

"Then what do you think *is* influencing people?"

Two well-dressed portly men, whom Morehouse knew to be Brooklyn city councilmen, stopped in front of the bench to pay their respects to Paul Epperly. The councilmen, who sported impressive whiskers befitting their political status, were indeed most respectful—to Epperly only—knowing that he was still a man of considerable influence. Neither of them even acknowledged Morehouse's existence or excused themselves for interrupting the conversation; they behaved as if Epperly had been sitting alone.

After the councilmen moved on, Epperly cackled, "Neither one of those two has the brains to be a dogcatcher, never mind run a city." He shook his head. "If that's the kind of politician we're getting in Brooklyn, I suppose we might as well merge with New York."

Morehouse reminded him that he'd asked about what was bolstering the pro-independence forces.

"I think it's the news about New York and Tammany," answered the old man. "Not so much the corruption, probably, as the fact that they got caught." He smiled, not a pretty sight with his sagging lower lip. "I am of the definite opinion that the public doesn't mind a little graft and corruption.

If a police officer charges a little for his services, or maybe avails himself of free beer or merchandise from the local businessmen, it's really nothing more than a gratuity for a job well done."

That was exactly Morehouse's view—although he never did accept cash "gratuities" himself—and he made a sound of agreement.

Epperly went on, "But if you take too much, like they were doing in New York, and you're so blatant about it that the damned legislature starts investigating you, well, then the public thinks you're both greedy and stupid. And they don't want to be run by incompetent thieves."

"So the Lexow Committee is having more of an effect than Joshua Thompson, you think?"

Epperly nodded. "I believe so. Can't say for sure, of course, but I've been in politics a long time—a *long* time—and I'm usually pretty good at reading what the public thinks."

"So you think consolidation is going to fail?"

"Oh, too early to tell. Three months until the election—opinions can change a dozen times by then. Plus there are other influences to take into account."

" 'Other influences'?"

"Certainly. Public opinion, one way or another, only accounts for a certain number of votes. The rest of the votes—in some wards most of the votes—are cast under instructions of the party bosses." Epperly chuckled. "Hell, down in Coney Island John McKane counts every summer visitor who signs a hotel register as a registered voter! Come November, there'll more votes cast in Coney Island than there are residents—and they'll all go the way McKane wants them to."

"How *does* he want them to go?"

"Right now, for independence. But there are other forces—powerful forces—eager for consolidation."

"Such as?"

"Some of the mobs. They figure Tammany is weak, and so is the New York Police Department, with all the charges being filed by the Lexow Committee and those police captains being booted off the force. Some of the Brooklyn mobs are looking at New York as a place they can move into. And maybe take over."

Morehouse considered that. "If there are Brooklyn mobs who *want* consolidation, any chance one of them had Joshua Thompson killed for opposing it?"

Epperly knitted his bushy eyebrows. "There's a chance—but only a small one. Killing a man is a bad political move."

"Why? He's the leading opponent to consolidation. Killing him is a good way of shutting him up."

Epperly shook his head. "Too risky. There could be a backlash of sympathy that helps his cause." He smiled slightly. "It's not so bad if you make a political opponent *disappear.* Back in the old days, especially, a man might be made to disappear to shut him up. Then you could start a rumor that he ran off with a mistress—even if he was really at the bottom of the East River. But if you shoot a man the way Joshua Thompson was killed, there's too much chance of stirring up sympathy for him."

Morehouse thought some more. Just to be sure he understood Epperly's position, he asked, "You don't think Joshua Thompson was killed because of his politics—by either side?"

"No, I don't. Not by anyone with any sense at least. It *is* possible some madman got so caught up in the battle that he resorted to killing. But I don't believe there was any *organized* effort to kill Joshua Thompson."

"And you don't think the shot was intended for Marshall Webb."

"The writer? No. Again, not by an organization at least."

Morehouse thought it over for a minute. So far, all he was getting was opinions on who *didn't* fire that rifle from the Lantigua Hotel.

The detective stood. "Thank you for your time, Mr. Epperly. If there's anything I can do for you, just let me know."

Epperly smiled. "You know I will." He lowered his head until it rested on his hands folded over the head of the cane.

Morehouse had taken a few steps down the hall, when he heard Epperly call after him, "Pattillo's on Fulton Street!"

Morehouse turned back to him. "What's that?"

"Pattillo. Best tailor in Brooklyn. He'll fit you out for a nice suit." Epperly scowled slightly. "Then you can give that thing you're wearing to the ragman."

The detective promised he would visit the tailor, and left wondering if he could get the suit as a "gratuity."

The oak door of the Thompson brownstone in Brooklyn Heights swung slowly open by an old stiff butler in an equally stiff black suit. He didn't bother to say, "Hello" or even "Yes?" His only greeting was a lifted eyebrow.

"Marshall Webb, with *Harper's Weekly.*" Webb held out his calling card. "Mrs. McCutcheon is expecting me."

The butler stepped aside to let Webb into the foyer. "Yes, Mr. Webb. I've been instructed to show you to the study."

As Webb followed the slow-moving butler through the hallway, he looked about at the décor. The Thompson home wasn't up to the standards of what one would find on the more affluent stretches of Fifth Avenue in Manhattan, but for Brooklyn it qualified as a mansion. From what he could see, the place was decorated with taste—a few oil paintings in the style of the old masters, a couple of marble sculptures, and several well-crafted tapestries. There was nothing ostentatious and there was ample space to avoid having the cluttered look that so many wealthier homes had.

Webb almost stepped on the heels of the butler when he drew up short at the entrance of the study. The old man went inside and formally announced the writer as if he were presenting him to a royal court.

The study was furnished with several leather armchairs, a horsehair sofa, one bookcase with a few books on it, and a polished wood desk so magnificent with its inlays and carving that it almost made his editor's desk at *Harper's* look like a packing crate. A thick burgundy carpet covered the floor and several framed maps, brown with age, hung on the walls. Above the flagstone fireplace was a portrait of Joshua Thompson, looking every bit the patriarch of an important family.

His daughter was seated behind the desk. "Wel-

come to our home, Mr. Webb." The greeting had
little warmth in it.

There was little warmth in her appearance, either. Mrs. McCutcheon was a slim woman in her
mid-forties. Her brown hair was pulled tightly back
from a face that was not unattractive, but rather
sharp and rigid. The long-sleeved black mourning
dress that cloaked her figure was of a severe, trim
cut; instead of conveying sorrow, it somehow gave
the impression that Mrs. McCutcheon had adopted
the style as her business attire. Webb was reminded
of her father and the black suit he had worn the
night he was murdered.

"Thank you for seeing me," Webb said, making
a slight bow. He turned to Sam Floegel, standing
to Catherine McCutcheon's side a step behind her
like an attentive waiter. "Good to see you again,
Mr. Floegel." It was also a surprise; when Webb made
the appointment to meet with Thompson's daughter, nothing had been said about Floegel joining
them.

Floegel returned the greeting with just a nod.
The general manager of Thompson Manufacturing
made quite a contrast with the new president of
the company. The rather pudgy Floegel was en-
cased in a pumpkin-colored checked suit that no
aristocrat would ever wear. While Mrs. McCutcheon's
fair face appeared composed to the point of stern-
ness, Floegel's ruddy face was damp with perspira-
tion from the top of his balding head to the jowls
hanging loose beneath his beard.

"You've met Mr. Floegel, I believe," said Mrs.
McCutcheon.

"Yes. He was kind enough to show me around

the shoe factory in Williamsburg. Quite an impressive facility."

"Thank you. My father always insisted on having modern equipment and providing good conditions for the workers."

Webb noticed that Floegel was nervously tugging at the white patch of hair that seemed to split his otherwise black beard. So far, the man hadn't said a word—a complete change from the garrulous nature he'd exhibited when he'd spoken with Webb at the factory. Webb wasn't sure if Floegel was simply deferring to Mrs. McCutcheon or if he was worried that Webb might reveal that Floegel had told him something that he shouldn't have when they'd last spoken. Webb decided that to be on the safe side, he would refrain from mentioning anything specific that he'd learned from the general manager—that way, if Floegel believed he could trust Webb's discretion, he might continue to be a source of information.

Without looking at him, Mrs. McCutcheon said to her subordinate, "Thank you, Mr. Floegel. I will finish reviewing these papers later." She slid a leather-bound portfolio to the side of the expansive desk.

"Very good, Mrs. McCutcheon." He hesitated, as if unsure whether he was being dismissed.

He was. "I'll call you at the office if I need you," she said. "On your way out, could you please ask Henry to bring us a couple of sherries?" As an afterthought, she said to Webb, "I assume you can use some refreshment."

Webb said that he could, and that sherry would be fine.

Floegel said to his boss, "Please do let me know

if there's anything more I can do, Mrs. McCutcheon."

"I shall." She then glanced at him and added in a pleasant one, "Thank you, Mr. Floegel."

Webb noticed that Floegel reacted with a somewhat awkward smile. Something passed between Floegel and Thompson's daughter in that look. Not romantic, Webb thought, but he sensed there was some kind of friendship or trust between the two of them. Perhaps it was just that Catherine McCutcheon was truly grateful to the man for helping to keep her father's company running smoothly.

After Webb and Floegel said their good-byes, too, Mrs. McCutcheon asked Webb to have a seat and he settled into an armchair set several feet away from her desk. Between the size of the desk and his distance from it, Webb felt almost like a child at the feet of a department-store Santa Claus.

Catherine McCutcheon began with a tight-lipped smile. "I was beginning to feel neglected, Mr. Webb. You've already spoken with Mr. Floegel and with my brother—I was wondering why you hadn't contacted me."

Webb wasn't about to admit that, based on his conversation with Buck Morehouse, he thought the men would be forthcoming. "I didn't want to intrude on your grief," he replied. "As I mentioned, *Harper's Weekly* has assigned me to write a story on your father and his company. I thought I would try to get information from other sources before troubling you at this sorrowful time." He also thought that, other than the color of her dress, she wasn't showing any signs of sorrow—but then he had learned over the years that people reacted to death in different ways.

She nodded. "I appreciate your consideration, Mr. Webb. It *has* been a very trying time. My father's death leaves such a void in our family and the company. And in the community."

"My condolences, ma'am."

"Thank you." She sighed. "But we will persevere. Our family is strong, and in another week I'll return to the office myself so that I can supervise the company's affairs directly. It's a bit unseemly to go back to business so early in the mourning period, but my father would have wanted it that way." She reached out and laid a pale, slim hand on the portfolio. "Until then, Mr. Floegel is quite competent to take care of matters. He also keeps me apprised of any matters of importance and brings me any documents I need to read or sign."

Webb said, "That was my impression of Mr. Floegel—a most capable manager. And he was a gracious host during my visit to the company."

The butler entered with the sherry. Webb had no place on which to rest his glass so he kept it in his hand.

When the servant left them alone again, Mrs. McCutcheon asked, "Did Mr. Floegel tell you much about the business?"

"He provided me with a history of the company. I could tell that he thought your father was quite a man."

"He was. But I must say my father was at least as important to the city as he was to the business or the family."

Careful not to spill his drink, Webb fished a notebook and pencil from his pocket. "That's why *Harper's* is so interested in a profile of him. Please tell me anything you'd like our readers to know."

Pausing now and then for a sip of sherry, Catherine McCutcheon proceeded to do so. Webb balanced the notebook on his right knee and dutifully recorded almost every word she said. There was little he didn't already know, though. She provided essentially the same history of the company that he had already heard from Sam Floegel. And she mentioned what a devoted family man her father was and how close the Thompson clan was, although her brother received barely a passing mention. She concluded by asserting that her father had earned a place in Brooklyn history as a bona fide hero for his lifelong support of the community and for his more recent efforts to keep the city independent of "those conniving New York politicians."

While he'd been writing, Webb had been paying attention not only to her words, but to her tone. He agreed with Buck Morehouse's perception of the woman: she was controlled in her demeanor and selective in what she chose to reveal. As far as Webb could tell, she hadn't really revealed anything and hadn't said anything that didn't serve to bolster her father's public image. There was no mention of the ruthless business practices to which her brother had alluded, nor did she mention that the business was suffering from the current depression.

She'd been so controlled that it caught Webb by surprise when Mrs. McCutcheon asked, "Mr. Webb, can I confide in you?"

He hesitated. "About?"

"About my father." She reached for the leather portfolio, slid it closer to her, and folded her hands over it. "I realize that you came here to get information from me about my father. But part of the reason I agreed to see you was that I wanted to meet you for myself and determine whether or not I can trust you with some rather, uh, sensitive information."

"And what *is* your determination?"

Catherine McCutcheon came close to smiling; with her rigid features, a full smile might have cracked something, thought Webb. "The fact that you did not immediately agree to maintain my confidence—in fact, you still haven't—is in your favor. You are a deliberative man and want to know the facts before making a decision."

Webb nodded. What she said was true.

"Also," Mrs. McCutcheon continued, "I am familiar with the series of articles you wrote on Tammany Hall. You supported your charges against Tammany with solid evidence—so solid that the Lexow Committee in Albany is using the results of your investigations to take action against criminals you wrote about. Again, an indication that you are not from the sensationalistic school of journalism."

Webb muttered his thanks at the compliment, but didn't see where she was leading with this.

Mrs. McCutcheon fixed her eyes on his long enough that he became uncomfortable. She finally said, "I have decided to trust you." She unzipped the portfolio, flipped through a number of documents, and withdrew half a dozen creased sheets of paper. "This might lead to some terrible embarrassment for our family—and for the company—but I believe the importance of this information outweighs any other considerations. I will not ask you to keep it confidential, because I do not believe you would make such a promise blindly. I *do* ask that you consider the possible ramifications of what you write and omit anything that might cause undue harm to innocent people."

Webb did feel comfortable making that promise. "It is not my habit—nor *Harper's*—to put the innocent at risk or to damage reputations that deserve to be protected."

She nodded, apparently satisfied. "Very well." She held out the papers for Webb to take.

He had to get up from his chair to reach them, so he put his notebook on the carpet and rested the empty sherry glass on top of it. Then he settled back in his seat to look over what turned out to be letters sent to Joshua Thompson.

There were actually five letters, dated from April to July of this year. All were signed by an "Ezra Gisclar" of Belchertown, Massachusetts. The writing paper was cheap and the penmanship poor; Gisclar wrote in childish block letters. The content, however, was explosive.

In one letter, Gisclar wrote:

> *I read that you done awful good for yourself. All that shoddy you sold the army made you rich did it? Thanks to you I been livin in hell with half my face blowed off and meanwile your living like a king. Hope you die and burn in hell Thomson you bastard.*

Another letter went beyond expressing the hope that Thompson merely die; Gisclar suggested that Thompson ought to be killed because "you cost so many good men their lives wile you lined your pokets."

"According to Mr. Gisclar," said Webb, "your father sold the army bad equipment." Webb knew that there had been a scandal during the War Between the States over profiteers selling substandard material that came to be known as "shoddy" to the War Department.

"Those are the rantings of an angry old man!" Color had come into Catherine McCutcheon's cheeks. "My father did this country a service. Many New Yorkers sided with the rebels, you know."

Webb nodded that he was aware of that historical fact.

"My father made goods to help preserve the Union—he never sold a thing to the Confederates."

"And they were all quality goods?"

She hesitated. "Perhaps not all. But not due to any negligence on my father's part. There was just such a pressing need for equipment that some manufacturing might have been rushed in order to supply the army as quickly as possible."

And to make money as quickly as possible, thought Webb. He recalled, but didn't mention, Sam Floegel's comment that government contracts during the war had given Thompson Manufacturing its greatest growth. "Whether or not your father was culpable," he said, "this Mr. Gisclar certainly blamed him—and threatened him. When did you find these letters?"

"Mr. Floegel gave them to me. My father never mentioned having received them, so I doubt that he took them seriously."

"They certainly seem serious now."

"After what happened to my father, yes. But they still might amount to nothing—this Ezra Gisclar could be nothing but a crackpot."

"Yes. But a crackpot who certainly held a grudge against your father. Have you shown these to the police?"

"No." She pursed her lips. "To be frank, Mr. Webb, I've felt torn about what to do. I want justice for my father, and if this Ezra Gisclar was responsible for his death, I want him brought to trial and hanged. On the other hand, if all he did was make idle threats, I would prefer that the allegations about my father's business during the war not be made public."

"I'm sure the police would be discreet." It had been Webb's experience that the police could be discreet to the point of covering up when it came to the wealthy and influential. Even though Joshua Thompson was dead, Thompson Manufacturing would remain a powerful force in the city.

"I was interviewed by the detective investigating my father's assassination, a Mr. Buck Morehouse. With all due respect to the detective's position, to be candid I must say that neither his approach nor his demeanor inspired any confidence in me."

Webb refrained from smiling at Catherine Mc-Cutcheon's assessment of the detective. He had no intention of relaying her opinion to Morehouse when he saw him next, although he would tell him about the letters.

"There's another consideration," she said. "I don't know Mr. Morehouse's politics. To some in Brooklyn, my father is a hero. To others—those who are willing to be subservient to masters across the river—he was an obstacle. If there are some in the police department who disagreed with my father's cause, they might reveal the contents of the letters if only to embarrass our family." She leaned forward. "Mr. Webb, I would feel much more confident of fair treatment if you would look into this Ezra Gisclar yourself."

"If Gisclar did murder your father, I don't see how his motive for doing so could be kept from the public."

"If it means bringing him to justice, I am willing for you to reveal why he bore an irrational grudge against my father."

Webb was intrigued. "I'll see if I can find this Ezra Gisclar," he promised.

CHAPTER 15

There was that dreaded noise again, echoing up through the stairway and into the sanctity of Rebecca's bedroom.

The knocking at the front door of Colden House continued while Rebecca rolled out of bed and into her dressing gown. "I'm coming," she muttered sleepily, knowing that her voice couldn't be heard all the way downstairs but somehow hoping that the words might work as an incantation to make the incessant pounding cease. It worked; the knocking stopped and Rebecca was so surprised that she hesitated in the middle of tying the robe's belt.

By the time she stepped out of her bedroom, however, a fresh assault was launched against the door. Rebecca raced down the steps, hoping it wasn't someone in urgent need, because there wasn't a bed to spare tonight. Even the infirmary had two girls sleeping in it.

Rebecca turned the lock and opened the door.

She was taken aback to see Stephanie Quilty standing alone on the front stoop. "What are you doing out?" she asked. "Come on inside."

The young girl remained where she was. "I was in Chinatown, ma'am." She was breathing heavily and her eyes were wide. "There's a carriage there that might be the same one Miss Robatin was in."

"And it's still there?"

"I don't know. When I saw it, I came right here—jumped on the back of another carriage to save time and ran the rest of the way."

Rebecca quickly decided to check it out. "All right. Hail a hansom cab while I get dressed and we'll go see."

"Yes, Miss Davies."

Rebecca ran upstairs and hurriedly put on a dress that had a minimum of laces and buttons to fuss with. As she dressed, she noticed the time on the clock: two-fifteen. She made a similar choice in shoes, opting for oxfords because of the low cut with no thought about whether or not they went with the dress. After grabbing her purse, she went back downstairs just as quickly.

Stephanie Quilty was no longer on the front stoop. Rebecca stepped out into the cool night air; she looked in both directions along State Street, struggling to see by the feeble street lamps. The street was quiet at this time of night, and there was no one to be seen. Rebecca felt a pang of concern.

In a minute, the young woman came running around the corner of Bridge Street. She raced up to Rebecca, panting for air. "I'm sorry, Miss Davies. I don't see a cab anywhere."

"We'll find one." Rebecca locked the door of

Colden House behind her. She should have realized that she'd given Stephanie an impossible task; there was no chance of finding a cab on this street at this time of night. She took the young woman by the hand as if she were a little girl and led her at a fast pace to Broadway.

At the foot of Broadway, they found a hansom cab and climbed inside. "Chinatown," Rebecca said to the driver. "And hurry."

"Pell Street," Stephanie said quietly.

Rebecca relayed the additional direction to the driver, then the two of them settled into their seats and tried to catch their breath.

They were almost to City Hall Park by the time Rebecca had recovered enough to ask, "What were you doing in Chinatown?"

"I was sorry we didn't learn anything about Miss Robatin when we went with Mr. Webb last night. So I thought I would go to Chinatown tonight— maybe her friends go there every Friday night. I was there for a couple of hours before I saw the kind of carriage you said Miss Robatin was in. Some young men and ladies got out and went into an opium den."

It had been exactly two weeks since Lucy Robatin had come to Colden House. What Stephanie said made sense, Rebecca thought. It was certainly a more sensible plan than Rebecca's idea of simply stopping in at opium dens and asking questions about the missing woman. "Next time please tell me if you're going to do something like this," Rebecca said. "It's dangerous for you to be out on your own at this time of night. I don't want you getting hurt."

"I've been out on my own a long time, Miss Davies." The girl shrugged her slim shoulders. "I don't really think about it."

Rebecca urged her again to be more careful and Stephanie agreed that she would in the future. During the rest of the ride, Rebecca again considered giving the young woman a regular job at Colden House. As much as she wished Stephanie had told her what she was doing, Rebecca did have to admire her initiative.

As soon as the cab turned from Mott Street onto Pell, Stephanie Quilty shouted, "There it is!" She pointed a thin finger at a shiny black brougham hitched to a pair of stalwart horses.

"Wait for us," she said to the cabdriver, who didn't bother to help them down from their seats.

Although it was a Friday night, the street was nearly as quiet as it had been the evening before. There were few pedestrians on the sidewalk, and not many carriages or wagons in the street. Certainly none were as fine as the one that Stephanie had pointed out.

Approaching the brougham, Rebecca became convinced that it was the same carriage that had let Lucy Robatin off at Colden House. There was no single identifying characteristic, but there were probably few carriages in all of New York fitted out as elegantly as this one and with horses that looked like thoroughbreds capable of winning the derby.

Hunched on the driver's seat was a powerfully built man in gray livery with black lapels and trim. At least she thought the colors were gray and black—the street was so faintly lit that it was difficult to tell for sure. She could tell that he appeared to be dozing, with his head on his chest.

Rebecca approached the driver, with Stephanie keeping pace beside her. She stepped as close as she could to the carriage, about to address the driver, when his head suddenly tilted back. His hand was close to the front of his mouth and there was a glint of silver in it. Rebecca didn't realize what it was until she heard the driver smack his lips; then she realized he was sipping from a pocket flask.

"Excuse me," she said.

The driver coughed and tried to tuck the flask out of sight in his jacket pocket. "Yes, ma'am?"

"I am looking for a young lady," Rebecca said. "I believe you know her—or at least drove her."

"I'm sorry, ma'am. Can't help you."

"I haven't even told you her name."

"It won't matter, ma'am. I don't know any girls." He coughed. "In fact, I don't know much of anything—all I do is drive."

Rebecca's eyes were becoming acclimated to the dim light and she searched his moon face for some expression. He appeared totally impassive—a quality highly prized in servants, she knew. She persisted. "I'm looking for Miss Lucy Robatin."

The driver shifted in his seat, but made no reply.

"Two weeks ago, you let Miss Robatin off in front of Colden House. She was traveling with a number of her friends."

"Can't expect me to remember two weeks ago, miss."

Rebecca tried to think of a way to loosen the driver's tongue. She knew she didn't have enough in her purse to give him much of a bribe. She thought of mentioning that she was a Davies, since he would certainly recognize the name of one of the city's best families, but why would he believe that a Davies lady would be standing in the street of Chinatown on a Friday night? She even thought of threatening to tell his employer that he was drinking on the job—but she didn't know who his employer was. Finally, she asked in a gentle voice, "What's your name?"

He looked away, hunched his shoulders, then turned back to her and answered, "Dawson, ma'am."

"Mr. Dawson, do you have a daughter?" He appeared old enough that he might even have granddaughters, Rebecca thought.

"It's just 'Dawson,' ma'am. Not 'mister.' And, yes, I have three darling girls, bless 'em."

"If one of your daughters was missing, how would you feel?"

"That's an awful thing to say, ma'am! I don't even want to think about anything happening to my girls."

"I don't mean to upset you, Mr. Dawson." Rebecca had decided to give him the title anyway as a courtesy; she wanted to appeal to him as a man, not a servant. "But I run Colden House and I know the kinds of awful things that can happen to girls. I hope nothing ever happens to your daughters, but think about how you would feel—and then think about how Lucy Robatin's family is feeling."

He did appear to think about it. "My girls are *good* girls," he finally said.

"And Lucy Robatin wasn't?"

Dawson shook his head. "Some of these young people are so wild. They get themselves into trouble."

"That's why you're here. Her friends like to visit Chinatown and smoke opium, right?"

He looked about to be sure no one was nearby

listening. "Yes, ma'am. I don't know what it is with them—they can have anything they want, but what they want is to go into the worst parts of the city and engage in the vilest behavior." He shook his head. "The young gentlemen used to go to the Bowery and gamble, but kept getting into fights. That's why I have to wait out for them wherever they go—in case they have to get away quickly."

"Who do you work for?"

He hesitated.

Rebecca said, "There aren't half a dozen families in New York with a carriage like this. You think I can't find which one?"

"I work for the Mues family," he said. "The youngest son, Robert, is in charge of these, uh, excursions."

Rebecca then tried to steer his attention back to Lucy Robatin. "And Miss Robatin used to go with them?"

Dawson nodded. "Never to the Bowery that I can recall. But Miss Robatin did enjoy visiting Chinatown."

"Have her friends said anything about her disappearance?"

"Not that I heard."

Rebecca recalled how noisy Miss Robatin's friends had been when they'd dropped her off at Colden House. "You must have heard *something*."

"Truth to tell, ma'am, I try *not* to hear them. To my ears, when those high-spirited youngsters get to talking and laughing, it's just noise."

"Was there anyone Miss Robatin was particularly friendly with?"

"Like I said—"

"Yes, I know, you try not to listen. But you must

have noticed or heard something during these outings."

Dawson sighed. "Ma'am, I honestly don't know anything about what happened to Lucy Robatin. And I haven't heard anybody say they knew anything, either." He reached into his pocket and put his hand on the flask but didn't take it out. "My employer pays me not only to drive this carriage, but to hear nothing and say nothing." He looked at Rebecca. "But, miss, if I knew anything that would help the Robatin family find their daughter, I would say so."

Rebecca believed that he meant it. "Thank you, Mr. Dawson. I'm sorry to have bothered you."

"No bother at all," he muttered. "I might be sitting here all night anyway, while they're in there smoking themselves senseless."

Rebecca turned to Stephanie Quilty and touched her elbow to lead her away.

The driver then called, "Miss!"

"Yes?"

"Honest, I've gotten so good at not listening that I can't say this for a fact. But I believe there was one fellow who was kind of sweet on Miss Robatin: Thomas Eubanks. He only came along once or twice, but I thought he was rather attentive to her—in a decent way."

"Thank you, Mr. Dawson."

He touched the brim of his top hat. "I hope you find the girl, ma'am."

Rebecca again began to lead Stephanie back to the hansom cab. She noticed that the girl was looking at the building that fronted the opium den. It was a wistful look, Rebecca thought, perhaps one of longing.

Although she was pleased to have gotten a couple of names tonight, Rebecca wasn't feeling happy on the ride home. She found herself wondering if Stephanie Quilty had indeed been staking out the area as she said or if she might have gone to Chinatown for another reason. Rebecca remembered the effect that the smoke-filled opium parlors had had on her the night before. It must have had even more of an effect on a girl who'd been addicted to morphine.

CHAPTER 16

Buck Morehouse felt an urgent need for a soft bed and a plump pillow. He'd been up all night and had hoped to be home asleep by now. Instead, he would have to wait until he got back from Manhattan before he could go home and go to bed. He was so tired that he briefly dozed off on the trolley over the Brooklyn Bridge; to his embarrassment, his head had slumped onto the shoulder of the matronly woman seated next to him and the annoyed woman slapped him awake with her purse. It was not an auspicious start to the day for the detective.

Morehouse perked up slightly when he walked into Marshall Webb's office at *Harper's Weekly*. He felt no more awake than he had on the streetcar, but it cheered him to see how modestly the writer's office was furnished. Morehouse had assumed a publication as prestigious as *Harper's* would provide its staff with the finest accommodations. He was happy to see he was wrong.

The office was small for the number of people who had to work in it. Although there was little furniture—four plain oak desks and a couple of file cabinets and bookcases all with matching stain that had largely faded away—it seemed cramped. A calendar, telephone, and some old framed *Harper's Weekly* covers were all that adorned the beige-painted walls. Meager sun coming through the room's one window was filtered through a layer of dust and the air was stale. The austere surroundings made Morehouse feel better about his own poor office at the Second Precinct.

It would have seemed even more cramped if the rest of the staff was there, but Marshall Webb was working alone at a desk in the rear of the room, so absorbed in what he was doing that he hadn't noticed the detective's entrance. The writer was too concerned with appearance, Morehouse thought; although he was toiling away in a rather bleak office with no one else around him, the man wore a suit and cravat that old Paul Epperly at City Hall would envy and his impressive Franz Josef whiskers were carefully sculpted.

Morehouse squeezed his body through the narrow aisle. "Mr. Webb," he said to get the writer's attention.

Webb glanced up and stood. Morehouse would have preferred that he remained seated because of the disparity in their heights. "Thank you so much for making the trip over," the writer said. "I'm sorry I couldn't see you in Brooklyn, but I have to finish an article and get it in by this afternoon." He gestured to the vacant desk next to his, offering its chair.

"Quite all right," said Morehouse, availing himself of the seat. He looked around at the otherwise empty office, hoping in vain to see a coffeepot or something to eat. "You the only writer *Harper's* has on a Saturday?"

Webb chuckled. "No. The editor doesn't come in until the afternoon, though, so the other writers seldom arrive much before he does. I would do the same, but I'm behind on this deadline."

Morehouse nodded. "You sounded eager to meet on the telephone. You've learned something?"

"I'm not entirely sure what I've *learned*, but I have had some discussions." Webb slid his swivel chair back from his desk and stretched out his legs. "I met with Eugene Thompson on Thursday. He doesn't seem to be in mourning for his father, but he didn't display any animosity for him, either. Eugene told me he didn't have the 'ruthless' streak it took to succeed in business as his father had. So he contented himself with living on an allowance and pursuing his sports."

"Was it enough of an allowance?" Morehouse asked. "Or did he need to bring about an early inheritance?"

"One of the things that surprised me about Eugene Thompson was that he seemed quite candid. He admitted to being a disappointment to his family because of his lack of interest in business, he openly said that his only real interests were tennis and golf, and he said he knew that people assumed him to be a wastrel. But he denied having any gambling or other costly vices."

"You believe him?"

Webb nodded thoughtfully. "I've spoken with so many political hacks and other criminals in the last couple of years that I'm used to people lying to me. I didn't have that sense from Eugene Thompson." He shrugged. "But that's only my opinion. I suggest we check further to learn about his personal habits. He mentioned that he lives in an apartment at the Hotel Margaret in Columbia Heights . . . perhaps a conversation with his doorman or maid might be revealing?"

Morehouse took the hint. "I'll check into it." He took a notebook and pencil from his jacket pocket to write down a reminder. Morehouse's memory was excellent, but for some reason he wished to appear official in front of the writer; it seemed that Webb was taking charge of matters, and Morehouse wasn't used to that—except from Captain Sturup.

"And then—"

"I've learned something myself." Morehouse cut him off, trying to get the upper hand in the discussion. Perhaps it was because he was so tired, but the detective was feeling distinctly irritable.

Webb appeared unperturbed at the interruption. "Yes?"

"I've done some checking—with a very credible source—and it appears that Joshua Thompson *was* the intended target."

"Your source knows that somebody wanted Thompson killed? Any chance we can find out—"

"No, no." Morehouse immediately regretted that he might have overstated what he'd found out from Paul Epperly. "I meant that there were no plans to have *you* killed. That must come as some relief to you."

The writer didn't seem affected at all; instead of relief, he looked indifferent. He answered dispassionately, "Yes, that's good news. Thank you." After a moment, Webb added, "Have you found any leads in Thompson's death?"

Morehouse didn't have anything else. He'd actually been working more on the jewel robberies lately, and hadn't even been focusing on the Thompson murder. It was his experience that after this amount of time, it would require a lucky break in order to make progress in the case. "You got any coffee here?" he asked.

"No, I'm sorry. There's a coffee shop on the corner, though. I could take a break if you'd like to go there."

Morehouse looked at the clock on the wall: a quarter to eleven. "That's all right," he decided. He might as well wait until he was done with Webb and then find a bar with a free lunch spread.

Webb seemed to be waiting to hear if Morehouse had anything more to tell him. Then he ventured, "I've also spoken with Joshua Thompson's daughter."

Now Morehouse wanted Webb to tell him quickly so he could get his lunch and then go home to bed. "Learn anything?"

"I had the same impression as you: she was very controlled, very careful not to let anything slip. One thing of interest was that Sam Floegel—the general manager at Thompson Manufacturing— was with her. I had the sense there was something between them."

"Something improper?"

"Not necessarily. Perhaps the two of them are just learning how to work together to fill in the void that Joshua Thompson left. Catherine McCutcheon is clearly in charge; Floegel almost acted like her servant."

"How long did he work for Thompson?"

"More than thirty years, he told me."

"Must be a helluva thing to work for the man that long and now have to answer to his daughter."

"He seems accepting of it. The first time I spoke with him, he said the company was always going to be run by a family member. Thompson had already been grooming his daughter to take over."

Morehouse briefly considered that. "Any chance Floegel was angry about that? Maybe he expected to take over for Thompson some day. Then, Thompson brings his daughter in instead. Could be Floegel felt he owed him a chance to run the company himself and killed Thompson for denying him that chance."

Webb shook his head. "Doesn't make much sense to me. If he knew that Catherine McCutcheon was going to take over, killing her father would only put her in charge even sooner. Would have made more sense for Floegel to kill *her*—if Thompson had no family competent to assume control, then he might have had no choice but to let Floegel take the reins."

The detective had to concede that Webb had a point.

"Catherine McCutcheon did reveal something that might prove important," Webb went on. "She had letters from a fellow named Ezra Gisclar in Belchertown, Massachusetts. They were threatening letters—this Gisclar had a grudge against her father and sent them to him earlier this year. Gisclar even wrote that Thompson should be killed."

Suddenly, Buck Morehouse felt wide awake. This could be the break that he was beginning to think might never come. "Why did he have a grudge against Joshua Thompson?"

Webb hesitated. "Something in the past."

"Do you have the letters?"

"No. She let me read them, but didn't want to relinquish possession."

Morehouse thought for a moment. "Why did she show *you* the letters? She never even mentioned them to me."

Webb hesitated again. "She might not have known about them until after you met with her and after she had a chance to go through his correspondence. They were sent to her father, and he might not have told her about them."

The detective didn't like being left out of important developments, but what Webb said sounded plausible.

"If you think it's worth pursuing, I could go up to Belchertown and see if Mr. Gisclar will speak with me."

Morehouse wasn't sure he liked that idea; it seemed he was being pushed further out of the investigation. But the truth was, the department was unlikely to spring for a railway ticket for him to go Massachusetts. And he was convinced that a breakthrough on the jewel heists could come any night. "May not be worth it," he said. "Thompson was a rich and powerful man. *A lot* of people probably had grudges against him."

"I expect you're right."

"May not even *be* an 'Ezra Gisclar' in that town."

Webb answered promptly, "There is. I already telephoned the postmaster in Belchertown; he confirmed it."

This writer did seem competent, Morehouse had to concede. And he would probably do almost as good a job of interviewing Gisclar as the detective would. "I'm awfully pressed for time myself—don't see how I can get out of Brooklyn with all I have to take care of. But if you're willing to chase a lead like this, I don't see how it could hurt."

"Very well, then. I'll go Monday."

"You will let me know if you learn anything?"

"Of course."

Morehouse had to admit to himself that so far Webb did seem to be forthcoming. Although the writer apparently had already decided to see Gisclar, he had done Morehouse the courtesy of speaking with him about it first. And he did report on his meetings with Joshua Thompson's children. Still, he was convinced there was *something* that Webb was holding back from him. Morehouse just hoped it wouldn't prove to be anything important.

The orchestra was playing superbly, as if all the instruments were in the control of one master musician playing them simultaneously with a hundred hands. The colorful costumes were tailored for each character, and the sets were works of art. The featured baritone, Russell Franks, had a magnificent, resonant voice and a commanding presence. But Marshall Webb understood no Italian, so he had no idea what the opera star was singing about.

The language barrier in no way diminished Webb's enjoyment, however. In fact, it might have added to his pleasure because he didn't have to follow the story or try to understand anything. He simply allowed himself to savor his surroundings. And they were plush surroundings indeed.

The Academy of Music on East Fourteenth Street, not far from Webb's apartment, was a luxury facility and a New York landmark. When it first opened in 1854, the Academy of Music was the largest opera house in the world, able to seat four thousand people comfortably, thereby surpassing the rival Astor Place Theater. Now in its fortieth year, the opera house had an aura of history and tradition that only added to its charms, making it a cultural oasis where one could forget about the noise of the city streets and the turbulence of city politics.

The charms of the opera house paled in comparison to those of Webb's companion, however. Rebecca looked especially pretty tonight, and from the corner of his eye he focused on her more than the performance on stage. Soft wisps of blond hair curled over Rebecca's ear, her fair face was radiant, and her eyes had a sparkle to them that he hadn't seen lately.

Rebecca seemed relaxed and carefree, a state that was rare for her. Webb wished that she could leave the concerns of Colden House behind her more often, and spend more nights together like this. But then, even if Rebecca could free herself of the responsibilities of the shelter, Webb himself was often involved in troublesome matters himself—like the Joshua Thompson murder. Webb began to review again his conversation with Detective Morehouse this morning, then caught himself. No, he wasn't going to allow those thoughts to intrude on him now.

So, while the opera went on, Webb settled back and appreciated the fact that he and Rebecca couldn't even talk about serious matters during the performance. He kept an eye on Rebecca's lovely face as she watched the stage, content to have her so close that he could smell the faint scent of her jasmine perfume.

The pleasant escape from the realities of their daily lives lasted only until intermission.

The spacious lobby of the opera house was as much a work of art as anything presented within the auditorium. There was a massive crystal chandelier that reflected light almost as intensely as a fireworks display, thick carpeting of an oriental design, ornate carved woodwork, and several enormous gilt-framed paintings of characters from famous operas.

During the intermission Webb and Rebecca went out to the lobby where he got them each a glass of champagne.

As the two of them moved to the edge of the crowd, Rebecca spoke enthusiastically about the first act, and Webb murmured in agreement although he was only vaguely aware of what it had been about.

Then she asked, "Will you be coming to dinner at my parents' tomorrow?"

"I went last Sunday!" Webb instantly regretted that he sounded so horrified at the idea of having dinner with her parents two weeks in a row.

Rebecca laughed brightly. "So you've done your duty for a while?"

Webb actually hoped that he wouldn't have to make another appearance with the Davies family until 1895. "Well, I thought . . ."

"I'm just teasing you." Rebecca put her hand on

his arm. "You're off the hook until . . . oh, let's say October?"

"Agreed." Webb could endure one more dinner at the Davies mansion before the new year.

"I would skip going tomorrow myself," said Rebecca, "except I'm looking forward to speaking with Alice."

"About the missing girl?" Webb was somewhat saddened by the fact that they couldn't have a conversation for very long before it would take a serious turn. But then, he would rather discuss the most unpleasant subjects with Rebecca than have lighthearted chats with anyone else he knew.

"Yes. I telephoned her with the name of the family that owned the carriage Lucy Robatin had been in. I also told her about Thomas Eubanks, the young man who might have had an interest in her." Rebecca smiled. "Alice has become committed to finding Miss Robatin. I'm sure she's been speaking with servants and anyone else who might be able to give her information on the young lady's whereabouts."

Rebecca had told Webb over dinner about her return trip to Chinatown with Stephanie Quilty. He wasn't happy about her going to such places in the middle of the night, but he did admire her courage and determination. "I hope Alice is successful," Webb said. "The longer she remains missing . . ." He didn't have to finish; Rebecca knew as well he—better, actually, because of her experience at Colden House—what could befall a young lady alone in New York City.

"I know." Rebecca's expression was no longer as cheerful. "But we'll find her." She smiled wryly. "My

sweet little sister is becoming quite the little bulldog. She—we—won't give up until Lucy Robatin is
found."

Webb drained the rest of his champagne glass.
"I'm looking to find somebody, too. Monday, I'm
going to Massachusetts."

Rebecca frowned slightly. "Why?"

He told her about Ezra Gisclar. "What I thought,"
he said, "was that you might like to come with me.
It's a long trip but it might be nice to get away
from the city . . . together."

"It would," Rebecca answered wistfully. "But to
leave for an entire day, as busy as we are at Colden
House . . ."

"Miss Hummel can take care of things. And
what about the new girl—Miss Quilty? You said you
were thinking of giving her a position. Between
the two of them, I'm sure the house can do without you for a day."

Rebecca appeared to consider it. Then she
brightened with her decision. "You're right! They
can do without me for a day."

The lobby lights flicked off and on, signaling that
the next act would be starting soon. Webb gave
Rebecca his arm and the two of them filed back to
their seats. But he found himself looking forward
to Monday much more than the rest of the opera.

CHAPTER 17

Rebecca hung up the receiver and took a deep breath. A five-minute conversation with her sister had just changed her plans. Now she had to tell Marshall—and she found herself reluctant to do so.

It was strange. One of the things she cherished about Marshall Webb was that she felt so free to speak with him about anything. He wasn't like so many men, who felt themselves superior to women. She never worried about what he might think of her because he never gave any indication that he felt anything for her but admiration and respect. She felt a closeness with him that she'd experienced with few other people in her lifetime.

So why was she so hesitant to telephone him now? He would understand, certainly. But he'd seemed so eager for her to join him on his trip that she just hated to have to disappoint him. Especially after he'd been so sweet at the opera; she knew that he endured such music only for her

238   *Troy Soos*

sake. And she'd noticed that he'd spent much of
the performance studying her—which led her to
spend much of the performance trying to read the
thoughts that were running through his mind.

Rebecca took another breath. It was seven-thirty
Monday morning, and she had to telephone him
now before he left his apartment to come and pick
her up. She placed the call.

Webb answered on the fifth ring.

"Marshall?"

"Yes. Rebecca?"

"I am *so* sorry. But Alice just telephoned me and—
and it turns out I won't be able to go with you
today." Rebecca had rushed to get the bad news
out and get it over with.

"Oh. Well, I'm sorry to hear that."

Despite bursts of static in the line, Rebecca could
hear the disappointment in his gentle voice.

He then added, "I hope there isn't anything the
matter."

"No, no. It actually might be good news. Alice
thinks she knows where Lucy Robatin is. And she
asked me to go with her to see if we can find her.
I'm sorry, Marshall, but I told her I would." It
sounded as if she'd chosen her sister over Marshall,
Rebecca knew, but she simply *couldn't* say no to
Alice.

"When are you going?" Webb asked. "Perhaps
we could still travel to Massachusetts tomorrow."

It was a reasonable question, and Rebecca regretted that she couldn't answer it. "I don't know.
Alice said she thinks the girl is in Atlantic City, and
she's trying to get more information now. She isn't
sure when we might leave to go see her—it might
be today, it might be in a day or two. Honestly, Alice

isn't very good at planning things, and that's part of the reason I agreed."

There was a pause at Marshall's end. "I'd better not wait then. I really should speak to Ezra Gisclar as soon as possible."

"I *am* sorry."

"I understand."

Strangely, Rebecca would have preferred that Marshall sound more perturbed than he did.

As the passenger train of the New York, New Haven & Hartford Railroad pulled out of Grand Central Depot, its wheels squealing harshly on the iron tracks, Marshall Webb was convinced that the trip would seem interminable.

He missed Rebecca; it seemed cruel that she canceled at the last minute—not cruelty on her part, but because of circumstances. Even realizing that he would have done the same in her position, it pained him no less.

On the way to Connecticut, Webb seriously considered making a change in his life. It seemed that with both him and Rebecca having such unusual and trying occupations, there was little chance of them spending more time together. He knew that Rebecca would never abandon Colden House, so perhaps he would have to resign his position with *Harper's Weekly.*

Webb had once made a handsome living by writing dime novel adventures. It was an occupation few knew about, since he used a pseudonym to protect his family from the embarrassment of having a lowly adventure novelist among its members. But he had enjoyed writing such tales, and they sold well enough that he made far more money from them than he earned from *Harper's*. And it was an easy profession; he wrote of cowboys and Indians, and cavalrymen and battles, all from the comfort of his New York apartment and with only his imagination providing the material. He had never once traveled to the West or fought in a war. And if he returned to writing dime novels, he wouldn't have to leave Rebecca as he did today.

But then he considered that if he left *Harper's* he would be giving up a reputable occupation. Although Rebecca's family didn't consider journalism quite respectable, it would make him a bit more palatable to them in case he were ever to ask Rebecca to marry him.

Once the train crossed into Connecticut, Webb allowed himself to relax and tried not to think much at all. The rocking of the car was soothing and the air coming through the open windows helped clear out the stale smell of human bodies and the smoke and soot from the locomotive.

Although he was a city man who loved the theaters, libraries, and museums so readily available in Manhattan, Webb did enjoy an occasional excursion to the country. The passing countryside was green and thriving, and the rolling hills were a welcome change from the sight of concrete and steel. It was a view that Rebecca would have enjoyed, too, Webb thought. Then, for the twentieth time this morning, he tried again to put her out of mind for a while.

Webb switched to another train in Hartford, which took him north across the Massachusetts border, through Springfield and to Holyoke. Then, after an hour-long delay during which he ate a bad lunch of fatty ham and undercooked potatoes, he caught a slow moving two-car train east.

After about ten miles, Webb caught the first sight of Belchertown. A white church spire poked the sky from atop a green hill overlooking the Connecticut Valley. At almost the same time that Webb spotted the spire, the train's conductor passed through announcing the impending arrival at the town.

From the goods loaded on trucks and flatcars near the small railroad station, Webb could tell that farming and lumber were the town's main industries. There was also a large factory, with a sign advertising Smith's Cigars, not far from the depot. The first place Webb headed was for the post office.

There was certainly an advantage to searching for a man in a small town instead of in a city like Manhattan. Everyone seemed to know everyone else. As soon as he asked about Ezra Gisclar, the postmaster gave him directions to the man's house without having to check any records.

Unfortunately, Gisclar's house was several miles north of town, so Webb went to the livery stable to rent a horse and buggy.

The stable's owner wasn't willing to let the rig out for money alone; he wanted answers first. "Where you gonna be taking her?" he asked.

"To Ezra Gisclar's house. I'm told it's about three miles out of town on Lincoln Road."

"Hell, more like four miles." The burly owner wiped the back of his thick neck with a handkerchief. "You a friend of Ezra's?"

"Never met him."

"Oh yeah? Where you from?"

"New York."

"That right? Ezra went to New York a couple weeks ago."

Webb was on the verge of becoming annoyed at the questions that were keeping him from proceeding on his journey. Now he was happy at his good fortune. "Are you sure? Do you know exactly when he was in New York?"

"Of course I'm sure. Nick Lloyd, over at the depot told me—he sold Ezra the ticket." With a chuckle, he explained, "This is a small town; somebody goes to New York—especially a fellow like Ezra, who hardly ever steps foot off his own land— and we all know about it."

Webb repeated his other question. "What day did he go?"

After a moment's thought, he answered, "It was two weeks ago. Don't remember the day exactly."

"Did he say where he was going in New York?"

"Hmm. Don't believe so. Leastways, not as I heard."

"Do you know Mr. Gisclar well?"

"Oh, everybody knows Ezra. Been down on his luck for some time, and folks try to help him out now and then, with him being a war hero and all."

"War hero?"

"Yup. Fought against the rebels." He gave Webb a defiant look. "We're mighty proud of that here. Belchertown sent most of its able-bodied men to the war, but not many of them suffered like Ezra Gisclar did."

"What happened?"

"A Confederate shell tore off a good part of his face, and he took a couple of bullets besides." He paused. "You'll see."

Webb paid the man for the horse and buggy

and, after a warning about some bad ruts in the
road, took off for Gisclar's home.

The sluggish nag pulled the buggy so slowly that
Webb began to think that he would have made better time by walking. By midafternoon, though,
with the sun beating down on the dusty road, he
pulled into a dirt path that ran a hundred feet or
so to a run-down frame house that had no nearby
neighbors.

The house, which could more accurately be
called a shack, was weathered and bare of paint except for a few streaks of dull green that clung tena-
ciously to some of the more protected planks. The
sagging roof was patched and a broken window-
pane had been replaced by a piece of cardboard.

Webb knocked tentatively on the front door; too
hard a blow was likely to have shattered the frail
wood. He tried twice, and when there was no answer he walked around to the back of the house.

There was a lean-to with no sides and a roof pre-
cariously support by two crooked timbers. In its
shade sat a man on a milking stool painstakingly
sharpening a scythe. Farm implements and machine
parts lay scattered all about the backyard, most of
them rusted and beyond the point of usefulness.

"Mr. Gisclar?" Webb called.

The man stopped from his work and looked up,
tilting and twisting his head in a peculiar manner.
"What you want?"

Webb walked closer. The man was about fifty,
with shaggy dark hair and a bushy beard. His body
was compact and sinewy—and it was easy to see the
muscles because all he wore was a pair of ragged
dungarees. It was also easy to see that Gisclar could
use a good meal; his ribs were jutting from skin

that was as dark and weathered as the house. The reason for the strange twist of his head, Webb could see, was that he only had one eye. The other was scarred over with an ugly patch of white flesh. "Ezra Gisclar?" he asked.

"Yeah, that's me," he answered impatiently. "What you want?" When he spoke, he revealed that he had only a few teeth remaining in his mouth, and his lips were pulled in at the gaps.

"My name is Marshall Webb." He was close enough to shake hands—and to see that part of Gisclar's right cheek was caved in, as if the facial bones were missing. The way the wound had healed left his thin nose crooked. Gisclar had probably let his hair and beard grow so long in order to cover as much of his shattered face as it could, but it was insufficient to conceal the fact that this man had suffered a horrible injury. "I'm with *Harper's Weekly.*" Webb tried to focus on the man's one good eye, and avoid staring at the shattered side of his face.

Gisclar quickly let go of the proffered hand. "You're wastin' your time here. I can't afford no subscriptions."

Webb smiled. "I'm not selling any. I'm a writer. I came up from New York to speak with you—about Joshua Thompson."

Gisclar dropped the sharpening stone. He looked down at it on the ground but made no move to pick it up. "I figgered somebody would come for me eventually. You gonna take me back to New York?"

It hadn't occurred to Webb that Gisclar might confess to him; if so, he had no authority to take the man into custody. "I'd just like to talk to you first. Would you tell me what happened?"

Gisclar nodded. "I been thinkin' ever since I came back, and I believe I ain't done nothin' wrong." He reached for a tin cup resting on a butcher's scale that was missing its dial. He brought the cup to his lips, took a swallow, and held it out to Webb. "Well water, but that's all I got."

"Thank you." Webb drank some himself and had to keep from gagging on the foul taste.

Gisclar gestured to a packing crate. "Sit down if you want."

Webb did so. Then he said, "You were in the war, right?"

"Yes, I was." He sat up a little straighter. "The Massachusetts Tenth Volunteer Infantry Regiment, Company D. First action I saw was Antietam." He pointed to a round scar below his protruding ribs. "Took a rebel bullet. But I stayed with my company, and fought in almost every big battle the army of the Potomac got itself into—Fredericksburg, Chancellorsville, Gettysburg." He hesitated. "And then there was Spotsylvania. That's where—" He brought up his right hand and touched the injured side of his face; Webb noticed that he barely made contact with the skin, as if it was still tender.

"You wrote to Joshua Thompson," Webb said. "You blamed him for what happened to you."

"That no-good bastard." Anger flared in Gisclar's eye. "It was his goddamned fault that I got hurt like this. And others got even worse—we lost some good men because of that bastard Thompson."

Webb didn't understand. "How do you figure he was responsible? What did Thompson *do*?"

Gisclar took another swig from the water cup

and calmed himself. "Joshua Thompson was only interested in making money. While men like me was fightin' and dyin' to save the Union, Thompson was gettin' rich off gov'ment contracts. Nothin' wrong in that, I reckon—we all *needed* uniforms and guns and equipment. Can't fight a war without 'em. But Joshua Thompson sold shoddy—he got gov'ment money for providin' us with *garbage.*"

Webb had a long interest in the War Between the States, in part because his own father had fought in a New York regiment and been killed in the battle of Cold Harbor. Webb had read about the scandals over greedy merchants who got rich selling poor-quality goods known as "shoddy" to the army. The term originally referred to "wool" blankets and uniforms that had been made from recycled rags and fell apart upon use, but became more broadly applied to the various substandard materials provided by unscrupulous manufacturers. The underhanded practice was so widespread that it led to a congressional investigation. After Catherine McCutcheon had shown Webb Gisclar's letter in which he accused Thompson of selling shoddy, Webb had checked the back issues of *Harper's* and read the reports of the investigation. "I've checked the records," he said to Gisclar. "Joshua Thompson was not one of the manufacturers accused of selling shoddy during the investigation."

"Of course not. How do you think he got his contracts? He paid off somebody in the gov'ment. Whoever it was wouldn't want that comin' up in an investigation, would he? So Thompson was protected."

"You know that for a fact?"

"Stands to reason, don't it?"

It did, except that other merchants *were* named in the investigation. Perhaps Thompson had simply paid more substantial bribes. "How do you *know* Joshua Thompson was selling shoddy?"

"Wasn't a secret at first. We got his blankets, which wouldn't hold together good enough to blow yer nose. Was a joke around the camps. Then we got Thompson boots, and it wasn't so funny anymore. The soles would come off after a mile or two of marchin'—had to tie 'em back onto the boots with rags. May not sound like anythin' serious, but if you're in the army you're marching all the time— feels like torture on the feet if you ain't got decent boots." Gisclar's already twisted features contorted in something like a sad grin. "You know what that bastard Thompson said when the army complained about them boots?"

"No, what?"

"Said the *army* made the mistake by givin' them to infantrymen. He said they was *cavalry* boots— cavalrymen rode instead of walked, so they didn't need the boots to hold together so good."

Webb could sympathize with Gisclar over the hardship Thompson had caused but didn't see how it led to the businessman being killed thirty years later. "How did bad blankets or boots cause your wounds?" he asked.

"Oh, they didn't. Thompson started makin' anythin' the army might buy. Even cartridges. That's what did it." Gisclar shook his head sadly. "Spotsylvania. May of sixty-four. Bloodiest goddamn fightin' I'd ever seen, and it went on for days. On the fourth day, me and ten or twelve others got cut off from the rest of our company. Had to fight our way back—and we would have, too, except we could hardly ever get our rifles to fire. The cartridges we had were mostly duds—made by Thompson Manufacturing. We was sittin' ducks for the rebels." He paused to collect himself. "Only three of us got out alive, and I come out like this—barely alive."

Webb had no words to express how sorry he was for Ezra Gisclar, or how angry he was to hear what Joshua Thompson had done.

Neither of them spoke for a few moments. During the silence, Webb heard the clop of hooves slowly approaching.

Ezra Gisclar stood up at the sound. "That'd be Denny Cepero." He then burrowed through some of the junk stored in the lean-to, and came out with a plowshare.

A farm wagon drawn by a stout workhorse pulled around the corner of the house. Its sole occupant was a short man, as stout as the horse and tanned nearly as brown, wearing a red flannel shirt and faded overalls. He climbed down from the seat. "Hey, Ezra. You got that—"

Gisclar held the implement out to him. "Good as new."

Cepero took it and looked it over. "Sure is. Don't know what I'd do without you—my land's so damn rocky, it just tears these things up." He dug into his pocket. "Same as usual?"

"Yup. Two bits."

Cepero put a coin in Gisclar's hand. He looked at Webb. "Who's your friend, Ezra?"

"Oh. This is Marshall Webb. He's a writer. Come all the way up from New York just to see me." He sounded quite proud of the fact.

Webb and Cepero exchanged brief greetings.

The farmer said, "Well, better get back to the

farm. Always too much work and too little time."
He turned toward the wagon, then back to Gisclar.
"Say, Ezra, my corn sheller ain't workin' right. You
think you can come out and take a look at it later
today? Reckon it won't be cheap to get it fixed, but
if you can get it workin' again for me it'll be worth
it."

Gisclar said that he could.

"Fine, I'll come by for you later then. We'll have
supper at my place. The wife's fixin' a ham if that's
all right with you."

Webb could see by the way Gisclar was already
moving his mouth that the meal sounded just fine
with him. Webb also had the sense that the offer was
an example of what the livery stable owner had referred to when he mentioned that the neighbors
often helped Gisclar out.

When the two were alone again and had seated
themselves, Webb asked, "Why did you wait so long
to contact Joshua Thompson? It's been thirty years."

Gisclar tugged at his long chin whiskers. "Well,
at first I was just tryin' to stay alive—the army doctors didn't think I'd pull through. Then I come
back home and was takin' a long time to heal.
Couldn't do much—certainly not what it took to
keep the farm goin'. My folks was dead—mother
died of consumption while I was in the army—and
I didn't have no brothers or sisters. So there wasn't
nobody to work the land." He looked around the
rolling farmland behind his ramshackle house. "I
had to sell it. Kept just a couple acres, so I'd still
have a roof over my head."

"You've been here ever since?"

"Yep. Never found a wife. What woman would
want to look at a face like this ever' day? I get by

though. Do repair work for the farmers around here. Keeps a little food on the table." He sighed. "But that's about it. That's been my life for years now—if you call that living."

Webb still wasn't following how this led to Thompson's murder almost thirty years after the end of the war. "When did you decide to write to Thompson?"

"Early this year. I go to the town library every week and look at the illustrated papers." He lips twisted in an ugly grin. "I'd take up drinkin' if I had the money. But I don't, so I read—it's free. The library gets some of the New York papers, and I was seein' stories about Joshua Thompson all the time—how rich he was, how important he was, how respected he was." He shook his head, causing more of his unruly black hair to fall over his forehead. "If folks only knew what he really was. So one day I decided to write him a letter—to let him know there was one man who *did* know what he really was."

"You did more than that. You threatened to kill him."

"Oh, I wrote something 'bout how he *deserved* to be dead for what he done, but I don't think I actually said *I'd* kill him."

"But you carried through with it."

Gisclar twisted his head sharply to stare at Webb. "You think *I* killed him?"

That was precisely what Webb thought. "Didn't you?"

"No. The more I think about it, though, the more I wish I did."

Webb didn't understand. He thought Gisclar was going to be confessing. "You wrote a threatening letter to Thompson and you went to New York the day he ended up being shot to death."

"I know all that. I also know I didn't have nothin' to do with killin' the son of a bitch. But tell you what: you find out who did, and I'll give him my medals." Gisclar picked up the scythe and resumed honing its blade.

Thoroughly puzzled, Webb asked, "What were you doing in New York then?"

"I was supposed to meet Thompson."

" 'Supposed to'?"

"Yep. Got a letter from him a month ago. Never expected to hear from him. I just wanted to let him know that he couldn't hide what he really was—no matter how 'respectable' other people thought he was."

"What did he say?"

"Said he knew he done wrong. Told me to come to New York and he'd make things right—he was gonna 'compensate' me, he said. The letter told me when to come, and that there'd be a hotel room already paid for."

"You still have the letter?"

"Nope. What happened was, I was supposed to check in to the Lantigua Hotel but sign in under the name 'J.C. Fullerton'—Thompson said he wanted to keep our meeting secret 'cause otherwise he'd have a thousand war veterans claiming injuries and wantin' money from him."

"You agreed to keep it secret? Didn't you *want* people to know what he'd done during the war?"

Gisclar stopped in his work. "Look at me. I got nothin' an' never had nothin'. If it wasn't for good people like Denny Cepero pretendin' to need somethin' fixed so they can give me enough money to

get by, I'd be starvin'. Sure, I would have liked
ever'body to know what Thompson done, but the
idea of havin' some money and maybe livin' a little
easier sounded even better."

Webb couldn't blame him, and nodded to show
that he understood.

The war veteran went on. "So I borrowed some
decent clothes, and enough money for a railway
ticket to New York. Got there on a Friday mornin'
and checked into the hotel just like I was supposed
to. And I gave Thompson's letter to the desk clerk—
told him to leave it in the box of another guest,
'Solomon,' I think the name was."

"Why did you do that?"

"The letter said I was supposed to. That way
Thompson would know I'd arrived. Didn't understand it, but I did it. I was real careful to do exactly
what the letter said so's I wouldn't lose my chance
at gettin' 'compensated.' "

"What happened after you checked in?"

"Not much. I went for a walk, but was awful hungry. And you have all those pushcarts there, smellin'
so good of sausages and oysters—there was even
fellers sellin' ice cream. So I went back to the hotel
and waited in my room. I knew the room was paid
for, but didn't know if I could charge a meal to it.
Figured soon as I saw Thompson I'd have all the
money I'd need anyway, so I could hold out. Then
in the evenin' I went to a saloon—Grady's Saloon
on Myrtle Avenue. I was supposed to wait there for
Thompson. He said he was making a speech that
night, but he'd meet me at Grady's soon as it was
over. Bartender there was a decent feller. First he
didn't like the fact that I wasn't orderin' anythin',
but then he asked how my face got to look like it

did. I told him and then he give me a couple beers on the house—even let me help myself to the pickled egg jar. Must have ate a dozen of them while I was waitin' for Thompson."

"But he never showed up."

"No, I waited and waited. No Thompson." Gisclar shifted uncomfortably on the milk stool. "The news came into the bar soon enough though—Joshua Thompson was shot. Some of the men in the place ran out to go to the place where he'd been killed and see for themselves what happened."

"You didn't?"

"I was shocked. Here I was so close to gettin' the first lucky break o' my life, and with him bein' dead it was gone." He snapped his finger. "Just like that. So I had another beer, knowin' it might be my last for a while. By the time I tried to go back to the hotel, the police had the street sealed off. I couldn't get there. I tried to tell one o' the cops I had a room there, and he told me to beat it or my next room would be a police cell."

That certainly jibed with Webb's experience of what had transpired that night. "Where *did* you go?"

"I walked the streets for a while. Dunno where exactly. I stayed away from the cops and just wandered around, collectin' my thoughts. As the night went on, I started to get real uncomfortable. Seemed so strange, Thompson gettin' killed just before I was supposed to meet him. And I started thinkin' somethin' was wrong about that—didn't know what, and I still ain't sure—but it sure made me feel uneasy. I decided the best thing was for me to get out of the city. So I come back here."

"You never went back to the hotel?"

"Nope. Like I said, cops had the area sealed off. I wasn't about to get myself throwed in jail."

"What about your luggage?"

"Didn't have none. All I come to the city with was the clothes I had on my back. Figured it's all I needed till I saw Thompson and got some money from him. Turned out I couldn't even buy a ticket home. Had to hop a freight car to New Haven, then a couple others to get back to Belchertown." He shook his head at the memory. "Was a rough night, that was. Thinkin' 'bout how close I come to havin' a better life, and how there was somethin' fishy 'bout Thompson gettin' killed while I was in Brooklyn. And I was tryin' to keep my clothes clean so I wouldn't have to be owin' anything to the fella who lent 'em to me."

Webb tried to absorb all that Ezra Gisclar had told him. As strange as the man's story was, it had a ring of honesty to it. One more question occurred to Webb. "You do any hunting, Mr. Gisclar?"

"I got a shotgun and go after rabbits now and then. But I ain't the shot I was in the war." He brought his hand near the blinded eye. "I was pretty damn good when I could see. But with this one gone, and the other only good for close-up, about the only time I get rabbit for dinner is if one of them happens to run in front of the shot."

"Thank you for speaking with me, Mr. Gisclar." Webb stood and was about to say good-bye when he thought of something more. "Do you mind if I report your story in *Harper's?*"

"I don't have no reason to object. I ain't done nuthin' wrong."

"In that case, I should tell you that it's *Harper's*

policy to pay for interviews that get used in the publication." Webb drew a ten-dollar gold piece from his vest pocket and handed it to the war veteran. "Again, thank you for your time."

Webb wasn't sure if Gisclar believed him any more than he believed the local farmers really needed their plowshares repaired so frequently. But one thing was sure: Gisclar wouldn't have to go hungry for a while.

CHAPTER 18

Alice certainly traveled in style, Rebecca thought. It was a style into which Rebecca had been born, too, but had long since abandoned.

Although the trip was only going to be a few hours, Alice had packed a trunk—actually her maid had packed the trunk—containing several changes of clothes with accessories. She'd also insisted on a first-class private compartment; since the train was already fully booked, that meant the railroad had to attach an additional Pullman car—but they did so willingly to accommodate an Updegraff.

At first Rebecca had been embarrassed by the fuss. She was used to traipsing alone through Bowery tenements and Hester Street sweatshops, picking her way through piles of rubbish and climbing rickety fire escapes. But as they proceeded on their journey, Rebecca found herself enjoying the luxury.

The plush compartment was like an elegant cocoon, with furniture and fixtures as stylish as those that could be found in the Updegraff or Davies mansions. Alice was on a velvet lounge while Rebecca sat on a divan that dripped with knotted fringe. They had been served a lunch of duck salad and squab soon after boarding. The plates were china, the service was sterling silver, and there were fresh flowers in a crystal vase. An attentive porter quickly responded every time Alice rang for him—which was far more often than Rebecca would have.

Rebecca forked a piece of duck. "I certainly hope Lucy Robatin is going to be there."

"So do I. But if not, at least we'll have a lovely trip to Atlantic City." Alice smiled brightly. "I know it's rather vulgar, but I do enjoy the boardwalk there."

Rebecca hoped that she wasn't going to waste the entire day just for a stroll on a New Jersey boardwalk. "Tell me again why you think Miss Robatin is staying down there." Alice had already given her a brief explanation on the telephone when she'd asked Rebecca to accompany her, but Rebecca hadn't found it convincing. The only reason she had agreed to come was as a favor to her sister, not because she had any real expectation of finding Lucy Robatin.

Alice dabbed at her lips with a satin-finished napkin. "I had my parlor maid speak to the upstairs maid of the Eubanks. Apparently, young Mr. Thomas Eubanks was indeed rather smitten with Miss Robatin. They were actually childhood sweethearts—almost inseparable when they were young." She paused. "That must be a wonderful feeling, to be young and innocent and in love."

It was something that neither Alice nor Rebecca had experienced. Alice's marriage had been more a matter of joining two wealthy and powerful families; as a dutiful daughter, Alice had allowed herself to be pressured into marrying Jacob Updegraff and learned to become content with being his wife. As for Rebecca, she had always been a headstrong girl, a trait that discouraged most young suitors. "But why do you think they're together now?" she pressed.

"Because Mr. Eubanks hasn't been home, either. He told his family he's at Princeton."

"In *August?*"

"He will be starting his junior year there in the fall, and he said he was going down early to do some research with a professor of natural history." Alice rang a bell, and the colored attendant promptly appeared.

"Yes, ma'am?" He made a slight bow and sounded courteous, but Rebecca thought she could detect an exasperated "What do you want now?" in his eyes.

"I would like some tea," Alice said. "Darjeeling." Once he'd gone to fulfill her request, she turned her attention back to Rebecca. "It seemed curious to me that Lucy Robatin and Thomas Eubanks were both away from home at the same time. So I telephoned Princeton and spoke with every natural history professor there—not one of them has seen Mr. Eubanks during the summer recess, nor do any of them plan for him to be doing research with them." She leaned back, positively beaming, obviously proud of her detective work.

"I understand that," answered Rebecca. "And perhaps they are together. But why Atlantic City?"

"The Eubanks have a summer home there. But it's nearly abandoned." Alice gave a laugh that would

have been called a "giggle" in a younger woman.
"They're a respectable family, but not nearly as
well-to-do as they would like people to think. They
spent a fortune building a magnificent new summer home in Newport—thought it would elevate
them in society—but now they can't afford to keep
up some of their other houses. Mr. Updegraff tells
me they even had to sell off one of their proper-
ties."

"Did you try telephoning the Atlantic City home?"

"It's been disconnected. As I said, it's nearly
abandoned."

The porter arrived with Alice's tea. After serv-
ing her, he asked, "Will there be anything else,
ma'am?"

She scanned the dining cart before. "Oh! Yes.
More toast, please."

"Right away, ma'am."

When he left, Alice continued to look over the
meal, as if there was something more she wanted
but couldn't remember.

Rebecca thought over what Alice had told her.
Her sister's logic wasn't unreasonable, but Rebecca
remained skeptical of finding Lucy Robatin. Perhaps
it was because of her experience with missing women. Alice could believe that a vanished girl could
simply be staying at the summer home of a wealthy
young gentleman. Rebecca knew that Lucy Robatin
might have met a much worse fate; far too often,
Rebecca had been called in to the New York morgue
to identify girls who had once stayed at Colden
House.

* * *

Overlooking the Atlantic Ocean on the north end of the city, the Eubanks's summer cottage was a sprawling, two-story frame dwelling with a wrap-around porch. There was little sign that the family had abandoned the place; coats of pink paint on the clapboard and white on the shutters were intact with little fading or chipping. The lawn was a bit unkempt, but not overgrown.

Alice, who had changed from the traveling suit she wore on the train into a lovely summer gown of peach silk and white lace, ordered the carriage that had brought them here from the depot to wait in front of the house. She and Rebecca then went up the flagstone walk to the front door.

Alice rapped the brass knocker politely. It was loud enough to summon a butler standing near the door, but unlikely to get the attention of anyone farther inside the house, Rebecca thought. After trying again, and getting no response, Alice gave Rebecca a questioning look.

Rebecca took hold of the knocker and banged the door in a most unladylike manner. The sound caused Alice to flinch, but it did get a response from within. A curtain was pulled a few cautious inches to the side in a window near the door. It closed quickly, but Rebecca had spotted the movement.

She banged again, and called through the door, "Mr. Eubanks?"

No answer. Not even the sound of footsteps.

Rebecca called the name again, adding, "It's urgent that we speak with you. Please, Mr. Eubanks!"

Still no response.

Cupping her hands to amplify her voice, Rebecca

pressed close to the window, thinking the sound
might carry better through it. "Mr. Eubanks! If you
do not let us in, we will call the police to search the
house!"

Footsteps came quickly now. The door cracked
open and a young man's voice asked, "Who are you?
What do you want?"

Rebecca gave her and Alice's names. "We are
concerned about a Miss Lucy Robatin. Is she here?"
It should have been a simple enough question to
answer, so when she received no prompt reply, she
asked him in a gentle voice, "You *are* Mr. Thomas
Eubanks?"

"Yes."

Alice spoke up. "We are only here out of concern for Miss Robatin's safety, Mr. Eubanks."

The door opened fully. Standing with one hand
on the knob was a slender clean-shaven young man
of about twenty with close-cropped sandy brown
hair and intelligent eyes. He wore a blue-striped
seersucker jacket with white duck trousers and a
red bow tie. There was sadness in his otherwise
handsome face. "This is the only place she *is* safe,"
he said quietly. "Please come in."

Rebecca and Alice did so, and he motioned to a
tidy sitting room sparsely furnished in rattan and
pine. It was a bright, airy room bathed in sunlight
from all the windows on two of its walls.

After the three of them were seated, Thomas
Eubanks said, "Miss Robatin is here. I took her out
of New York."

"Why?" Alice asked.

"Because I thought she was going to die if she
kept on the way she was."

Rebecca wanted a clear story from the beginning. "You've known Miss Robatin for some time?"

"Yes. Our families had always been friends, and Lucy and I practically grew up together." He suddenly stood. "My apologies. I haven't offered you anything. Lemonade?"

Rebecca would have preferred information, but Alice accepted his offer with enthusiasm, so they had to wait until the young man returned with a tray holding a pitcher of lemonade and several glasses.

After Alice was occupied by taking dainty sips of the beverage, Rebecca continued the questioning of Eubanks. "You said Miss Robatin is here. Will she join us?"

"She's resting right now. And the way she's been feeling lately, I'm happy for her to get some sleep."

Rebecca didn't press him to see the young lady, but she certainly intended to before she and Alice left. "I have a shelter—Colden House—in New York. Miss Robatin appeared on my doorstep in the middle of the night a couple of weeks ago in a terrible condition. Intoxicated, I believe, and smelling of opium. I have since been told that she was a visitor to the opium dens of Chinatown—is that true?"

Eubanks nodded sadly. "I'm afraid it is."

"I also understand that you accompanied her to Chinatown on more than one occasion." Rebecca tried not to make it sound like an accusation.

"I did." He looked up. "Only to protect her, though. I never used the stuff myself, and I didn't want her to."

"How long had she been using opium?"

"I'm not sure exactly." Eubanks ran his fingers

back through his hair, leaving locks of it sticking up. For the first time, Rebecca noticed that his expression of sadness was also a tired one. "About a year ago, Lucy fell in with a different group of friends. Wealthy, and of good families, but rather wild." He looked at Rebecca earnestly. "I'm not an innocent myself. I've tried some things that I'm not proud of—but nothing that most of my classmates haven't also done, and nothing that would shame my family. Lucy got carried away—developed quite a fondness for champagne and brandy although she could handle neither."

Alice spoke up. "I don't remember many young ladies who *didn't* enjoy champagne to excess from time to time."

"She was coming home drunk almost every night. Had some awful rows with her parents about it. Then her friends took her to Chinatown to try an opium pipe—it's become the fashionable thing to do lately." He took a swallow of lemonade. "It only took one outing for Lucy and she was in love with the stuff. Then she had a serious argument with her father—he threatened to throw her out on the street if she continued the way she was. She seemed to take it as a challenge—couldn't keep her away from drugs and drink. Believe me, I tried."

Rebecca asked, "The fight with her father was over her drug use?"

"I think there was more than that. She developed a real hatred for him, but never told me why."

Rebecca remembered the girl who'd arrived at Colden House and the condition she'd been in. "I believe Miss Robatin might have suffered some violence the night she came to me," she said. "There was skin and blood under her nails—as if she'd been fighting somebody off. Do you think her father beat her?"

Eubanks cringed slightly. "She never suggested that to me. It might have been some of the young men she was with in Chinatown. Just because they're from 'good families' doesn't keep them from trying to take advantage of a girl who's in no condition to defend her honor."

And here was Eubanks, a young man living alone with Lucy Robatin, away from both their families. Rebecca wondered what his motives might be.

As if he'd read her mind, Eubanks said, "She's *safe* here with me. I would never do her any harm."

"We really *must* see her before we go back to New York," said Rebecca. "Just to be sure."

Eubanks nodded and stood. "I understand. But please don't disturb her any more than necessary. She really hasn't been feeling well."

He then led Rebecca and Alice to an upstairs bedroom. It was painted pale blue, and sheer white curtains fluttered in the open window. The smell of salt water was invigorating, but Lucy Robatin, lying under a light blanket on a brass bed, showed no sign of life. She was curled on her side, facing the wall.

Rebecca went to the bed. Sitting down on the edge of the mattress, she reached for the young lady's wrist. Picking it up gently, she was about to feel for a pulse when Lucy groaned, "Leave me 'lone."

"My name's Rebecca Davies. Do you remember me?"

Without looking at Rebecca, she answered, "No."

Alice came over. "It's me. Mrs.—Alice—Updegraff. Surely, you remember *me*, Lucy?"

After a moment Lucy rolled over enough to direct her bleary eyes at Alice. Her fleshy, pale face was totally impassive and her thick lips were slack. "Yes, I remember you." Then she rolled back. "Now leave me alone."

Rebecca refused to, but she did postpone any questions. Instead, she studied the girl with a practiced eye. During her years at Colden House, she had seen just about every kind of injury and illness a girl could suffer. She peeled back the edges of the blanket, enough to see that Lucy Robatin was wearing a clean muslin nightdress; Rebecca noticed no signs of bruising or other injuries.

"I'm cold." Lucy snatched the blanket back and pulled it tight around her.

"We just want to be certain that you are unhurt," said Rebecca.

"Do you really want to stay here?" asked Alice.

"Might as well be here as anyplace else. Please go 'way."

Rebecca offered, "We can take you home if you want."

"Don't have one."

Both Alice and Rebecca repeated the offer and repeated their questions as to her well-being. They received no further replies—at least not any verbal ones. After Lucy Robatin made a gesture that caused Alice to gasp, they did as the young woman had repeatedly asked and left her alone.

Back downstairs, Thomas Eubanks said, "I apologize. Lucy has been like this for some time."

Rebecca asked, "You have *no* idea what is wrong with her?"

"No. And I've had two doctors in to examine

her. One of them said it was withdrawal—she hasn't had a drink since I took her out of New York. And, of course, no drugs."

"She should be over that by now," said Rebecca.

Eubanks nodded. "That's what the second doctor said. He attributed her behavior to 'malaise.' "

" 'Malaise'?" Rebecca repeated. She had never heard that as a legitimate diagnosis for anything.

Slumping in his seat, Eubanks nearly broke down. "I don't know what to do! I *love* Lucy—that's why I brought her down here. I thought I could save her. I know if she stayed in New York, she would die."

Alice said softly, "You did the right thing."

Rebecca wasn't sure that that was true, but she was starting to lean toward that opinion.

Eubanks appeared grateful for Alice's words. "My family will probably disown me if they find out about this, but I don't believe there were any other options. There were two things in New York that Lucy had to be taken away from: her father and the opium dens."

"You don't know what the problem was with her father?" Rebecca asked.

He shook his head. "He claimed she was a disgrace to the family. And Lucy said the same thing about him—but she never told me why. I know he never offered to help her—he only threatened her with being disowned if she didn't change."

"Maybe you should take her to another doctor," suggested Rebecca.

"She won't go. All Lucy does is lie in bed. It's all I can do to get her to eat enough to stay alive and take an occasional bath." He looked up. "And she bathes *herself*. I have *not* taken advantage of her."

"Then have another doctor come here," said Alice. "And perhaps a maid so that she can be properly looked after."

Eubanks looked stricken, as if he'd been reprimanded for his own efforts to care for her falling short. "I'll get another doctor," he said. "I've already used most of my college expense money for this coming year, though—I don't believe I can afford a maid."

Alice began to argue that everyone should have a maid.

Rebecca cut her off. "I believe you are caring for Miss Robatin as well as anyone can, Mr. Eubanks. May I ask a favor of you, though?"

"Yes, certainly."

"Please telephone me at Colden House in a few days and let me know how she is faring."

"I will."

"Also, I believe it only fair if you permit Alice to tell her family that she is alive and well."

He agreed, but said he doubted that they would care.

CHAPTER 19

Buck Morehouse's legs were cramping. He struggled to resist the urge to stretch them out, but the more he tried to keep from doing so, the greater the pain became and the stronger the urge to relieve it.

The only thing that kept him from giving in was the conviction that it was only a temporary inconvenience. He had done everything he could to ensure a successful outcome, and it had to pay off.

He only hoped the payoff would come tonight. This was the fifth night that he was spending crouched next to an ash barrel in the dark alley behind Namm's Department Store. The thief *had* to come soon.

Morehouse had deliberately dangled the bait in front of Frankie Lew at the Wild West show, telling him about a nonexistent jewel delivery at Namm's. And he'd deliberately antagonized the burglar, to ensure that Lew would want revenge against him. He knew that Lew couldn't have committed the earlier crimes, since he'd been in Sing Sing, but he had no doubt that Lew would want to tip off his friends about the jewels—it would both earn Lew a few dollars and, perhaps more importantly to him after their recent encounter, humiliate the detective.

Still trying to ignore the pangs in his legs, Morehouse kept his attention focused on the rear wall of the department store. No thief would try to go through the front door on Fulton Street, and the store abutted other buildings on its sides so there was no way to get in there.

A soft drizzle began to fall, only adding to Morehouse's misery. Every other police officer with Morehouse's years of experience was either off duty, playing poker at a station house, or in a saloon. And here he was, a detective with the Brooklyn Police Department, breathing in the foul smell of refuse that had been dumped in the alley, his suit grimy with soot from the ash barrel, and his entire body aching from remaining motionless for hours.

The rain fell a little harder. At least, Morehouse thought, it would keep down the ash that had been blowing onto him. And it should help with the smell. Besides, it couldn't be another hour or so until dawn. If the thief didn't show up by then, at least Morehouse could go home.

Please let it be tonight, he silently wished. Even the prospect of going home to bed wasn't all that appealing knowing that he would only have to come back again tomorrow night.

The rain made it even harder to see, though, and the back of the store was already in nearly pitch-blackness. He began to blink frequently, trying to keep his eyes clear of the rain that collected on his eyelashes.

Just when Morehouse was beginning to think he might like to leave the police department entirely and find a job as a bartender, he thought he spotted a shadowy movement at the top of the wall. He blinked several times and tried to focus his eyes as if straining them could cut through the dark and haze.

Yes! It was the figure of a man descending from the roof of the department store. His movements were slow, fluid, and silent.

Morehouse brought his police whistle to his lips, ready to blow when the moment was right. He had two young patrolmen, so inexperienced that they still wanted to prevent crimes, ready to answer his call. Christopher Nulph was positioned on the roof of the bank next to Namm's and Mike Sprigg was at the end of the alley. Either one of them could easily outrun Morehouse; he hoped they were also fast enough to snare a second-story man.

From the man's movements, Morehouse could tell he was lowering himself by a rope. The detective waited until he had lowered himself to a point midway between the roof and the window.

Morehouse blew the whistle hard and low, and tried to hop up. He almost fell when his sore legs failed to comply. He blew again and yelled, "He's comin' down from the roof! Get 'im!"

He could hear running footsteps and was glad the younger men had no trouble moving. Finally, he got his own legs to function and walked as quickly as he could to a position behind the wall.

The burglar had hesitated, apparently unsure whether to try to go up or down to attempt his escape. He started to go up, then stopped when Christopher Nulph looked down at him from the roof, his helmet giving away the fact that he was a police officer.

Nulph held a nightstick above his head, ready to strike. "Freeze!" he cried. "Right where you are!"

Morehouse groaned at the rookie's words. *We don't want him to freeze,* he silently reprimanded the patrolman. *We need him down from there.*

Meanwhile, Mike Sprigg, a tall skinny officer, had joined Morehouse. He was jumpy with excitement. "What do we do?" he hissed.

Morehouse continued to look up. "He's either got to go up or go down. Either way, we catch him."

"What if he goes in the window?" Sprigg asked.

"Then he's trapped inside the store." Morehouse had a brief sense of worry, though. If the thief did decide to go through the window, there would be a hundred places to hide inside a store as vast as Namm's. The police would have to search—and while they were searching, their man could dart away.

Fortunately, the thief apparently didn't think of that option. The sight of Nulph's nightstick was enough to send him downward, the rope sliding through his hands as he came down.

As he approached, Morehouse could see he was wearing tight-fitting dark clothes, like little more than a union suit, and a knit cap. A small leather satchel, which no doubt either contained burglary tools or was intended to carry away stolen jewels, dangled from a belt.

Morehouse moved to grab the man as soon as he was within reach, and thought Sprigg would do the same.

The younger officer had taken a cue from Nulph,

though. He, too, grabbed his nightstick and swung it, delivering a sharp blow across the man's back.

With a yelp of pain, the wiry man fell the rest of the way and crumpled to the ground.

In his excitement, Sprigg delivered more blows to the man's legs and didn't appear about to let up.

Morehouse grabbed his arm. "That's enough, Officer."

"Don't want him to run away."

The way the man was writhing, there was little chance of that.

"You are under arrest," Morehouse informed him. He called up to Nulph, "Come on down! We got 'im!" He then lit the wick of his police lantern to provide adequate light.

"Detective?" Sprigg said in a strange voice.

"Yeah?"

"Sounds like he's cryin'."

That was no surprise considering the blows that Sprigg had administered. But what *was* peculiar was the sound.

Morehouse reached around, pulled the cap off, and shone his lantern at the man's face. He was stunned to see that it was the face of a young woman.

CHAPTER 20

Wednesday morning, Marshall Webb arrived at the Second Precinct station house in downtown Brooklyn. A uniformed officer escorted him to the office of Detective Buck Morehouse.

"Detective?" Webb said from the doorway.

Morehouse swiveled around in his armchair. "Oh yes," he replied in a weary voice. "Come in, Webb."

The detective looked as exhausted as he had sounded on the telephone when Webb called about coming to meet with him. Morehouse's fleshy face always sagged a bit; now it seemed to droop almost to the crooked bow tie around his yellow collar. His eyes were red and half closed, and his jowls were dotted with heavy stubble. Even the detective's suit was in worse repair than usual; in addition to the ever-present food stains, the brown sack suit was streaked with soot.

Webb sat down in the tiny office's other chair and faced the detective. "Looks like I came at a bad time," he said.

Morehouse looked down at some papers on his desk. "It's a good time, actually. We made an arrest in the jewel heists last night." He glanced up at the small clock atop the chipped pine file cabinet. "This morning, actually. And I haven't been to bed yet, with all the damned paperwork."

"Congratulations!"

"Thank you, but I'm not celebrating."

"Why?"

The detective handed him a sheet of heavy stock paper. "This is our thief," he said with a tired sigh.

Webb looked at the document. It was an arrest report for one "Sara Jaeger," aged twenty-two, and a small photograph of an attractive young woman with frightened eyes was attached to it. "Women are moving into all sorts of new professions, I suppose," he said.

"It was her father's line of work." Morehouse took the paper back. "Remember when we were at the Wild West show and I went to speak with somebody?"

Webb said that he did.

"His name is Frankie Lew. Used to be a helluva burglar himself—one of the very best. He was doing time in Sing Sing during the earlier robberies, or I would have pegged him as the thief. Turns out it was his daughter, carrying on the family business. Jaeger is her married name."

"Is her husband in it, too?"

"No. He was killed in a ferry accident soon after they were married." Morehouse shook his head. "Poor girl had a father in jail, and a husband in the grave. Told me she took to robbery to make a living."

Webb didn't buy that excuse. "There are a lot of people struggling to live without turning to crime. She didn't have to steal."

"I know." Morehouse continued to look at Sara Jaeger's image in the photograph. "Still, I don't like putting a woman in jail."

Having been in jail himself, Webb knew that it was a miserable experience, and must be even more so for a woman at the mercy of guards and other inmates. Still, he had come because of another woman who was following in her father's footsteps, and he wanted to speak to the detective about it before Morehouse succumbed to exhaustion and fell asleep.

"I visited Ezra Gisclar on Monday," Webb said.

"Was it a wild-goose chase?"

"On the contrary." Webb then told the detective everything about his conversation with the Civil War veteran.

Morehouse appeared to grow more alert as the story went on, and when Webb had concluded, he said, "Damn! What do you make of it?"

Webb had given that a lot of thought on the train back from Massachusetts. And he mulled it over some more yesterday, while Rebecca was away in Atlantic City. He'd come to some definite conclusions. "First," he began, "I believe what Gisclar told me—I do not think he killed Joshua Thompson."

"He admitted having an old grudge against him," said the detective. "And he admitted he was in Brooklyn—at the Lantigua Hotel."

"Yes. He admitted many things that could be incriminating for him. I don't believe he held anything back. If he *had* killed Thompson, I have the feeling he would have said so."

Morehouse snorted. "You don't have much experience with murderers, then."

Webb replied quietly, "As a matter of fact, I do."

The detective spread his hands, as if conceding the point.

"If Gisclar wanted to claim innocence," Webb said, "he wouldn't have come up with a story so complex. I believe he was set up to take the blame for Thompson's murder—and if the police hadn't prevented him from getting back to the hotel, he might have gone back to his room, which had the murder weapon in it. No doubt there would have then been an 'anonymous' tip to the police giving them his room number."

Morehouse said morosely, "The real killer was counting too much on the competence of the Brooklyn PD, then. The officers we had searching that night probably wouldn't have found Gisclar even *with* the room number."

That might have been true, but Webb chose not to agree with Morehouse's assessment of his colleagues. "There are two important questions to be answered," he said.

"Who was it that tried to lure Ezra Gisclar into a trap?" said the detective.

"That's one of the questions. It had to be somebody who had access to the letters Gisclar sent to Thompson."

"Sam Floegel? Catherine McCutcheon?"

Webb nodded. "Both possibilities. But also anyone else who might have handled the company's mail."

"Oh!" Morehouse appeared to have remembered something. "I did go to the Hotel Margaret. Spoke with the doorman, a maid, and a bartender. According to them, Eugene Thompson lives a pretty clean life. Useless, but clean."

"Good to know." That was the sense Webb had after his meeting with the younger Thompson, too.

"So what's the second question?"

"What?"

"You said there were two important questions about Ezra Gisclar," Morehouse reminded him. "The first was, who tried to set him up?"

"Oh yes. The second question is, why did Catherine McCutcheon show me his letters?"

"Because he threatened to kill her father." Morehouse made it sound like the obvious conclusion.

"I don't think so." This was the point that Webb had given the most thought to. "I think it was to distract us."

Morehouse frowned, obviously puzzled.

"The timing struck me as curious," Webb went on. "Catherine McCutcheon showed me those letters after she knew I had spoken with Sam Floegel and her brother Eugene. And, of course, you had already spoken with her. I think she was concerned that we were going to learn something either about her father or about the company that she didn't want known."

"But then why reveal her father's war profiteering during the war? Surely she would want that kept secret."

"Not if there was a more incriminating secret to maintain."

"Like?"

"Remember, whoever lured Ezra Gisclar to Brooklyn was most likely connected with Thompson Manufacturing."

Morehouse stretched his portly body, leaning back so far in his chair that he almost toppled over. He caught himself just in time. "So she put you onto Gisclar as a distraction. That's all she hoped to gain?"

"Not necessarily. She might have thought that Gisclar would still be arrested for the murder of her father. That would put an end to everything, and the only embarrassing information to be made public is a thirty-year-old scandal. Gisclar did admit to enough that you could easily arrest him if you wanted to—it would close the case for you." Webb didn't add that, judging by Catherine McCutcheon's low opinion of Morehouse, it might have been exactly what she expected the detective to do. Possibly the only reason she hadn't shown the letters to Morehouse directly was that she didn't think he would take the initiative to travel all the way to Massachusetts to check out the lead.

Morehouse studied Webb for a while. The writer could tell he was trying to make a final determination about whether to trust his judgment. "I have to admit," he finally said, "that I am very tired, and I'm not sure I'm thinking straight. But what you've said makes sense. I see no reason to arrest—or even bother—Ezra Gisclar."

Webb nodded his appreciation at the answer.

"So what's next?" asked Morehouse.

Webb didn't have a clear answer to that question, but he did have an idea. "I think it would be helpful to know if there is something else going on with Thompson Manufacturing. The business was built on the suffering of men like Ezra Gisclar. Perhaps Joshua Thompson didn't change his business practices much after the war. Perhaps that's what Catherine McCutcheon still wants to hide."

"I thought you said she was protecting whoever it was that brought Gisclar to Brooklyn."

"I said it's a possibility. This is another possibility. One way to narrow them down might be to get a look at Thompson Manufacturing's books. You think you could get a court order to see them?"

"Not easily. We'd have to convince a judge—and by the time we did, you better believe somebody will have tipped off Catherine McCutcheon." He dug into his pocket and popped several gumdrops into his mouth. He chewed for a while, and Webb could almost see the thinking process grinding away behind his furrowed brow. "I think you're right though—it would be worth looking at their books."

"So how do we get them?"

Morehouse chewed some more. "I might know a way. But even if we got the books, what good would it do? I don't know how to read a financial ledger any more'n I know how to read Greek. How about you?"

Webb admitted that he didn't. It was his turn to mull the situation over. "You sure you know a way to get the books?"

"Maybe. But the way we'd get them, we wouldn't have more than a few hours with them."

"Well then, I might know somebody who could review them for us." Webb wasn't sure if the man he was thinking of would want to get involved though.

Both of them agreed to speak the next day. Webb found himself looking forward to it—Buck Morehouse was turning out to be a reasonable man for a police officer.

CHAPTER 21

Newly released ex-convicts generally didn't live in the toniest neighborhoods, and that was certainly true of Frankie Lew.

Lew's address was a four-story apartment building on Van Brunt Street in Red Hook, a stone's throw from the Brooklyn waterfront. Judging by the look of the building, it might indeed have been the target of stone throwers. About half its windows were broken and many of the dull red bricks of its facade were chipped and cracked. One of the railings on the front stoop was missing and a board had been placed over a front step that had collapsed.

Judging by the number of children playing in the filthy street, darting between the horses and the wagons, the interior must have been even worse—at least it held no attraction to keep the youngsters indoors.

Inside the entrance hall, Buck Morehouse found that he was right. The hallway was used as a garbage dump. After a few steps, he discovered to his disgust that it was also used as a toilet.

On the second floor, he rapped on the door of an apartment at the dark end of the hallway.

"Get the hell out o' here!" was the greeting from within.

Morehouse recognized Frankie Lew's voice. He wondered how Lew knew it was him at the door, then realized it was likely just Lew's standard response. He knocked again and called, "I gotta talk to you, Frankie!"

The door soon opened, and the wiry burglar looked up at him with fire in his small dark eyes. "I oughta kill you for what you did to my little girl." His body was tensed and his fists clenched.

Morehouse had to fight off a fear that the little man might do just what he'd said. "That's what I want to talk to you about."

"Too late for talk. Sara's in jail."

"Maybe we can work something out."

"You gonna let her go?"

Morehouse held up hand. "Let's talk first. I got a proposition for you, so let me in and listen to what I got to say."

From his fierce expression, Lew would have clearly found more satisfaction in killing the detective, but he took a backward step. "All right. I'll listen. But I ain't saying for how long."

"Fair enough." Morehouse took off his derby and stepped inside.

To his surprise, the small apartment was clean and neat. It was in poor repair—the ceiling sagged, strips of wallpaper had been torn away, and the electric light flickered, but those were most likely the fault of the landlord, not the tenant.

"Go ahead. Sit down if you want."

Morehouse accepted the offer and took a seat on a threadbare easy chair. "Thanks."

"It's more'n you deserve, you bastard." Lew took a straight-backed dining chair and turned it around; he sat down using the backrest to support his folded arms. "How could you do that to my little girl?"

"First off," said Morehouse, "I didn't even know your daughter was in the business. When did she start?"

"While I was away. She needed the money."

"And when I talked to you at the Wild West show, I tried to get you riled at me. I figured you'd know who was doing the robberies and pass on the tip about Namm's just to make me look like an ass. I assumed it would be somebody else—not you or anybody in your family."

"Well, you was wrong."

"Yes, I was. But *you* must have told your daughter what I said. Why would you let her go out there and try another robbery?"

Lew was slow to answer. "I wish I hadn't. But she was gonna do one more heist—just to get enough money so she could leave town and start over some place else." He smiled grimly. "And I did like the idea of my girl makin' you look like an ass. Guess I'm the ass now."

"As I see it," said Morehouse, "what's done is done. But maybe we can help each other out."

"How?"

"I need you to steal something. Just for a while."

Frankie Lew looked as if he'd been hit by a brick. It was a long moment before he replied, "What the hell are you talkin' about?"

"It's an easy job. A man with your skills will have no problem."

"What is this? You want me back in jail too?" He waved his arm toward the front of the building. "I got two boys playin' outside. Should I call 'em so you can put our whole family behind bars?"

"No, no," Morehouse quickly said. "Let me explain. I need some books taken from certain business for a while—and then put back."

"What business?"

Morehouse wasn't about to share that information before he had to; he didn't want Lew to go tip off Thompson Manufacturing in the hope of getting some payment. "You find out when we get there."

"You said we can help each other. What's in it for me?"

"If it's successful—you get the books out and back in with nobody being the wiser—maybe things go easier for Sara."

"*Maybe* don't count for much."

"Okay. She was caught with burglary tools—a jimmy and everything else those of your profession use. You do this for me, and the tools disappear from the evidence room. That'll make for a weaker case against her. Maybe she gets off with trespassing instead of attempted burglary."

"How you gonna guarantee that?"

"I sure as hell ain't putting it in writing. But you got my word, the tools will disappear."

"Your word," Lew said mockingly.

"I know you're mad at me, but think about it—ask your friends if you like. My word is good." Morehouse added, "And if Sara returns the jewels she stole to the other stores—even if she only has some of them left—maybe she can make a deal on those charges."

Lew mulled it over, not an easy process for him, the detective could tell. "So you're gonna take me some place, and I'm supposed to break in—"

"No 'breaking.' You gotta get in clean."

"Okay, so I get in, grab some books for you, then put 'em back." He smiled with genuine amusement. "Be the first time I ever tried to put something back!"

"You willing?"

Lew nodded. "But if you're tryin' to trap me, I *will* get you."

Morehouse was more concerned that, if it didn't work, Captain Sturup would get him. "One more thing, Frankie: this is unofficial. Neither one of us says anything about this."

Lew agreed. "Sure wouldn't do my reputation any good if this gets out," he said. "What would my buddies think if they heard I stole something as useless as books and then went and returned 'em!"

Marshall Webb found Al Napoli's Barbershop on Bleecker Street in Greenwich Village with little trouble. The only other time he had been to the place was about a year earlier, but his memory served him well.

Before he opened the door, Webb could hear the marvelous singing within. He walked in quietly, hoping to avoid disrupting the quartet that was harmonizing "In the Evening by the Moonlight."

He definitely didn't disturb the barber. Napoli was leaning all the way back in one of his two chairs, a newspaper over his face. Judging by his soft snoring, he wasn't enjoying this evening's rehearsal by the Village Four.

Webb did, though. He stood, breathing in the scents of bay rum, brilliantine, and pomade, and listening to tight harmony sung in tune.

As the four men continued the song, a couple of them nodded in greeting to him. Webb had sung a song with them the other time he was here, and recognized the bass, Chris Flynn, and the lead, Bob something. He didn't recall seeing the baritone before.

The tenor, a bespectacled sharp-faced man named Nicholas Bostwick, was staring at Webb with a look of trepidation. His voice became strained as the song went on, and his pitch began to waver, earning him a couple of glares from the lead. Stump! That was the man's last name, Webb remembered: Bob Stump.

When the last chord rang, Webb applauded. "You gentlemen sound even better than you used to."

In his deep voice, Flynn said jokingly, "Even with Bostwick doing his impression of a rusty gate?"

Bostwick, blinking rapidly behind his thick glasses, had moved slightly behind the others, as if worried that Webb had come to see him. If that was his assumption, it was entirely correct.

"Good to see you again, Mr. Bostwick," Webb said, offering his hand. "I thought you would be here on a Thursday night."

"Regular as clockwork," said Flynn. The bass laughed. "Or should I say 'regular as a calendar'?"

Bostwick shook Webb's hand weakly and muttered something polite about how good it was to see the writer again, too. He then introduced Webb to the others, including the quartet's new baritone, Burt Szabo.

Flynn asked, "Have you come to try another song with us, Mr. Webb? We've been hoping you'd be back."

"I'm afraid I've actually come to speak with Mr. Bostwick, if you can spare him for a few minutes."

"We were about to take a break anyway. But first"—Flynn flashed an easy smile—"do you remember the rule?"

"Yes." Webb chuckled. "Any man who comes in here has to sing."

"At least one song. What'll it be?"

Webb had given thought to the selection on his way to Napoli's. "Good Night, Ladies," he answered.

"Good choice!" said Flynn. "Go ahead. You take the melody and we'll harmonize around you."

They did, and they actually made Webb sound fairly good, he thought. After the song, he regretted that he only had time to sing one. But he did have to speak with Nicholas Bostwick.

The other three men left Webb and Bostwick alone in the shop—except for the sleeping barber—while they went to the saloon two doors down to wet their whistles. Bob Stump explained as they left that beer was an essential part of keeping the voice in proper condition.

Webb and Bostwick walked over to the waiting chairs on the other side of the shop from the barber and sat down.

The nervous Bostwick said, "I suspect this is not a social call."

"I'm afraid you're right. And I do apologize for intruding. But I need your help with something."

"*My* help?" He pushed up his spectacles. "Not something dangerous again." Bostwick was chattering faster as he spoke. "I couldn't do that. I have responsibilities now. Miss Schulmerich and I—do you remember her?—she is now my fiancée. We will be getting married."

"That is wonderful news. Congratulations."

"Thank you." Bostwick still appeared to be bracing himself for whatever Webb was about to ask of him. The concern was justified. Last year, a banker who worked at Jacob Updegraff's New Amsterdam Trust Company, where Bostwick was an accountant, had been murdered. Bostwick and Webb worked together to solve the case, and it was work that Bostwick clearly had not relished.

"There is no danger involved," Webb assured him, hoping that would turn out to be true. "It is a simple financial matter."

"What kind of financial matter?" Bostwick remained suspicious.

"We would like you to look over a company's books and determine if there is anything suspicious in its practices."

"What company?"

Webb evaded a direct answer. "We don't have the books yet."

Bostwick appeared to be considering the request. "All I have to do is review the accounting?"

"Yes." Webb considered stressing the importance of his cooperation by telling him that his efforts might help solve a murder, but that would most likely scare him off. He chose a different approach. "Of course you would be compensated. I suppose some extra cash could come in handy with your marriage plans."

"It would," the accountant conceded. Then he looked at Webb. "Who is the 'we' to whom you refer?"

"Oh. A Brooklyn police detective."

"So there *is* something criminal about this."

"There might be. But you have nothing to fear. We will simply provide you with some financial ledgers to review. You will look them over and tell us anything that looks suspicious to you. That's all. We will take it from there, and your name will never be made known."

Bostwick took a neatly folded handkerchief from his pocket, shook it open, and proceeded to clean his spectacles with it. Looking at Webb with his myopic eyes, he said, "I have to admit that there were aspects to our previous encounters that made me rather uncomfortable. However, I also have to say that I admire what you did in solving the murder of my colleague." He put the glasses back on his nose. "I will help you in what you are asking."

"Thank you," said Webb, with genuine gratitude. Then he added, "Can I impose a bit more for one more favor?"

"What is it?"

"When the others get back, can I try singing another song?"

For the first time since Webb had stepped into the barbershop, he saw Bostwick relax and crack a smile.

CHAPTER 22

Rebecca Davies wasn't sure what Marshall's reaction would be when she arrived unannounced at his apartment. For one thing, she suspected that he didn't much care for surprises of any kind. For another, she worried that he might be harboring a disappointment that she'd had to back out of the trip to Massachusetts with him. Part of the reason she was here, late Friday morning, was to make it up to him.

There was indeed a look of surprise on his handsome face when he opened the door, but Rebecca was happy to discern from the smile that soon grew that he took it to be a pleasant surprise.

"I am taking you hostage," she announced. She lifted her arm, over which she'd hooked the handles of a wicker picnic basket.

He looked at the basket, then into her eyes, and raised his hands in mock surrender. "I'll go willingly."

A short time later, they were munching on cold

chicken and potato salad by the pond at the south end of Central Park. The sun was high and bright in a cloudless sky, but a soft breeze blew across the water, making the temperature perfectly comfortable. The thick grass under the plaid blanket on which they sat was soft, making the bank of the pond almost as good a cushion as a velvet sofa.

Rebecca and Marshall weren't the only ones taking advantage of the fine weather and the resources of the park. Boys in knickers sailed toy boats in the pond and flew simple kites, some girls were playing jump rope, and there were several young couples picnicking on the lawn much as she and Marshall were.

Their conversation had taken a predictable course. So far, Marshall had told her about his visit to that unfortunate Civil War veteran in Massachusetts, and she had reported on her trip with Alice to Atlantic City. She'd also had more recent news about Lucy Robatin that she shared with him.

Alice had visited Lucy Robatin's mother and told her that her daughter was alive and unharmed. Mrs. Robatin, relieved and grateful, had broken down in tears and confided to Alice what had caused the rift in their family. Lucy had learned that her father's real estate holdings included buildings that housed opium dens in Chinatown. Every time her father reprimanded her for late nights or unacceptable companions, Lucy would accuse him of profiting from vice and drugs—she said if he would change his ways, then she would too. Eventually, the girl seemed to think she was punishing her father by spending the family's ill-gotten money on the opium that her father seemed to think was all right for others.

Rebecca looked over at an attractive young couple walking along the edge of the pond, talking and laughing. They made an adorable picture.

Rebecca suddenly laughed. She wondered if any of the other couples had noticed her and Marshall and assumed they were engaged in sweet talk—if so, they were certainly wrong.

"What's so funny?" Marshall asked.

"Oh, nothing. I was just thinking how nice it is to be outside here." That hadn't been the thought that triggered the laughter, but the sentiment was one that she genuinely felt.

"I hope we can do this more often—and we should, now that you have extra help. How did Miss Quilty react when you offered her the job?"

Rebecca smiled, recalling the young girl's reaction. "She cried—with happiness. And then she went right back to work. I think the hard thing will be to convince her to take occasional breaks." Yes, Stephanie Quilty would certainly be an asset to Colden House, and give Rebecca some much-needed relief.

Maybe she and Marshall *would* be able to spend more time together. And then maybe they would have more romantic conversations.

As he paced outside the Fields Hotel on Bushwick Avenue in Williamsburg, Buck Morehouse considered the strange similarities to the nights he'd spent staking out Namm's Department Store.

It was again shortly after midnight, and he was

again waiting for a burglar to strike. He'd also taken precautions, although this time they didn't involve any other police officers—he didn't want anyone in the department to learn of his arrangement with Frankie Lew.

The main difference this night was that Morehouse was hoping for the theft to succeed.

He had checked, and found that Thompson Manufacturing had no night shift in operation, something that the depression had put an end to more than a year ago. He'd also learned that the company's night watchman was a retired Brooklyn police officer who had been pushed into retirement because excessive drinking had prevented him from carrying out his duties. Morehouse doubted that the man's habits would have improved since leaving the force, so he was probably in a drunken stupor by now, giving Lew one less thing to worry about.

Morehouse did worry, though. Things could go wrong with any plan, no matter how well thought out.

He was relieved when Frankie Lew approached him with a satchel tucked tightly under his arm.

"Got 'em," the burglar announced in a low voice.

"Any trouble?"

"No. Easy in and easy out."

"Good." Morehouse took the satchel. "Be back here in four hours to do the rest of the job."

"I gotta kill four hours?"

Morehouse dug into his pocket and found a dollar. "Here," he said, giving the coin to Lew. "Find something to do. Just don't drink too much and be sure you're here in time. The job's only half over."

"And when it's all done, you lose the evidence on Sara?"

The detective promised that he would carry through on his part of the agreement. To his mind, trading a burglary conviction for a murderer was a good deal.

Morehouse carried the heavy satchel into the hotel and up to room 412. The hotel room had been Marshall Webb's idea; he'd said the accountant would need a place to review the books.

The Fields Hotel wasn't a flophouse but it was far from luxurious. It provided small rooms, plainly furnished, at an affordable price. Most importantly, it was the kind of place where staff and guests minded their own business.

Webb answered the door and Morehouse handed him the satchel. The writer carried it to a cheap pine writing table and took out the canvas-bound ledgers it contained, placing them before the nervous young man seated at the table.

"You want me to review all this in just *four hours?*" Nicholas Bostwick asked. "Do you have any idea how long it takes to do a proper audit?"

"We're not looking for a penny-by-penny accounting," Webb answered. "All we want is for you to look these over and see if anything stands out as peculiar about the Thompson company or the way it operates."

" 'Peculiar' as in illegal?" asked Bostwick.

"Illegal, immoral, or unusual. You know how a business should operate; you tell us if anything gets your attention."

"Very well." Bostwick made a production of removing his suit jacket, sliding a couple of elastic bands over his shirtsleeves, and cleaning his spectacles. Then he went to work, occasionally jotting notes on a large pad of yellow paper.

Morehouse and Webb sat down on a hard couch and watched Bostwick work. Neither of them spoke, so that they wouldn't distract the intense accountant.

After he'd been studying the books for about ten minutes, Bostwick made a murmur of disapproval.

"Find something?" Morehouse asked.

"Somebody forgot to use blotting paper on this page. The ink smudged, and I can hardly make out the numbers." Bostwick shook his head with disproval. "Terribly sloppy. It defeats the purpose of keeping records if no one can decipher them. Thompson's bookkeeper should be fired." He looked the page over and scowled. "Oh, this page is from 1882—probably too late to fire him now."

Morehouse had to restrain a groan. He'd been hoping for something more incriminating than poor penmanship that was more than ten years old. "Keep looking," he said grumpily.

Bostwick shot him a look that indicated that he didn't appreciate the detective's tone.

Morehouse and Webb then watched in silence again, while Bostwick skimmed through all the books, then began to review parts of them more carefully. The detective soon discovered that perhaps the only thing more boring than reviewing financial ledgers was watching somebody else review them. It was a struggle to remain awake, a struggle that became more difficult as the time began to pass by.

* * *

Webb was shaking Morehouse awake. "It's time," he said.

Morehouse looked at him and tried to clear the slumber from his head. "Huh?" The question took the form of a yawn.

"Four hours is gone, and Mr. Bostwick is finished with the books. You have to get them back now."

"Oh yeah, right." Morehouse pulled himself up off the couch. It took a moment to get his balance. He asked the accountant, "Whatcha find?"

Webb said, "Why don't you take these downstairs? Mr. Bostwick can give us his report when you get back."

Morehouse agreed, and hurried downstairs with the satchel. He was happy to see Frankie Lew waiting for him.

"You're late," Lew said.

"You got time to take them back." He passed the ledgers on to Lew. "Get the job done, and your daughter will thank you for it."

As soon as Lew left, Morehouse returned to the hotel room and immediately asked Bostwick again if he'd found anything suspicious.

The accountant answered in a measured voice. "Of course, I only had time for a cursory examination, but I believe I did find something that may be of interest."

"What's that?" asked Webb.

"Thompson Manufacturing actually includes some affiliated companies." He looked over his notes. "Money and equipment is transferred back and forth between Thompson's companies and these affiliates."

Webb asked, "Who are the affiliates?"

The accountant showed them a list of names that he'd written down.

When Morehouse saw the names, he recognized them as some of the most notorious sweatshops in Brooklyn. Even after hearing about Joshua Thompson selling shoddy during the war, he found it hard to believe a man of such prominence could be involved with places like these. "Are you sure about this?"

"Absolutely," Bostwick answered.

Webb spoke up. "When Sam Floegel gave me a tour of the factory, I noticed that some equipment seemed to be missing. Maybe it was moved to one of these other companies."

Bostwick said, "That appears to be how they operated. If there was any slowdown with his major companies, they shifted the same equipment to produce cheaper goods in one of these other facilities—quite an effective cost-saving measure. And these companies were often of short duration, operating in vacant warehouse space also owned by Thompson."

"Anything else you can tell us?"

"I can give you some numbers, but without the time for a detailed examination I was rather limited in what I could determine."

Morehouse didn't want to hear numbers. "You did great, Mr. Bostwick" he said. "Thank you."

The accountant almost beamed with pride. "There is one other thing that might be of interest."

"What's that?" asked Webb.

"The name you mentioned—Sam Floegel."

"What about him?"

"Although Joshua Thompson's equipment and facilities were used by these other companies, the majority owner was a Mr. Samuel Floegel." He cleared his throat and corrected himself. "I mean he *is* the majority owner—the companies are still in operation."

CHAPTER 23

The lawn tennis courts of the Knickerbocker Field Club were empty this afternoon, sodden from a heavy morning rain. Marshall Webb wouldn't have thought to try finding Eugene Thompson there, but the doorman at Thompson's apartment house had told him that's where he had gone.

Webb found Thompson on the veranda of the wood-frame clubhouse. The darkly handsome sportsman was sitting and chatting with two other men, all of them dressed in white tennis flannels.

"Mr. Thompson?" Webb said when there was a pause in the conversation.

Eugene Thompson looked up and an easy smile crossed his face. "Mr. Webb! How good to see you." He stood, shook hands enthusiastically, and introduced Webb to the other two men. "What brings you out here again?" he asked.

"I was hoping to speak with you—if you can spare me a few minutes."

Thompson laughed. "Why, certainly. All we're doing is watching the grass dry anyway."

The other men chuckled. From the color in their faces and the glass tumblers on the table, Webb suspected that watching grass dry was a thirst-inducing occupation. "Can we speak in private?" Webb asked.

"I believe we can get a table inside," said Thompson, provoking another chuckle from his friends.

Webb and Thompson excused themselves and went into the clubhouse. *Every* table was available. The only other men in the place were two uniformed waiters who stood along the wall almost as motionless at the sporting equipment hung upon the dark wood paneling.

The two of them took a seat at a corner table, and were almost pounced upon by a waiter apparently eager for something to do. Thompson ordered two gin rickeys, then explained, "Not many club members come out when the ground's so wet. I wouldn't be here myself, but I thought it would be a good time to have my racquet restrung. And, of course, it's always a good place to enjoy a drink or two."

Webb waited until the drinks were served before proceeding to the reason he'd come. He leaned toward Thompson and reminded him, "When we spoke last, you told me your father had a ruthless streak, a 'killer instinct,' you said."

The cheerful expression on Eugene Thompson's long chiseled face turned down a bit. "Did I say that?"

"Yes."

Thompson shrugged. "Well, it *is* true."

"And you don't have the same ruthless streak."

"Only on the tennis courts."

"I've learned some things about your father," Webb said. "Not the kinds of things he would have wanted to become public. But I think you know about them."

"I told you I'm not involved in the business. Haven't been for some time." He drained his glass.

"Yes. But I'm guessing there was some reason you dropped out of the family business."

Eugene Thompson smiled wryly. "It simply wasn't for me."

"There wasn't some particular reason you left? Wasn't there something that led you to believe your father had a ruthless streak?"

Thompson waited until the waiter had taken his empty glass away before responding. "Mr. Webb, my father is dead. Can't we let it be?"

"Your father is dead, but his business practices are continuing."

"Yes. And they continue to provide me with my livelihood. Why should I jeopardize that by telling you anything?"

Webb had thought about what Rebecca told him regarding Lucy Robatin, and how she hated the way their family had earned its wealth. He hoped that Eugene Thompson had such a conscience, too. "I can understand you not wanting to give up the comfortable life you lead," said Webb. "But if you know that the people financing it are the poor men and women slaving away in sweatshops, do you really want to continue this way? Can you live with that?"

"I have so far," was the sad reply.

Webb said nothing while the waiter returned with a second drink for Thompson; he shook his head no when the waiter asked if he was ready for another too.

Thompson took a long swallow of the fresh drink. "I know how my father made his money. He told me about how he got rich on government contracts during the war. He was actually proud that he'd boosted his profits by selling the army garbage that wouldn't be of use to anybody." After another lift of the glass, he said. "But that's ancient history now."

"Some people are still living it." Webb proceeded to tell him about Ezra Gisclar and what the veteran's life had been like since the war.

"That supposed to make me feel guilty?"

"No. Your father was the one who ran a crooked business, not you. I just want you to know that it's not 'ancient history.' In fact, Thompson Manufacturing is still associated with sweatshops and shoddy businesses."

"Yeah, I know about those."

Webb wasn't sure if Thompson would; according to Nicholas Bostwick, Eugene's name hadn't appeared in the ledgers.

Thompson went on, "Those were mostly Sam Floegel's operations, though."

"He was directly involved?"

"Oh yes. I think part of the reason that my father wasn't too disappointed about me not going into the family business was that he had Sam. The two of them worked together since early during the war—and they saw eye to eye on things. As my father got rich, though, Sam got the itch to try doing the same for himself and start his own business. My father didn't want to lose him, though, so he helped him acquire some down-on-their-luck operations. That way Sam had something of his own—with my father as a minority partner—and my father still had Sam to run his major operations."

"And you never had anything to do with them?"

"No. I'm not greedy and, as I told you before, I'm not ruthless. I couldn't take advantage of people the way they did." He hesitated. "I was tempted once, though."

"When?"

"About a year ago, my father came to me. He said he couldn't run the company forever, but he wanted it to stay in the family. He wanted me to come back and learn the business so I could take over someday. I told him I couldn't—not the way he operated the business. He told me he was going to be making a change; said he was going to cut off Floegel's businesses."

"Sounds like he really did want you back."

"It wasn't to win me over. It was because he'd become so obsessed with being 'respectable.' My father didn't want any associations that could damage his public image."

"Is your sister still going to divest the family interest in those companies?"

"I doubt it. She wants to *grow* the family empire, make even more money."

Eugene Thompson spoke awhile longer, but had no more useful details.

Webb thanked him for his time and stood to leave.

Thompson said, "Can I ask you a question now, Mr. Webb?"

"Of course."

"What's it like to work for a living?'

308   *Troy Soos*

Webb considered that. "Hard sometimes. But sometimes very satisfying."

Thompson nodded thoughtfully. "I have the feeling I'm going to be finding out for myself soon."

CHAPTER 24

Buck Morehouse eyed the writer across his desk in the station house. He had come to respect Marshall Webb's judgment and now he felt he had to rely on it—because Morehouse wasn't sure what the best course of action was now.

"What do you suggest we do now?" Webb asked.

Morehouse was hoping that Webb had a suggestion. "You're confident about what Eugene Thompson told you?"

"Yes. Everything fit. He didn't seem to be hiding anything." Webb had already given Morehouse an account of his conversation with the Thompson heir.

"If Joshua Thompson was going to divest the other companies, Sam Floegel would be the one to lose the most," said the detective.

"According to what Nicholas Bostwick tells me, Floegel would be out of business without access to Thompson's facilities and equipment."

Morehouse said, "All things considered, I would

have to say that the most likely suspect in Joshua Thompson's murder is Floegel. He had to stop Thompson from putting him out of business."

Webb nodded. "I agree. But there is no direct evidence. And although he's the most likely suspect, I still wonder about Catherine McCutcheon."

"You think she was involved in killing her own father?"

"Honestly, no. But she stood to lose a great deal also. According to her brother, she's maintaining the relationship with Floegel's companies. If her father had lived, that relationship would have been severed and Mrs. McCutcheon would lose a considerable part of her business. She wants to grow the family fortune, and I don't think she has any more scruples than her father as to how she does it."

Morehouse considered that argument. "I think what it comes down to," he finally said, "is that Sam Floegel *had* to be involved. Catherine McCutcheon *may* have been involved."

"Yes," said Webb. "That's the conclusion I've come to. And my question remains: where do we go from here?"

The detective knew there wasn't much else they could do without approaching Floegel directly. There had been no witnesses to the Thompson shooting, and the killer had apparently covered his trail. All they had was a possible motive—and the only one who could confirm that motive was Floegel himself.

Webb leaned back in his seat and pressed his fingers together waiting for the detective's answer.

"I think we have to confront Sam Floegel," Morehouse finally decided. "Tell him what we know and see if he breaks."

"If he doesn't break," said Webb, "then we have nothing. He'll clam up and you'll have no grounds on which to arrest him."

"Do *you* have a suggestion?"

Webb hesitated. "Yes. Instead of telling him everything we know, drop just enough information to tease him."

"What will that accomplish?"

"It might motivate him to try and prevent any more incriminating information from coming out."

"You mean—"

"Try to get him to act."

Webb already had thought of a plan, Morehouse could tell. "What do you have in mind?"

The writer sat up straight. "If Sam Floegel thought I was about to publish an article revealing his business practices, don't you think he would want to stop it?"

"Yes . . ."

"I do, too. If it were to be made public that Thompson Manufacturing was associated with Floegel's sweatshop, Catherine McCutcheon would have to divest them. And she could easily claim that she had known nothing about that part of her father's business. Thompson Manufacturing's reputation would be damaged, but the company would no doubt survive. Floegel, on the other hand, would be destroyed—and he has to know that."

"And he would think he could stop *Harper's Weekly* from publishing such an article?" Morehouse was skeptical.

"No. But he might think he can stop the article from getting to the *Harper's* office."

"You mean—"

"Make me a target and see if he'll come for me. If we can arrest him for attempted murder, at least that's something—and maybe he'll admit to his involvement in Joshua Thompson's death."

"That's too dangerous."

"We'll take appropriate precautions."

"The department has no way of guaranteeing your safety," Morehouse said. "I can't let you do that."

"I don't expect a guarantee. I only ask that you do your best—keep a tail on Floegel and have some men on hand in case he tries to kill me."

Morehouse considered the proposal. Then he asked, "Why is this so important to you?"

Webb answered simply, "I want to know what happened."

The detective suspected there was more to it than that. And he still wasn't sure he would go along with such a plan, but they did begin to discuss how it might be carried out.

CHAPTER 25

Marshall Webb was having second thoughts about the plan. Unfortunately, it had already been set into action. So Webb continued to wait, alone in his apartment, to see what the result would be.

If Buck Morehouse had carried out his role correctly, he'd informed Sam Floegel that Webb was turning in an article to the *Harper's* office tomorrow morning. The detective also would have led Floegel to think that Webb's article would be exposing something about the Thompson business operations.

All Webb had to do now was wait until business hours tomorrow morning. After that time, Floegel would think it was too late for Webb's story to be stopped, so if he took no action by then there should be no attempt on Webb's life. Until that time—well, Webb simply had to endure some anxious hours.

Although there was no convenient place across the street for a gunman to hole up, Webb didn't pass near his window; he'd even turned off the light nearest it.

While he waited to see if Sam Floegel would take the bait, Webb passed the time trying to read an old *Police Gazette*. He barely noticed the lurid illustrations, though, and wasn't able to focus on the words.

At ten-thirty there was a knock at the door.

Webb stood, tied the knot of his dressing gown, and cautiously approached the door. "Who is it?"

"Sam Floegel, Mr. Webb. Sorry to come by so late, but I'm here on a matter of some importance."

Webb cracked the door open with his left hand while keeping the right in the pocket of his robe. Floegel looked much the same as he had at Catherine McCutcheon's. Light from the hallway bulb glistened on his sweaty face from his balding head to his droopy jowls. Hair on his beard was matted together. Floegel was dressed in a bulky sack suit that might have contributed to the warmth, but Webb was sure there was more than that behind the sweating. Importantly, though, Floegel's hands were empty.

"Come in," Webb said. "Can I get you something?"

Floegel stepped inside. "No, no. I don't want to be any trouble."

Webb motioned to an armchair, and Floegel took the seat. Taking care not to turn his back on the man, Webb sat down across from him. "What did you want to see me about?"

"This is really quite embarrassing," Floegel stammered. "I understand you have some information on Thompson Manufacturing that you're planning to publish in *Harper's.*"

"Yes. I'm giving the article to my editor tomorrow morning."

Floegel fidgeted in the chair. "That could prove damaging to our company. Do you realize that?"

"Yes. I considered that. But I believe the public has a right to know how a major business like Thompson Manufacturing operates."

"Do you think that's fair to Mrs. McCutcheon? She has just taken over the company and had nothing to do with the way her father ran it."

"But *you* did."

"I hope you don't have any personal animosity for me, Mr. Webb." Floegel was maintaining a controlled voice, but he was growing visibly more nervous.

"No, I'm just a reporter."

"Well then, if there's nothing personal, perhaps we can come to a business arrangement. I can offer you a much more handsome price for that article than *Harper's* is paying you." He added, "Of course I would need your assurance that you would drop the matter entirely."

Webb pursed his lips as if considering the proposal. Actually, it had come as a surprise to him; he hadn't expected to be offered a bribe. "I'm sorry, Mr. Floegel. If it was just the story about the company, I would be tempted to take you up on the offer. But I have a couple of leads that I'm convinced will lead me to solving Joshua Thompson's murder. That's a story I *have* to pursue."

"I'm sorry to hear—" Floegel reached into his jacket. He tried to move quickly, but in his nervousness it ended up clumsy. By the time he pulled out a revolver, Webb already had his aimed at the man's chest. It was much easier to draw from a loose dressing gown pocket than from a suit.

"Drop it," Webb said.

Floegel's hand fell weakly to his lap, but the gun remained loosely in his grip. "I was just going to threaten you," he said. "I wouldn't have shot you."

Webb kept his eye on Floegel's right hand and his revolver aimed at his chest. "How can I believe you? You knew Joshua Thompson for thirty years, and you killed *him.*"

Floegel was slow to reply. "It's *because* I gave that man thirty years of hard work that I killed him."

"You were going to be out of business if he had his way."

Floegel nodded sadly. "He was going to cut me loose. Thompson was more interested in being *respectable* than making money lately. So he was going to drop the companies that I had majority ownership of. I told him I couldn't survive without them, and he said I should just start a new business all on my own. In these times, even good companies are going bankrupt—how could I start a new one?" His right hand moved slightly.

"Drop it," Webb warned.

Floegel looked down at the weapon in his lap as if hadn't even realized it was still there. "Thompson made *his* fortune; *his* family was going to be fine. I got a wife, and boys in college, to pay for. I can't afford to go broke."

Webb said, "Did you set up Ezra Gisclar?"

"Yes. Thompson showed me the letter Gisclar wrote; he told me it was part of the reason he was cutting his interest in the other businesses we were in—not because he felt guilty, but because if people started looking into his company he wanted it to be clean.

"Gisclar's letter gave me an idea. I thought I could kill Thompson and get away with it by setting up Gisclar to take the fall. It was a good plan—I held out a carrot and Gisclar came to Brooklyn." He frowned and a bead of sweat dripped from his ear. "But it didn't work out the way it should have. It was a shame. I figured Thompson would be dead, Gisclar would be caught, and Mrs. McCutcheon and I would be free to continue running our companies."

"Was Catherine McCutcheon in on the plan?"

"On killing her father? No, that was me. Strange thing: I worked with the man for so long and I always liked him. Then he betrayed me. You'd be surprised how fast a hatred can develop. And by the time I killed him, I did hate him."

"Does Mrs. McCutcheon know about your sweatshops? What if she wants to close them down—will you kill her too?"

"She's her father's daughter—the way her father *used* to be. She has her companies, and I have mine. And we both make money. Like I said, I got a family to support."

A strange look came over Floegel's face, and he appeared on the verge of crying. "I can't take care of them now, can I?"

"You're going to jail," said Webb. He omitted mentioning that jail would no doubt be followed by the electric chair.

In a hoarse whisper, Floegel said, "What's my wife gonna think of me?" Then he slowly lifted his hand.

"Stop," Webb warned, ready to pull the trigger.

Floegel tilted the barrel of his revolver straight up.

Webb hesitated, not wanting to shoot unless Floegel was taking aim at him.

Floegel quickly lifted the gun higher, straight up, and pushed the muzzle under his jaw, right behind his beard. Then he made his wife a widow.

CHAPTER 26

Harry Hargis strode into the office waving an illustration. "Got another one, Webb!" He put the drawing on Webb's desk, while the other writers tried to look busy enough to please the editor.

Webb looked over the drawing of a mustachioed New York police officer. "Who's this?"

"Captain James J. Deighan. He's going to prison for ten years for accepting bribes, neglect of duty, and—and I don't remember the other charges. But it's all thanks to you."

"It was the Lexow Committee," said Webb.

"No need to be modest." Hargis picked up the drawing. As he walked out of the office he called back, "This will be front page in the next issue."

"Congratulations," said Keith Hopkins at the next desk.

"Thanks," Webb answered absently. He was already calculating how much more harm Deighan's conviction would do to the cause of consolidation. The vote was only a month away, and the continuing revelations about Tammany Hall and police corruption had scared Brooklynites to the point where it was unlikely now that they would vote in favor of merging with Manhattan.

In the past couple of months, there had been developments on other fronts, too.

Thompson Manufacturing's fortunes had been sinking to the point where Keith Hopkins was writing mock obituaries for the company. Webb hoped it wouldn't get to the point of bankruptcy; he remembered the workers he'd seen in the factory and didn't want them to lose their livelihoods.

There was some good news about Lucy Robatin. Although relations with her father remained strained, she had recovered from her opium habit and was enrolling in Mount Holyoke College; her father had agreed to pay for her school on the condition that she not come home again, a condition to which she readily agreed.

And Ezra Gisclar had finally gotten some compensation. Eugene Thompson had sent the war veteran money from his allowance and was even arranging to buy him a small farm.

For today, though, the best news was that Stephanie Quilty was working out well at Colden House. That meant she could cover the duties, giving Webb and Rebecca a chance to spend some time together.